THE EWE LAMB

THE EWE LAMB

Margaret Bacon

This first world edition published in Great Britain 1999 by
SEVERN HOUSE PUBLISHERS LTD of
9–15 High Street, Sutton, Surrey SM1 1DF.
This title first published in the U.S.A. 1999 by
SEVERN HOUSE PUBLISHERS INC of
595 Madison Avenue, New York, N.Y. 10022.

British Library Cataloguing in Publication Data

Bacon, Margaret, 1931-
  The ewe lamb
  1. Female friendship - Fiction
  I. Title
  823.9'14 [F]

ISBN 0 7278 5435 6

Typeset by Hewer Text Ltd
Edinburgh, Scotland.
Printed and bound in Great Britain by
MPG Books Ltd, Bodmin, Cornwall.

One

S omething was different this morning. Still half-asleep, she tried, by a process of elimination, to work out what it was. If she stretched her right leg down into the corner of the bed she could feel the torch which she'd used for reading under the sheet last night, after her mother had turned off the light. It felt just like it felt every other morning, hard and cold but somehow reassuring, promising safe reading for the night to come.

She could hear the familiar morning sounds as all the usual outdoor noises made their way through the open window: birds which had begun the dawn chorus with such enthusiasm two hours ago were now bringing it to a ragged, half-hearted close. The top branch of the pear tree which climbed the wall outside her bedroom scraped gently but persistently against the drain pipe as it always did and from the hillside opposite she could hear the gentle bleating of sheep; there was something casual about the way they called to their young now, quite different from the urgent summons they had given to their newly born lambs in the spring.

On the air that drifted in through her window was a faint smell of mignonette, recognisable from its stronger evening smell. The grandfather clock on the landing wheezed, hesitated as if drawing breath and began its slow chiming of eight o'clock. The little bedside clock, shaped like a cottage, which her father had given her last year on her eighth birthday and which her mother had condemned as frivolous, was already ten minutes slow. It never kept good time, a fact which she kept from her mother's censorious eye by adjusting it every night so that her mother would never know the failings of her father's gift.

1

Nothing, she thought, looked or sounded or smelled any different from yesterday morning or the morning before yesterday, or before that. Then suddenly she realised what it was – the missing sound. She hadn't heard the swooshing noise which the sliding door of the kitchen cabinet made when her mother opened it to take out cups and saucers for breakfast. Nor, come to think of it, had she heard the juddering of water in the pipes when her mother turned on the kitchen tap to fill the kettle. These sounds always preceded the striking of the grandfather clock on the landing. But today there had been only silence.

Alarmed, though she didn't know why, she got out of bed. The lino was cold against her bare feet, but she didn't stop to put on her slippers and went quickly to the top of the stairs. There she paused. Nothing stirred in the house. She crept quietly downstairs and into the kitchen, not wanting to disturb the silence. Everything there looked exactly as it had done the night before: the washing-up bowl upside down in the sink, the cover lowered on the cooker, everything wiped and cleared away; no sign of preparations for a new day, just the closing down of the old one.

The door into the sitting-room was open. As she paused in the doorway a trickle of soot fell down the chimney on to the newspaper in the hearth, sounding so unnaturally loud in the stillness of the room that she jumped and, for the first time, felt frightened. Still moving as quietly as she could, she ran upstairs and tapped on her mother's bedroom door. No sharp voice bade her enter. Feeling like an intruder, she pushed the door open. The twin bed her mother used was made. The one her father used when he came at weekends was likewise untouched.

She wandered aimlessly around the room. She made herself look under the bed. If someone had murdered her mother they might have hidden the body there, but all she saw was the trunk where blankets were stored in the summer.

The house seemed suddenly big and empty and she wanted to get out of it. She dressed quickly, not stopping to wash or to clean her teeth. But she did stop to make her bed, knowing the trouble she'd be in if her mother found it unmade. She'd been in trouble recently for not helping more in the house. 'You're no help to me,' her mother had said. 'You might as well have been a boy for all the consideration you've ever shown.' So she made her bed and then wiped her handkerchief across the top of the chest of drawers in a gesture towards domesticity.

There were two ways to get out of the house; she chose the back door first, turning the key easily, but the bolt was too high. She dragged a chair across the kitchen. Standing on it on tiptoe she could just reach the bolt, a big iron thing, rusty and unyielding, at which she pulled and tugged in vain. She just couldn't get enough leverage behind her fingers. Tears of frustration filled her eyes as she clambered down and made for the hall.

The front door was locked. Her mother must have locked it behind her, but the spare key hung on a nail next to the door. Of course, she should have tried that first, Judith realised as she unhooked it and put it into the lock. It turned halfway and then stopped. The door remained closed. She tried again but the key refused to turn. Again and again she tried but each time the key half turned and then slipped back in her fingers. Tears prickled her eyes again. "I'm not crying," she said aloud. "I'm just cross."

She heard footsteps on the gravel drive. It must be the postman. She would call to him, to Tommy the postman. There were no windows in the hall. Quickly, she ran into the dining-room, whose windows overlooked the drive. It wasn't Tommy; it was the vicar's wife, delivering the parish magazine. She had stacks of them in a basket on her arm. In the time it had taken Judith to run into the dining-room, the vicar's wife had pushed the magazine through the letter-box and started back up the drive. She had her back to the house.

"Please God, let her turn round," Judith prayed.

But the vicar's wife kept her back to the house and moreover was singing loudly so didn't hear Judith banging on the window. Although a timid little lady, much in awe not only of her husband but also of most of the parishioners, Mrs Trott had a surprisingly powerful contralto voice; when she sang she outdid any competition. Judith knew this and could only pray.

God intervened in the form of a pigeon. The dawn chorus

over, a large breakfast consumed, it flew over the garden, swooped and deposited a creamy white splodge on Mrs Trott's dark hair. The vicar's wife turned, looking round to see where it had come from. Judith saw her lips open and close briefly to form what looked like an unholy word. In doing so she glimpsed a child at the window.

She waved. The child did not wave back. It beckoned, there was no mistaking the anxiety of the gesture. The child looked as if it might be crying. Mrs Trott, anxious though she was to deliver all the magazines by coffee time, turned back to the house.

They mouthed at each other through the window, Judith and Mrs Trott. It was hard to make sense of these mouthings through the glass. It was Judith who pointed to her right, suggesting that communication might be easier through the letter-box in the front door. Now that she was no longer alone, she ceased to be frightened. Talking through the letter-box was an adventure. Pyramus and Thingummy, she thought.

"Is your mother in, dear?"

"No."

"Where is she then?"

"I don't know. Not here. I have the key," she explained, "but I can't make it turn."

"Oh, dear. And I can't get in to help you."

"I could take the key out and push it at you through the letter-box. Then you could open the door from outside."

"What a good idea. Such a clever girl, you are. I'd never have thought of that," Mrs Trott enthused through the letter-box.

She turned the key easily. Once outside the house, Judith stood, not sure what to do next, except that she mustn't let Mrs Trott think she'd been scared.

"It wouldn't have mattered, being locked in, I mean," she informed her casually, "but of course I have to get to school."

"It's Saturday."

Judith's newfound confidence vanished. Mrs Trott might be a bit slow on the uptake, but at least she knew the days of the week, which was more than she herself had done. Then she thought of something.

"Saturday," she repeated. "Daddy will be here."

"What time does he come?"

"At eleven, usually. Sometimes I go up to the lane end to meet him."

"Well, now, let me see. The best thing is for you to come back to the vicarage with me. Yes, that's it, that's for the best. And of course we'll close this door and then I'll put a note through the letter-box for your father telling him you're safe with me at the vicarage."

Safe! Had she been in danger? The idea appealed to her so much that she had a sudden urge to be helpful.

"I can help you deliver the magazines," she volunteered, nodding towards the basket. "He won't be here for ages yet."

So they went on the rounds together, Mrs Trott either chattering in her haphazard way or singing snatches of hymns. Judith marvelled at the way the conversational voice was so hesitant, hard to make out with its sudden drops into a semi-whisper, often gabbling and inconsequential, and yet the singing voice was so full-throated and confident. Her father had once said that some actors were like this, shy in themselves, confident only in their roles. But Mrs Trott wasn't an actress. She put the idea to one side, ready to ask him about it.

The thought of her father filled her with joy. She began to skip and joined in the singing.

> *All things bright and beautiful*
> *All creatures great and small,*
> *All things wise and wonderful*
> *The Lord God made them all.*

So pronounced Mrs Trott in her rich contralto voice as they walked up the vicarage drive, and Judith sang happily along with her.

"Nearly all done now, with your help, dear," Mrs Trott said an hour later as they approached the Newboulds' house. "Of course the outlying farms are always a problem, but I shall pop along to

5

the whist drive in the village hall tonight and maybe find some of them there."

She was relieved to notice that the child had got over her initial fright at being left alone in the house by that mother of hers – not, of course, she corrected herself hastily, that she should ever be critical of Mrs Delaney, who was such a pillar of the church, such a one for doing her duty in the parish, such a support to the vicar (more of a helpmeet to him, she sometimes feared, than she was herself), but all the same she couldn't help contrasting that dutiful concern for others with the severity with which Mrs Delaney treated her own daughter; the hardness of her eye, the coldness of her voice when she spoke to the little girl. Mrs Trott had no children of her own, but despite that, or perhaps because of it, she felt deeply for the children of others.

"Well, now, would you believe," she remarked suddenly. "There's Mr Dowerthwaite from Sloughbottom Farm. I can give their magazine to him."

She crossed the road and accosted the farmer, which Judith thought very brave, because she was so small and mousy and the farmer was huge and didn't even pretend to look pleased to see her.

"If you don't mind, Mr Dowerthwaite," she was saying, holding out the magazine like a peace offering. "Perhaps you could be so kind as to take the magazine and save me a journey up to the farm? I'm sure Mrs Dowerthwaite will want to read it."

"I'll tek it," he said grimly. "And mebbee her'll read it."

"Dour by name and dour by nature," Mrs Trott remarked after he had gone. "But there, I shouldn't have said that."

"Why not?"

"Well," Mrs Trott floundered. "It wasn't a very charitable thing to say, was it? I mean, I'm sure he's a very good man and they say he isn't in the best of health. Farmers have so many problems," she concluded vaguely.

Judith stared after him. Funny that such a grumpy man should be Alice's father. Alice was three years younger than she was, three forms below her at school. She was little and pretty and still in the Infants' Class. Last year Miss Markham had

6

suggested that Judith should play with her, as part of a scheme to get the big girls to help with the little ones. She'd loved that; it was like being given a readymade younger sister. She'd helped Alice with her sums and protected her from the teasing of her contemporaries who were all much bigger and inclined to push her about.

Then one afternoon there'd been some sort of muddle and nobody had come to collect Alice from school. Judith had hung around as Miss Markham and her assistant conferred anxiously over Alice's head, saying what a pity it was that this had to happen on the one day that they should both be at a teachers' meeting in Pendlebury.

"She can come home with me," she'd volunteered and instantly regretted it, not knowing what her mother would have to say, but by the time she'd thought of that, her offer had been accepted.

"You're late. What have you been up to?" her mother had greeted her sharply. Then, seeing Miss Markham and Alice on the doorstep behind her daughter, her voice had softened and she invited them in.

There followed explanations about how Alice would be picked up later by her two elder brothers when they came in from Pendlebury. There was much gratitude expressed by Miss Markham, and Judith's mother said it was her pleasure as well as her duty to help them, and pointed out that we have all been put into this world for the sole purpose of helping each other.

It was a proposition which Judith never understood. If everyone was to help everyone else, surely it would all cancel out and you might just as well help yourself, which would be simpler because you'd know better than anyone else exactly what you wanted. But she knew better than to say this, especially at a time when her mother was busy getting them a special tea with dropped scones and sponge cake.

Afterwards, they went up to play in Judith's room and it was there that Alice, looking in bewilderment at all the books in the bedroom, suddenly said, "I'm the only one left in the top of the Infants who still can't read," and her eyes filled with tears.

Judith had been astonished by this revelation. Alice had done sums all right and surely reading was easier than sums?

"I'll show you how," she said confidently, as she put away the jigsaw and got out her own early reading books instead.

So they sat together on the bed with the books and by the time her brothers came to collect her, Alice was reading out the sentences, very slowly but quite correctly. At the time it had struck Judith as being perfectly natural, but now she did sometimes think it had been rather strange.

She'd expected Alice to rush up to her brothers when they arrived and tell them all about her new skill, but hardly a word was spoken as the three of them went off together into the night.

They were big, gloomy and rather frightening, those brothers of Alice. Derrick and Samson, the two who had collected her that evening, went to the big school in Pendlebury, but the eldest one had already left school to work on the farm with his father, who was even gloomier than his sons.

Poor Alice, Judith thought now, as she watched Mr Dowerthwaite trudge along the village street, head down and the parish magazine screwed up in his hand, poor Alice to have a grumpy father like that. Apart from anything else he was *old*. He wasn't a proper father like hers, who talked and laughed and wasn't old at all.

Two

"Can I go up to the road end to meet my father?" she asked when they had finished their morning cocoa.

"Does you mother let you?" Mrs Trott enquired anxiously.

Sometimes her mother did, sometimes she refused.

"Yes," Judith said, crossing her fingers and adding "sometimes" under her breath, in case God was listening.

The road wound in a leisurely way out of the village between high, dry-stone walls until it joined the main road up to the Lakes. She knew every corner of it, every bend, every grass verge. Her favourite house along the route was a cottage with a stream at the bottom of its long garden which ran alongside the road. It was overgrown and full of secret places and she thought it the most wonderful garden in the world. Her friend Susan had lived here and they had played for hours by that stream, imagining it to be a great river, but it was quite small really, narrow enough to jump across. If you didn't feel like jumping you could walk across a little slate bridge, which was warm to sit on in the summer and just the right height for dipping your feet into the water if you stretched your legs. But they'd gone away, Susan and her family, and an elderly couple now owned the garden and the stream and the little bridge. She hadn't been in the garden since, but as she walked along the road she could hear the water chattering over the pebbles as it had always done. Heartless, really.

That was the last house out of the village. After that there were just fields. The walls were lower here and she could see the sheep and lambs. The lambs seemed bigger now than their mothers, who had just been sheared and looked quite skinny and frail,

9

especially when their woolly offspring pushed up at them to feed, shoving and thumping and not at all like their younger selves who were all skittle legs and long, agitated tails.

She heard the cars on the main road before she reached it. During the war, people said, there had been no cars at all, only convoys. But her father said that as the sixties went on there would be thousands and thousands more cars and they'd have to build bigger roads. But for the moment it was just right, she thought as she settled herself on a stile at the corner of the field where the two roads met.

She fixed her eyes, as she always did, on the cars coming along the main road; about three every minute she'd worked out – counting up to sixty and putting a pebble on the wall for each car that passed. But all the time she was watching to see if a blue car slowed down and indicated that it was turning right into the village. At last one did and she jumped off the wall, waving. The car slowed but it was an elderly man who looked back at her, shook his head, scowling in disapproval, and drove on. Ashamed, she retreated back to the stile. So that was how her father found her when, a few minutes later, he turned the corner: a disconsolate little girl in an old-fashioned dress.

"You're looking very subdued," he said, as he opened the car door for her. "Where's my usual welcome? Anything wrong?"

She didn't want to tell him about her silly mistake with the wrong car so said instead, "Mummy's gone and I'm at the vicarage."

For some reason this dismayed him, she could see that. But he seemed to recover himself quickly and said, "Oh, well, I expect she'll be back soon," and asked her about school and other things, but she could tell that he wasn't really listening to her replies.

At the vicarage, Mrs Trott was waiting.

"I'm so sorry," he told her. "My fault entirely. I'd quite forgotten that my wife might be called away. I should have come last night. We're both very grateful to you for looking after Judith, aren't we, darling?"

Prodded into gratitude, she proffered thanks, but couldn't understand why he was taking all this blame on himself.

10

"You'll stay and have a meal with us, Mr Delaney?" Mrs Trott suggested.

"No, thank you, it's very kind but there is plenty of food at the house," he said inexplicably and, taking Judith's hand, led her firmly back to the car.

"I'll just take a look at the post," he said, going upstairs.

Her mother always left the bills on the table by his bed. Following him, Judith saw that on top of the pile of brown envelopes there was a white one with just his name on, no address. He picked it up, glanced at her and put it in his pocket.

"Nothing very important," he said. "Now, how about your being in charge of lunch? We could have it outside. It's a lovely day."

She thrilled at the words. The house felt so different now that he was in it, suddenly everything was warm and friendly and exciting and, best of all, he had put her in charge of this meal, just like a grown-up. She ran around the kitchen opening drawers, sliding cupboard doors back and forth, peering into the metal meat safe, surveying the marble slab in the larder. She found eggs and cheese and bread. This was better than playing houses with dolls. She carried two kitchen chairs outside, placed them on either side of the little table. She found a table-cloth. It was far too big and trailed on the grass, but it was pretty with red and white squares. She set out knives and forks, though she didn't quite know what they'd be eating, and side plates and two tumblers. She found a jam jar, filled it with marigolds and put it in the middle of the table. Then she went to find her father.

He was standing in the sitting-room, the letter in his hand. Lost in thought, he didn't see her. But she could see his face very clearly as he stood by the window and she stood in the shadow of the doorway. He was frowning and looked older than usual, and worried. She couldn't think why or what she had done wrong. She'd got the lunch all ready, hadn't she? But there must be something that she'd done wrong, for him to look like that.

He smiled when he saw her, put the letter in his pocket and came quickly across the room.

"How's the picnic going?" he asked, taking her hand. But he

11

spoke too cheerfully, as if he was trying not to think of something else. Why was he being so jolly?

"It's all ready," she said, leading him out into the garden and it all looked so good, the pretty cloth, the marigolds, and so correct with the bread on the bread board, the cheese on the cheese board, the butter in the butter dish, perhaps the lettuce and tomatoes not quite right in the roasting pan, but she hadn't been able to reach the glass bowl. She beamed up at him and he looked down at her and smiled a proper smile.

"Well done," he said. "What a feast! Oh, we shall manage, shan't we?"

"Of course," she said, handing him the butter.

"You're a practical person, like your mother," he said. "That's good."

She shook her head wondering why, if she was really like her mother, her mother didn't like her more.

He made his own coffee, though she knew she could have managed the kettle, then he sat back in his chair looking at her.

"We're going to have to make plans, little one," he said.

"Yes," she agreed, happy to be included in any plan-making.

"It is possible, you see, that your mother might not come back."

He seemed to think that she would be upset by this news so she tried to look sad, though at that moment she was blissfully happy, sitting quietly in the garden with him, having this grown-up conversation.

"It isn't that she didn't love you," he was saying. "You mustn't think that she went away because she didn't care about you."

Again she shook her head, not replying. There couldn't possibly be any other reason why her mother should have left. She'd often said that looking after Judith took up too much of her time. Why else should she have gone?

"She wasn't leaving *you* exactly," her father was explaining. "Really it was me she was leaving and—"

"But you weren't here much," she objected. "I was here all the time."

"Well, I don't mean just my presence, but being married to me. I think she wanted to get away from the whole situation."

Judith gazed down the garden; from her vantage point up here at the little wooden table with the red-checked cloth, she thought the situation looked pretty good. There was plenty of long grass, lots of poppies and an old apple tree in the corner. On the other side of the dry-stone wall was Mr Norman's nursery field where the sheep were brought down at lambing time. Last year there had been calves too. She couldn't imagine a better situation, nor why anyone should want to leave it. Her father must be wrong; it could only be because of her that her mother had decided to leave.

They sat quietly for a while, her father evidently trying to say something difficult.

"She says in her letter that she wishes to go and work among needy people, people she can help, possibly children abroad," he said at last.

That really did surprise her. She'd thought her mother had gone away to somewhere like Pendlebury. She wasn't sure where abroad was, but knew it was a lot further away than that.

"She's been in touch with an educational mission," her father went on, nodding towards the letter which he now held in his hand. "She mentions that she might help in an orphanage in Africa." He looked at her uneasily. "I can see that it might seem rather strange to you, I mean, that she should look after other children."

It didn't seem strange. She had often observed that her mother dealt more gently with other children. At Sunday School she never used the sharp voice she used at home. She seemed to like them; even if they did things wrong she didn't get cross, whereas at home she got angry even if Judith did things right. Just by being there, she seemed to annoy her mother.

She had never thought about it properly before, but she did now and understood why her mother might prefer to go and work with other children.

"What I really do want you to understand, Judith, is that she has gone out of a sense of duty to these children, not because she doesn't love you—"

13

"But because she loves them more," she put in cheerfully, trying to help.

Her father shook his head, said nothing for a while and then, "She writes here," he said, "that she feels she has a duty, an obligation – a calling, I suppose – to do this work out of consideration for those more unfortunate than ourselves—"

"Like the dustbin men."

He looked puzzled, but she said no more. It was too difficult to explain about the broken vase, though she remembered it vividly. She'd been in the hall; through the open door she had seen her mother at the kitchen sink, washing this glass vase, the special cut-glass one. As she stood there, she saw her mother lift it out, let it slip, saw it smash on the floor.

She had gasped in horror. Her mother had heard her, turned, and, as she looked at her daughter standing there in the doorway, her brown eyes had narrowed with anger.

'Now look what you've made me do!' she'd said.

There was cold accusation in the voice. Judith had stood speechless, knowing that the vase had fallen before she appeared, remembering exactly how it had slithered through the soapy fingers of the yellow rubber gloves. It wasn't fair to blame her, but still she felt guilty, overawed by the power of her mother's wrath.

'And you don't even apologise, just standing there like a stupid thing.'

'Sorry,' she had muttered.

She had gone on standing there all the same, watching as her mother with short angry movements wrapped the broken glass in newspaper and tied the bundle up with a piece of string, like a parcel. 'I do this,' she had said 'out of consideration for the unfortunate dustbin men who might otherwise cut themselves. I hope you will one day learn similar consideration.'

So she knew about her mother and consideration.

"Would you mind very much leaving here, leaving Netherby, I mean?" her father asked after a while. "Perhaps living in a town? Would you miss all this?" he added, gesturing vaguely at the garden and the countryside beyond.

She shut her eyes, trying to imagine what it would be like to live away from these fields and hills, not going down to the beck to play, not hearing the sheep. That was altogether a sadder prospect than being motherless.

"But I'd be with you, wouldn't I?"

"Of course, my darling."

"Then that's all right."

He seemed taken aback by her response, relieved even. For some reason which she didn't understand, it seemed that she had done well in this business of making plans.

"Luckily it's nearly the end of term and you'd have been changing schools next year anyway, so it's a good time to make a break."

She hadn't thought of that, of leaving school.

"We'll go and see Miss Markham this evening. Do you know where she lives?"

Of course she knew where the headmistress lived.

"In the first house in the row next to The Curlew," she told him.

They sent her out to play in Miss Markham's small back garden while they talked. It wasn't much of a garden, more a courtyard really, with flowers in wooden tubs and a patch of smelly vegetation which Miss Markham called her herb garden.

She could hear their voices droning through the open window but couldn't make out the words. At some point Miss Markham must have gone down to the school, which was just round the corner, because when they called Judith back into the house all her school exercise books were on the table.

Miss Markham explained that she would write a letter to Judith's new teacher and said she'd be sorry to lose such a good pupil. Then she gave a glass of sweet sherry to her father and a tumbler of Tizer to Judith. Now that the business of books and schools was settled nobody seemed to know what to say. Her father refused a second glass of the sweet sherry but Judith accepted another tumblerful of Tizer and then wished she hadn't because she tried to drink it so quickly that she gave herself hiccups. This made her feel silly and childish and that she had in some obscure way let her father down.

At last the wretched drink was finished and her father got up to go.

"We shall miss you at school, Judith," Miss Markham said as they stood in the hall.

She tried to think of a polite and grown-up reply but couldn't find the right words. The only person she would really miss was little Alice who would be looking out for her next week and would now have nobody to help her with her reading. But she couldn't bring herself to say this, so just stood in embarrassed silence at her father's side. He came to her rescue, putting his arm around her shoulders and thanking Miss Markham on her behalf.

They all shook hands and then, still hiccuping gently, she walked hand-in-hand with her father down the village street and back to the empty house.

Three

"I'll take our Alice down in the trap," Hilda Dowerthwaite told her sons on the first day of the autumn term. "I've groceries to fetch. Derrick, you help Edmund with the walling and Samson can get on with ploughing the bracken."

Since her husband's illness, Hilda Dowerthwaite had ruled the family. She looked older than her years, for her face was severe, heavy-jawed and she rarely had cause to smile. Her iron-grey hair was drawn back and pinioned in a tight little bun. As if in anticipation of widowhood, she always dressed in black, as her mother had done. Over her long thick skirt she wore a coarse hessian apron, which she now removed and hung behind the scullery door in deference to visiting Alice's school.

Alice sat quietly beside her in the trap enjoying the gentle morning breeze, warm against her cheeks, happy to think that soon she would see Judith again. She'd see more of her now that she was going up into the Juniors. There'd been a time when she'd been scared they would keep her down in the Infants because she couldn't read. She could still remember how awful it had been, how she had struggled to learn all those letters, and had managed to do so, but somehow couldn't make sense of them when they were all strung together in books. She wasn't used to books, they were strange things to her. There weren't any on the farm apart from the cash book, a forbidding dark red volume, which was kept in a drawer in the parlour except when her mother took it out, set it down on the kitchen table and, grim-faced, entered figures into it.

It was only when she'd seen all those story books in Judith's room that she'd understood the point of it all, realised that it wasn't just some strange exercise carried out in school; suddenly everything she'd been taught came together and made sense. It had been a marvellous feeling, the secret that she'd carried home with her that night, fearful only lest she might forget how to do it when tomorrow came. But she hadn't forgotten and every day it was easier to read aloud to Judith or to her surprised but gratified teacher.

She often wished she had an older sister like Judith, though Judith did seem to have a funny sort of family, with her father only home at weekends. Once Judith had shown her a book called *The Wind in the Willows* which, she said, her father used to read to her. It struck Alice as being a very odd thing for a father to do.

The schoolyard was noisy with Juniors playing hopscotch and chasing each other; they all looked very big to Alice who took her mother's hand tightly in hers. Hilda Dowerthwaite made as if to withdraw it, then hesitated and said, "I'll come in with you," and got down from the trap.

Knowing that the Dowerthwaite children either made their own way down the two miles of track and lane from the farm, or were dropped off and left at the school gate, Miss Markham was surprised to see her. Dowerthwaite adults never came in for a chat as other parents did. It had worried her when she first came to the village, but the unsociable ways of the Dowerthwaite clan were soon explained to her. Evidently the Dowerthwaites went neither to church nor chapel except for such necessities as funerals. Dowerthwaite women did not join the Mothers' Union or support the Women's Institute. Not for them the weekly outings to the village dance or whist drive. Apparently no Dowerthwaites had been seen even at the celebrations to mark the end of the war when the rest of the neighbourhood had dragged trees and anything else combustible up to the top of Westerbirt to light the great victory beacon.

So Miss Markham was pleased to see Hilda Dowerthwaite accompanying her little daughter into the school playground and went into the porch to greet them.

"Welcome to the Juniors," she said, taking Alice's other hand.

"She'll be walking down with her brothers after tomorrow, when their school starts," Hilda explained.

"It's a long walk for a little girl."

"She's accustomed," Hilda told her, releasing her daughter's hand and turning to go.

"Come along in, Alice," Miss Markham said. "I'm afraid you'll miss your friend Judith."

Alice stared.

"She had to leave rather suddenly – for family reasons."

Disbelief. Panic. Alice turned towards her mother, but Hilda Dowerthwaite was already getting into the trap.

Since the Dowerthwaites never discussed anything – it was not their custom – Alice had learned early the way of acceptance, so she didn't question Miss Markham about where or why Judith had gone, nor did she tell her family of her grief. She tried hard at school, but never did well except in craftwork.

"Alice's are best of all," Miss Markham declared at the end of term, holding up a length of paperchain.

It was true: splodges of glue, creases and uneven joins characterised the gaudy links made by other children; only hers were uniformly smooth, neat and spotless. She didn't know why it was; things just seemed to fall into place in her hands. She didn't think much of it; being good with your fingers was all very well, but being good with your brain was what really mattered.

She was lucky that that winter, and in the two that followed, the snow came early and lay a long time, which meant that she couldn't go to school – the snow plough which swept through the village street didn't venture up the dale. So she stayed at home, doing a few lessons at the kitchen table but mostly helping her mother with the baking, ironing and mending. The real joy of being snowed up was that she was free to do all the domestic tasks she enjoyed instead of the school lessons which she didn't. The farm seemed like a refuge, cut off from the world, warm with the smell of paraffin stoves and tucked up under its insulating blanket of snow.

But best of all was when her mother said, "Get yourself dressed up warm and you can go out now," and she was free to go and explore this new white world outdoors. The ridges in the farm track felt rock hard under her feet and the ruts between them full of ice which crunched and crackled as she walked. Once off the track, she used to stop and gaze about her, awestruck that the world could be so different; she would try to walk quietly and not disturb the peace of it, for the silence was intense as she made her way down to the beck, across what had once been green and bumpy fields and which was now a great expanse of snow, smooth and white as newly ironed linen sheets. She loved the orderliness the snow imposed, the tidiness of it all.

One of the streams that joined the beck, flowing under a little slate bridge, was always the first to ice over. Beneath its frozen surface the leaves of water plants drifted like ribbons in the current while long strands of moss moved gently in the water, reminding her of the silken threads in her sewing box. Icicles always hung from under the bridge; later they grew big and fat but at first were slender little things no bigger than darning needles.

She used to dread the first signs of a thaw: the tiny dark holes, no bigger than pin pricks, which began to mar the smooth perfection of the snow, the gradual softening and dimpling of its face, the little spikes of grass appearing, then whole blades breaking through with all the little giveaway sounds of the thaw. She watched miserably as the magic world melted and crumbled in front of her while she could only look on helplessly, though she did of course pray for another snowfall and more frosts. She knew better than to say anything of this to her father or brothers, for whom the snow was an accursed thing and the thaw a welcome relief.

Judith had loved the snow too, she sometimes remembered, though the memory of her friend faded as the years passed. The Judith who had once been a familiar part of her life had gone away and belonged to a different world now, leaving only odd memories, warm and comforting, of someone she would have liked to have as a sister and who was good at explaining things.

20

One of those memories was of standing together in the school porch watching the snow swirl down in an unexpected flurry; Judith had said that if it lasted and the lane was cut off, Alice would have to come home with her and sleep at her house. But it hadn't lasted, it had stayed only long enough for them to make a little snowman in the playground, with pieces of coal for eyes.

Such frivolities were not indulged in at Sloughbottom Farm, so this was the first snowman Alice had ever made and she loved him. But by the next morning he had melted away, leaving just a little heap of snow and two pieces of coal to mark the place where he had been.

Four

W hen her father had talked about her going away to school, Judith hadn't understood that it meant boarding school. She'd thought it just meant going away from Netherby to school and living with her father somewhere or other and going to school each day. She was dismayed when she realised the truth and he was dismayed that she was dismayed.

"I'm sorry, pet. I thought you understood. You see, I can't look after you properly here, in college. And sometimes I have to be away lecturing. You need someone to look after you all the time. You need women around you too. I'm sorry. I should have explained better."

He shouldn't be sorry. It wasn't his fault. If she'd been more grown-up she'd have understood in the first place.

"Oh, yes, well, of course," she said now. "I do understand all that. It's quite all right."

"And of course we'll be together in the holidays. If you like we can rent somewhere in Netherby and go up there and you'll be back in your old haunts. St Mary's is a very good school."

She spent the first term longing for the holidays. She hated everything about the school; there were always so many people around, you were never alone and it was noisy with bells and the sound of feet rushing along corridors. But most of all she disliked the flatness of the surrounding countryside. There were all these houses and streets where they had to go for walks when it was too wet for games in the afternoon. It rained a lot that first term, and as she walked miserably along the wet streets she thought of the fields and hills of Netherby, missed the sight and sounds and smells of it and was filled with a dull aching feeling. Afterwards

23

she realised that it was as well they didn't allow people to go home at weekends. If she'd been able to escape so soon, nothing and nobody – not even her father – would have made her go back.

The only consolation was getting such wonderfully long letters from him, which she hid away until she could read them alone, usually in the lavatory. He wrote several times a week, but she only replied on Sunday when they had an hour for letter-writing. She told him everything about school – except that she hated it.

It was never again as bad as that first term. Gradually she got used to being always in a crowd, never alone in classroom or dormitory. Being miserable, she worked hard and did well. If the others thought her a swot, she didn't care. She consoled herself with work and with reading. She found she could escape into a book and, living in its world, forget the misery of her own. The school library had all the classics; she read her way through Dickens, George Eliot, the Brontës, Jane Austen and many others beside. As she read, the characters became more important to her than the people around her, and the world they inhabited more real than that of school. She missed the people in the books so much that often when she'd finished the last chaper she went straight back to the beginning and started again in order to stay with them. Yet, familiar though she was with the plots, she always hoped that things would turn out differently: that Maggie Tulliver wouldn't drown, that Smike would get well, that Emily would marry Ham and live happily ever after, that Little Nell would recover or – failing that – not take quite so long to die.

Her father kept his promise; in the holidays they went up to Netherby to a rented cottage which, after a few years, was always reserved for them. There were few changes in Netherby; the Trotts left the vicarage to be replaced by a young man who upset everyone by introducing a newfangled service, which induced the older members of the congregation to take their custom elsewhere. The village blacksmith installed a pump outside the smithy and often broke off shoeing a horse in order to fill up a car with petrol. Not long after that men came and painted yellow lines along the high street and around the green because, as her father had predicted, there were many more cars on the roads, even in Netherby.

She used to break up sooner than the children in the village. Sometimes, when she was already on holiday, she saw Alice Dowerthwaite waiting for the school bus into Pendlebury, for she was at the big school now. They talked, but weren't quite at ease with each other as they had once been, as if in growing up they had grown apart. But they were still pleased to see each other, still shared memories: remembered the day Alice had come home with her when nobody had collected her from school; talked about Miss Markham, remembered making the snowman.

She'd have liked to ask Alice to come to the cottage, go for a walk with her, but now that she was older she knew that it wasn't the Dowerthwaite way of doing things and didn't want to embarrass her or get her into trouble. She saw that Alice was young for her years. Always slightly built, she was still quite small, unlike Judith herself who was five foot seven inches by the time she was fourteen. She knew she was, because she was weighed and measured, like everyone else at St Mary's, at the beginning and end of every term.

Her father always brought piles of books and papers to Netherby and worked on them in the little front parlour. Often when she went off by herself down to the beck or to walk on the hills, she wished Alice could have come with her, though sometimes, on very special days, her father abandoned work and they went off together for the day, taking a picnic lunch and in the evening concocting some kind of a meal in the cottage kitchen.

Neither of them was much good at cooking; after a particular disaster in which macaroni cheese turned into an inedible mucilaginous mess, she bought a collection of supposedly easy recipes for a healthy diet. But he was dismissive. "Mark Twain said never mind about diet, just eat what you fancy and let the food fight it out inside you," he told her.

"And there's always The Curlew," she suggested.

She loved going out to a meal with him, felt very grown-up as he pulled out her chair for her and handed her the menu. She was often puzzled at the way other couples ate in semi-silence; her father and she chatted non-stop. Whether they were walking on the hills, eating at the pub, cooking at home or just sitting by the fire, they talked of everything – except her mother. She was never mentioned; it was as if she had never been.

Gradually, she had more and more school work to do in the holidays. Usually she studied in her bedroom but, if it was cold, her father lit a fire in the cottage parlour and moved her table downstairs so that they could work together in the same room. She loved this arrangement. One day, she thought, when she'd finished with all this education, they would have a house together and live like this; only it would be permanent, their own home, for ever.

Her father had been right about St Mary's, she realised as the years passed, it *was* a good school. The elderly Miss Murray was a headmistress in the tradition of Miss Beale and Miss Buss: discipline was strict, slacking not tolerated, *excellence* the word most often on her lips.

"Excellent," she said to Judith as they discussed what subjects she should specialise in. "Excellent choices for an arts person: History, English and Latin. Plenty of time to decide which you will study at the university. Have you any idea about your career? I think you would make an excellent teacher. Of course, it must be your own free choice. And it's very early days to make a decision about that."

"But I have decided," Judith told her. "I want to read law."

Miss Murray was taken aback. Clearly she didn't approve. She wanted Judith to make her own free choice, but she also wanted that free choice to coincide with her own.

"I am told there will soon be too many lawyers," she demurred. "And while I can understand your wish to follow in your father's footsteps, I don't advise our girls to read law. Certainly nobody from St Mary's ever has."

"Then I shall be the first," Judith told her.

Miss Murray, who often lectured her girls on the need to be trail-blazers, didn't argue, but her disapproval was no less apparent for being unspoken.

Judith was less confident than she had sounded; she knew how her father valued the opinions of Miss Murray, who was, after all, the expert on girls' education. But she needn't have worried; he was on her side, as she should have known he would be.

"Of course there are plenty of girls going in for the law now," he said. "I'm afraid she's just a bit out of date. Have you any idea which branch of the law?"

"No."

"Plenty of time to decide that. The first stage is to get you to the university."

Miss Murray was magnanimous; once she saw that Judith had made up her mind to read law, she did everything to help her. When she won her university place, Miss Murray was the first to congratulate her.

"Well done," she said. "You'll be the first of many, I hope. You must ring your parents straight away."

It was one of her rare *faux pas*. Quickly she added, "Your father will be delighted for you."

Judith noticed the momentary embarrassment. Nice to think the Head was human and made mistakes like an ordinary mortal. She would have liked to reassure poor Miss Murray that she really didn't mind about not having a mother because, apart from anything else, her mother hadn't approved of girls having careers. Women, she had always said, should be homemakers. Which was odd considering that the home she herself had made was such a cheerless place and one which she had ultimately abandoned without, apparently, a backward glance.

Five

"Book us a week in the cottage in September," Judith instructed her father over the phone from Delhi. "It's ages since we've been back to Netherby."

"Whose fault's that? You're the one who's been backpacking around the world every long vacation."

She laughed. "Don't argue, just do it."

"I shall be knee-deep in lecture notes in September," he objected.

"Take it all to Netherby. You can just as well work up there. I don't mind going for walks by myself."

So, on that first day, she walked alone up to the dalehead, pausing now and then to look back on the way she'd come. She'd seen more spectacular views, she thought, in Europe, in India and Egypt, but none of them could ever move her as this landscape did; this land which still felt like home. Below her lay the little hills and valleys which surrounded the village, a gentle landscape of green fields divided by grey walls. Ahead of her the countryside was wilder, less marked by man, though even here the dry-stone walls clambered up mountains and clung to the sides of cliffs.

She could see the Dowerthwaites' farm in the distance, down to her right. She was alongside their copse now, a curious little walled wood, just below the farm, artificially created in this treeless landscape.

Sloughbottom Farm had none of the sunny openness of the other Dales farms which seemed, in fair weather or foul, to be happily at one with the green and grey hillsides. It lay in perpetual shade in a north-facing hollow, its approach muddy and unwelcoming. The Dowerthwaites were, of course, similarly inhospitable and, much though she wanted to see Alice again, she knew it would be unthinkable to call on them. She had glimpsed Hilda Dowerthwaite in the village as they arrived yesterday; solid and unyielding in her habitual severe black, she looked exactly as Judith remembered her twelve years ago when she sometimes came down to collect Alice from school. The unchanging and unchangeable mother.

Hilda Dowerthwaite's three sons, so everyone in the village said, worked ceaselessly, their parents not believing in labour-saving farm machinery. 'Why have it, when we've got our lads?' they would demand, as if machinery was an indignity that only the childless were reduced to. So the boys toiled and, if they cursed, it was under their breath.

The puzzling thing about the Dowerthwaites, Judith thought once again as she approached the spot where the track to their farm joined the lane, was Alice. It still puzzled her that this fair, slightly built girl, with her cheerful face and shy but open manner, could belong to such a family. How did this dainty petite creature come out of the dark and gloomy Dowerthwaite stock? With a mother like that, with brothers like that, how did she manage to seem so normal?

As she approached she saw that a cart had just turned off the track and into the lane. One of the Dowerthwaite boys was driving and Alice had jumped down to open and close the gate. Judith saw her hesitate, not sure whether to wait there until she herself drew level. Family lore decreed that she should return to her seat in the cart with no more than a curt nod, but other laws prevailed and she stood in the lane waiting until Judith caught up with her.

"Out walking then?" she asked.

"Yes, I'm going up Sawborough. My father and I are staying in the village for a week, but he has work to do. How's the farm? Has it been a good summer?"

"Oh, it was grand, was the hay harvest. We even had to take on a man to help for the first time ever. But it didn't work out," she finished abruptly, remembering that when her mother had found the labourer drunk and smoking a cigarette by the side of a haystack, she'd sacked him without notice and he'd gone off, vowing vengeance and still clutching the whisky bottle.

30

"And you're going down to the village are you, Alice?"

"Yes, I've some errands to do for Mam. Samson has to take the horse to the smithy so I've got a ride down."

Her face lit up, "Then I'm going to our Clara at the post office and she's taking me to a whist drive this evening."

"You'll enjoy that," Judith said, seeing how excited she was.

Then, hearing sounds of impatience from the cart, Alice said, "Must go," and ran off.

"City folk," Samson said in disgust, when his sister rejoined him.

"She's not city," his sister told him indignantly as she climbed back into the cart. "She was born here and was at school with me. She used to play with me even if I was just a little one and she used to help me with my sums. It was her that got me reading. I really missed her when she left."

"To go back to town where her folks all came from in t'first place," Samson said, as he rearranged some of the sacks in the cart behind him. "That's where she belongs."

"I don't think she does, not really. She loves it here. She's off now to climb Sawborough."

"There's no sense in it. Clambering about on hills for no reason."

"I'd like to climb it one day. They say you get lovely views from up there."

"Us as lives here have no cause to go looking at views. Push that other sack over, will you?"

"Samson, they're all filthy dusty," she told him, handing the sack over. "You should've given 'em to me to shake. And I'm sorry for her," she persisted, "not having a mother and all. Clara said her mam just went off and left her alone in the house when she was a mite."

"Clara's always got some tale to tell."

"No, Samson, it's true. Poor Judith, just think what she's missed, not having a family."

"They say you don't miss what you've never had."

"That's not true. Of course she'd miss having a mother, even if she didn't know what she was missing. How would we manage without our mam?"

31

Samson couldn't answer that, so she went on, "And she's still as kind as ever she was. I could see she was pleased that I'm having an outing tonight."

"I don't know why our mam let you," her brother said. He could only suppose that their mother deemed it right for Alice to meet someone to breed from. On the other hand, as the only girl in the family, shouldn't she stay home and be trained up to manage the house when their mother got too old? Probably that Clara was behind it, their second cousin once removed who kept the post office and was forever interfering. He cracked the whip and they set off along the lane down to the village.

Judith stood for a moment on the brow of the hill, watching them disappear round the corner, for the lane curved widely at this point. How pathetic, she thought, that a girl of Alice's age should be so excited at the prospect of going to a village whist drive, probably with a lot of old men and women. And not to have a career, never to travel, just to be stuck up here day after day. You'd think it was the 1870s, not the 1970s! And then to be treated so like a child. Really, in that blue-checked gingham skirt and little white blouse she looked about fourteen. Striding along in her fashionable flares, Judith felt desperately sorry for her. And the dreadful thing was that Alice didn't seem in the least rebellious; she seemed to accept her lot, to be quite satisfied with it.

It wasn't fair, she thought as she set off up the lane; all girls should have the opportunities she had had; all women should have a career and not have to depend on their menfolk. She shuddered as she thought of Alice summoned back to the cart by her oaf of a brother. If she'd been Alice, she'd have said, 'Get stuffed, I'm talking'.

But poor Alice would never say such a thing; she'd been conditioned not to. She needed someone to speak up for her. When she was qualified as a lawyer, Judith thought, she would fight for the Alices of this world; fight for their rights, whether they wanted them or not. Never having had them, they didn't know what they were missing.

32

Six

"Then there are trumps," Clara explained. "They're different for each game. They could be hearts, diamonds, spades or clubs."

Alice nodded, unsure. "The diamonds and hearts are the red ones?" she queried.

"That's right. You're cottoning on fast," Clara told her, reflecting that her own ten-year-old knew more about cards – and much else – than poor little Alice.

"And they, the trumps I mean, are stronger than the other cards?"

"Yes, but you mustn't play one unless you can't follow suit. I mean if hearts were led and you didn't have any, you could trump all the hearts to take the trick. But if you had a heart you'd have to play it."

"I see."

"But remember you're playing with a partner, not like we did when we were just practising. So if your partner's taken a trick, you mustn't go higher."

"I'm not quite sure—"

"Don't worry, love, you'll soon get the hang of it. There, there's another curtain finished for you to hem."

She pulled the material out of the machine and handed it over to Alice.

"You're ever so neat with your stitching," she said. "Mine are twice the size of yours."

"It's how they taught us at school."

"You were lucky. In my day it was called Domestic Science and we learned nothing useful. We spent hours studying how to

33

make a block knicker pattern and then we made these great bloomers – huge, mine were – big enough to cover the backside of an elephant, but somehow I couldn't sit down in them. My mam made them into dusters."

She laughed. She was a jolly, red-faced woman, with coarse features and a lot of frizzy fair hair. When she laughed, she opened her big mouth very wide and her stomach heaved and vibrated. She was naturally bossy and made all the decisions in the household, and many in the village. She had told her husband to manage the shop this afternoon while Alice came to help with the curtains, and had made up her mind that she was going to take the girl in hand and find some way of getting her down to the village more often.

"Oh, we made lots of things: pinafores, aprons, then skirts and blouses," Alice was telling her.

"Did you make what you're wearing?"

"Oh, yes, I made the blouse at school and Mam let me have a bit of material left over when I'd made the kitchen curtains last month to make the skirt."

"You might do some sewing for people in the village," Clara suggested. "Then you could earn a bit of money for yourself. Be a bit more independent like. Just simple things at first. You could come down to the village and see people in their homes—"

"Oh no, I couldn't possibly. I'm wanted at home all the time. And with our dad so often poorly . . ."

"Well, think on't," Clara suggested, realising that the time was not yet ripe. "And now we'd best get the little ones off to bed."

The two youngest, a boy and a girl, were two-year-old twins. Alice was put in charge of bathing them. She was in her element. At school they'd noticed she had an affinity with little children and had suggested she might be a nursery nurse. She'd have loved that. She'd have cared for them, played with them, sewn for them and wanted nothing else. But it could not be. She was needed at home. So she made the most of bathing the twins and telling them fairy stories until it was time to go to the whist drive with Clara.

The village hall was a great barn of a building with its own musty smell, compounded of oil stoves and dampness and the sweat of generations of dancers, card players and parish councillors. It was laid out now with twelve little tables with green baize tops, each with four chairs and a pack of cards. Since Clara was chairwoman of the village hall committee, they had come early, but soon the other players began to arrive and take their seats.

"What we do here," Clara explained to Alice, "is that the couple who win stay in their places, but the losing man moves one way and the losing lady moves the other. So you keep changing partners."

She laughed at Alice's puzzled expression and then said kindly, "Here, you sit opposite Mr Oldby as his partner and next to Mrs Peacock. They'll see you move in the right direction afterwards."

Mr Oldby, whose face was as expressionless as a dry-stone wall, stared at her and gave an almost imperceptible nod which might have been a nervous tic, but Mrs Peacock, who was a comfortable looking lady in a stiff and bumpy tweed skirt and orange jumper, smiled kindly. She had a long oval face and sheep-like look; an impression which increased when she popped a tablet in her mouth, saying, "It's for my acid stomach, you know," and proceeded to suck and chew with little rotary movements of her lower jaw.

"My start, I think," she said a little later and led a heart. Alice, still trying to sort out her cards while the other two played, saw that she had no hearts. None. She checked twice before carefully putting on one of her trumps.

She picked up the trick, as Clara had instructed, and glanced at her partner, expecting at least a glimmer of a smile. He glared.

"That was my ace you trumped," he said.

She blushed furiously.

"Never mind," the orange sheep told her, "just think of it this way; you won that trick twice over."

And she smiled and rotated her lower jaw like a Swaledale.

She had reason to smile; she took all the rest of the tricks and stayed put while Mr Oldby moved to the right and Alice to the left.

It was a baffling evening. It didn't seem to make much difference whom she had for a partner, she always lost. She was relieved when, at eight o'clock, Clara clapped her hands and announced, "Time for supper break," and led the way into a smaller room off the main hall.

On trestle tables covered with white linen sheets, an astonishing array of food was laid out. She saw neat little white triangles of egg sandwiches decorated with mustard and cress, trays of brown bread sandwiches from which thick slices of ham and tomato protruded, sausage rolls varying in shade from pale gold to dark brown piled up on thick white plates. Jam tarts, their pools of shiny red jam fringed with pastry so delicately incised that it might have been cut with pinking scissors, nestled on finer china. Then there were buttered dropped scones and sponge cakes, sprinkled with icing sugar and resting on doilies. Alice gazed at all this luxurious food, which seemed to go on and on as far as her eye could see.

"Take a plate, love," Clara prompted, "and help yourself. Then come and sit with me over there, because I doubt you'll know anyone. And I shouldn't take that Victoria sponge. It's Molly Truebody's baking and she allus uses margarine. That one'll be better," she advised, pointing. "Mary uses her own butter from the farm. And her best brown eggs too, you can tell by the colour of the cake. And I'd be wary of them big sausage rolls. The inside'll be all right but like as not the pastry's as hard as a brick. Take two plates, love, one for the sweet and one for the savoury."

So, holding her two laden plates, she followed Clara to the little group of women at the end of the room. She knew some of them vaguely by sight, all big comfortable women with floral aprons over their cotton dresses, wide-hipped and motherly. They welcomed her and then got on with their gossiping while she listened, interested but puzzled, for she was used only to the silent meals of Sloughbottom farm.

Clara, having seen that she had a chair, remarked, "I've warned her about Sally Wiggins' pastry; you can break your teeth on it."

"I broke my dental plate biting on her fruit cake last Christmas," one of the women said. "She'd left a date stone in it, would you believe that? I had to go into Braxton to the dentist."

"You know they've got a woman dentist there now?"

"Aye, it's Jane Prout's daughter, from over Highton way."

"I wouldn't go to a woman dentist. They don't have the strength. It's a man's job, is dentisting."

"And the Prout girl's only a wee bit of a thing with no meat on her."

"It takes strength to pull teeth. My old dad was a grand one at it."

"Oh, the Prout lass'd be no good for pulling teeth. She'd be all right for stuffing them, like as not."

"I don't know what her mam's thinking of, letting her go poking around in strange mouths."

"And what about when she gets married and has babies? You can't just go off and do all that drilling and suchlike when you've a baby to feed."

"Her mother wants the sense she was born with. And stuck up, with it. I was sat next to her on the bus going to market last week and she was on about her new fitted carpets: wall-to-wall, she called it."

"They never get taken up, them carpets. Never get given a proper beating outdoors. No wonder they're all getting these newfangled diseases."

"Nobody spring-cleans like they used to. That's the trouble."

"And she'd been on one of them package holidays."

"What, at her age?"

"She said it was all right, but she'd got diarrhoea and couldn't understand the language."

"That's the trouble with abroad."

As they returned to the hall for the second part of the evening's whist, Mr Oldby was waiting for her by the door. Very stern he looked as he stood there, his face impassive except for the little nervous tic which disturbed the granite surface of his jaw, like some portent of a possible earthquake.

"Why did you play the jack of diamonds if you didn't have the king?" he asked.

She didn't know what to say. She'd played the jack because she'd liked the look of him, but had a feeling now that the truth wouldn't please Mr Oldby, so just said, "I'm sorry if it was the wrong card," and was relieved when Clara came up at that moment and asked him to give a hand with moving a trestle.

Other similar questions were asked of her during the rest of the evening's play.

'Why didn't you follow my lead with spades?' she was asked. And, 'When you led hearts I thought it must be your strong suit,' an exasperated partner remarked before moving on after they'd lost the game. It seemed that there were hidden meanings in every move and that secret conversations were carried on between partners through their cards.

But she enjoyed the evening all the same; it was strangely agreeable to be part of this little community, to be treated like a grown-up, to listen to the women's gossip. When she was awarded a pretty glass butter dish as a booby prize, she blushed with pleasure and several people clapped, though probably not those who had been her partners.

"You did all right," Clara said kindly, as she helped to fold the tables and stack the chairs. "To tell the truth, there's some as takes it a mite too serious."

She laughed suddenly and went on, "By, but I could tell where you'd been by the trail of gloomy faces you'd left behind. Never mind them, love, you'll improve with practice. There now, I think all's done. And they've made a good job of clearing the supper-room."

She glanced around the hall, sharp-eyed and proprietorial, to make sure that everything was in order.

"We'll be off then," she said, picking up the keys. "When are you going to come again?"

Alice shrugged. Probably never, she thought.

Clara observed that forlorn look.

"I'll get a message up to your mam and see what we can do," she said, turning off the last of the lights and locking the door behind them. "You're all right for walking back, are you?"

"Oh, the walk doesn't bother me, and it'll not rain."

When the lights of the hall were turned off, the village seemed to be plunged into darkness, but that was only momentary. Once her eyes accustomed themselves to the night, plenty of light came down from the sky, illuminating the narrow village street. The road looked dark but the houses were silvery grey under the moon and, as she turned up the lane, it seemed to lie ahead of her like a pale highway beckoning her on. The way was as familiar to her as the rooms of the farm. She knew exactly when she would hear the first sound of water tumbling down Boar's Syke; she knew when she was likely to hear the bleating of sheep on the other side of the wall when, alarmed by her footsteps, they called briefly to summon their lambs. She knew the sound and sight of it, and she loved the feel of the very air on her face and bare arms.

She walked quickly, happily. She'd enjoyed the evening. True, there had been that grumpy Mr Oldby, but she was used to grumpy men. She'd do better next time. Maybe Mam would let her go down to Clara if she worked really hard all week.

At the brow of the hill she paused. Ahead of her the lane wound in a great curve before it reached the point where it was joined by the track to the farm. A shorter way was to climb this stile, cut across the field and through the copse and so across the next field to join the track lower down. It wasn't always quicker of course because you couldn't walk so fast, especially at night. But no, she thought as she climbed the stile, it's light enough now.

She loved the copse, planted long ago to provide timber and fuel for the farm. It was surrounded by a low wall with a little metal gate at each end and a rough path between the trees. When she was little she used to come here and play for hours, imagining herself in a different world; for this was her own little country. Here she would find imaginary babes in the wood, hidden beneath the pile of leaves which lay deep on each side of the path, winter and summer alike.

Once her brothers had set traps here and suddenly, as she played, she'd heard a terrible screaming. A baby rabbit, caught by its leg, was trying frantically to escape, hurling its little body

39

this way and that, so that the wire cut deeper and deeper into the flesh. She struggled to free it, but her six-year-old fingers weren't strong enough. She ran back, crying, to the farm, calling for someone to come and help her. But her mother made her stay in the kitchen and sent one of her brothers who, she said, 'Would know what to do with it'.

He must have freed it, because next time she went into the copse there was no sign of the rabbit or trap. In fact no more traps were ever set, but all the same she never forgot the panic, the terror in the animal's eye or the sound of its screaming. Her own eyes would fill with tears as she remembered the little trembling, blood-stained body and the torn flesh.

The metal catch echoed sharply as she shut the gate behind her now, disturbing the stillness of the night. She stood for a moment, almost apologetic for breaking the silence. Then something rustled and shifted in the leaves by her feet, moved swiftly, lifting up a peaky little face, surrounded by a circle of spines, so that it looked for a moment as it it was wearing an old-fashioned poke bonnet. But even as she smiled down at it, the hedgehog curled itself up into a ball, a perfect sphere of prickles, with no hint of the vulnerable being within.

She had walked only a few yards along the path when another noise broke the silence, a rustling sound, and then something like a great animal fell heavily on her shoulders, as if it had dropped from the trees. She felt a hand over her mouth, a big hand, a man's hand. She bit hard into it, heard a man's voice exclaim angrily and the hand moved away for a moment and she screamed. But then the hand came back harder than ever and she felt herself being forced to the ground, felt another hand pulling now at her blouse, now at her blue-checked skirt. The little glass butter dish flew out of her grasp and she heard it smash. She hit out wildly with her fists, flailing the air, but felt her arms pulled behind her back, torn almost out of their sockets as he forced himself down on top of her, pinioning them under her. She heard the sound of tearing cloth and horror overwhelmed her as she felt a rough hand on her stomach, grabbing and tugging at her, tearing at the tender flesh between her legs.

It was no good fighting. She began to beg, "Please let me go. I won't tell anyone, if you'll just let me go. I'll say I just fell, oh please, no, no, no."

She might as well have implored the wind not to blow on the fells on a wild winter night, she might as well have screamed at the water not to cascade down Boar's Syke. This savage thing that was tearing at her, wrenching her, skewering her, was as deaf and blind and merciless as nature. She expected to die, wanted to die quickly, but when he finally flung her aside and ran off into the trees, she still lived, a bedraggled, blood-stained little creature, scarcely able to crawl out of the copse, which scrabbled at the gate and then made its way, stumbling and sobbing, across the field to the safety of the farm.

Seven

"Go out and find him," Hilda Dowerthwaite told her three sons, as they stood lined up in the scullery. "And you'll know what to do when you've got him. There's no need to trouble your father."

They moved out, silent, stony-faced.

"And put on your boots with the steel caps," she called after them.

In front of a roaring fire in the kitchen, she had prepared the big bath, filling it with hot water from the copper, adding salt, testing the heat with her elbow. Then she walked slowly across to the couch where her daughter lay, wrapped in blankets.

As she looked down at the trembling heap, pity and tenderness transformed her face. Carefully and with gentle hands she lifted the girl up and carried her over to the bath. There she sat on a chair she had put ready and cradled her in her arms, before carefully removing the blankets and lowering her gently into the water to be cleansed. Alice clung to her mother as she had never done before, holding on to the marbled flesh of that powerful arm, biting back tears, shaken every now and then by uncontrollable sobs as grief and shame and disgust overwhelmed her, worse even than the pain.

As gently as she could, the mother wiped and dabbed with soft cloths at the torn and bruised flesh, then lifted her out and wrapped her in a big towel she had warmed at the fire and dried her on her lap as she had done when she was a little girl; holding her close, trying to still her shaking. She put plasters on the worst of the scratches and bandaged the gash in the girl's back where he had pressed her down hard on to the broken dish. Then she

43

pulled a nightdress over her head and with her big work-worn hands sorted out the tangled hair, all knotted with leaves and twigs and dirt. She brushed it as best she could.

"We'll leave this to wash tomorrow," she said. "It won't do to go to bed with wet hair."

Then she gave the girl a sleeping draught, made up from an old recipe of her own mother's, and carried her up the uncarpeted stairs to the little bedroom under the eaves. She took the stone hot-water bottle out of the bed and eased her burden down between the warm sheets. Then she sat by the bed holding her child's hand until at last she slept. She waited until she was sure the sleep was sound before gently removing her hand. But still she sat by the bed unmoving, as silently she wept.

Eight

"What a wonderfully peaceful place Netherby is," her father remarked that night, putting another log on the fire, for the summer evening had turned cold. "You just can't imagine crime or any other beastliness up here."

Judith nodded, remembering the serenity of the long walk over the grey and green countryside with only the occasional bleating of sheep and distant cry of the curlew for company.

"On the other hand," she pointed out, "you'd be out of a job if there wasn't any crime."

He had read for the Bar and practised for a while, but then, for reasons Judith could never quite make out, had given it up and taken an academic post instead. She always had an uneasy feeling that perhaps he still hankered after life in court.

"It'd be a marvellous fire for making toast," she remarked, watching him as he sat by the fire, which now glowed red and flameless.

He disappeared into the kitchen and came back with slices of bread, a packet of butter and a jar of honey.

"Whatever are you doing?" she asked, laughing. "You can't be hungry after all that pub supper?"

"No, but you're right; it *is* a good fire for toasting. It's a pity to waste it."

"Idiot," she said, taking down one of the two toasting forks which hung above the hearth. "You're as bad as old Mrs Paisley next door, who washes all the blankets, even when they're clean, if it happens to be a good day for blanket washing."

"I saw her when you were out. She told me her cousin is getting a blind dog."

"So you pointed out that it was her cousin and not the dog that was blind?"

"No, I refrained."

"There should be a word for it, some grammatical term for putting the adjective in the wrong place. We could collect examples."

"Well, here's one for your collection. I saw a sign outside a garage the other day which said 'disabled toilets'."

"I can beat that. I saw 'incontinent knickers' on sale in the chemist's."

"I don't believe it," he said, chuckling. "You're not allowed to make them up."

"It's true. And, after all, one always knows what people mean when they say things like 'blind dogs'. It's just that they don't actually say what they mean."

"It could get obsessive. Ernest Stroab – you know him, in the Philosophy department? – once told me he was worried by a sign telling him to put litter in a bin, because strictly speaking it wasn't litter until he'd first thrown it on the ground."

"Poor Dr Stroab, it must make life very complicated, being a philosopher."

They sat companionably by the fire, talking and laughing, Judith leaning against his knees while the slices of bread, which dangled precariously on the end of the toasting forks turned, with satisfactory little crinkling sounds, from gold to brown in the orange heat of the embers.

"We will have an open fire when we have a house of our own, won't we?" she asked.

"And when will that be?" he queried, looking down at her.

He had extraordinary eyes: limpid, blue-green eyes. Too often they looked sad, she thought, and resigned.

"It will happen when we make it happen," she told him firmly. "When I'm finished at college, I'm going to find a house for us and it will have a fireplace and we'll make toast and—"

"And in a few years' time you won't want to be stuck with your old father. You'll be wanting to set up house with some young chap . . ."

"No, I won't. Just you wait and see."

"Some young chap like that Cedric you went walking with last year—"

She laughed at him. "He's so boring. I'd rather have my old dad any day."

"Oh, I don't know, he seems a steady sort of young man—"

"Forget it," she interrupted. "On my walk today I've been thinking about what to do with my law degree."

"Yes, you must. You have three options: first, the Bar. You've covered that by joining an Inn and arranging a place at Bar School and I think there'd be no problem getting pupillage. I've spoken to Michael Moorgate about it. Second, a solicitor, and you've been looking at possible—"

"Three of us had a great time last term," she interrupted, "going through the London firms to see which we'd like to train with. The others gave them marks for who paid most and gave the longest holidays."

"And you – what did you give them marks for?"

"For which of them had appointed the most women partners, of course. What's the third option?"

"Well, you could become a dried up old academic like me."

She looked up at the young, boyish face, with its thick dark hair, and smiled.

"Why did you choose to be an academic?" she asked suddenly.

He hesitated. It was something he had never discussed with her. Instinctively she had known that it was an area of pain and shied away from it.

"I married very young, you see," he began at last. "And it's very tough at the beginning, at the Bar. you could earn almost nothing for a year or two. When I was still struggling, I was offered a university post, so I accepted it. It seemed the right thing to do at the time."

"Couldn't you have waited until you were established at the Bar? Before you got married, I mean?"

Again a long pause. Another area of pain; she shouldn't have asked.

"Sorry," she said, "Don't—"

"No," he interrupted. "It's something I should have talked to you about before. Your mother didn't want me to. In fact we agreed we never would. But maybe you have a right to know, so that you can understand her better."

He seemed to draw himself together and then went on more firmly, "Your mother was abandoned when she was a little girl by her own mother, who left her in a children's home and emigrated to America. She had a much older married sister, your mother's aunt, who was childless, but she didn't ask them to take care of your mother. Or perhaps she did and they refused. I don't know. But when she was thirteen, this couple decided to take your mother out of the children's home to live with them. She was useful by that age."

He paused and then went on, suddenly bitter, as he remembered. "I really do think that they just wanted her as cheap labour in the house. They seemed to take it for granted that in return for her keep she did all the work. They used her like a cheap skivvy. But she never complained. She seemed to accept it as a normal daughterly duty."

"How did you meet her?"

"At a friend of my mother's. The three of them were there. I felt sorry for her, she seemed so dominated by this ghastly old pair. I asked her out and she said her aunt wouldn't allow it. She was eighteen by then! I was a very romantic young man, Judith, so of course I saw myself as a kind of knight in shining armour, rescuing her from these fearful dragons. Do you know, they'd go on holiday and never take her with them?"

"Wasn't that your chance, when she was left alone?"

He laughed.

"I did try," he admitted. "But if I suggested we went out for an evening, she just said her aunt wouldn't approve. They were hundreds of miles away but she was still completely dominated by them. I knew that if her aunt had suspected anything she'd have had the Bible out to make her swear on. She'd have threatened hell-fire even for a harmless little outing to the pictures, evil-minded old woman that she was."

"Go on." Judith was enthralled. After all these years, to hear this story. "How did you break into this castle of despair?"

"They died. About three years after we met. The old man took ill first. He drank; I think his liver packed up. Your mother nursed him at home. Soon afterwards her aunt died too. So she was all alone."

His hand rested on her head; he stroked her hair gently as he said, "Oh, Judith, she was so young and pretty. I just couldn't bear to see her treated like that by people who should have looked after her. And then to see her all alone . . ."

His voice trailed off as he remembered, as he felt again all the pity he had felt then.

"I was twenty-three," he went on, "and had never been in love before. I just desperately wanted to make her feel loved, give her all the tenderness and affection she'd never had, give her a home."

She tried to imagine him, her father, as he was then: a quixotic young man, helplessly in love. Without the wisdom, the authority he had now. She couldn't. And her own mother in the clutches of drunken religious maniacs – that was hard to imagine too.

He was silent. Then, "I suppose," he said slowly, "it was hopeless from the start. We'd nothing in common. Her situation had blinded me to that. She'd been brought up without any interest in books or the arts or any of the things that I cared about."

"Some such marriages work, don't they? Attraction of opposites and all that?"

He smiled down at her, his hand resting on her shoulder.

"Yes, you're right. There was much more to it than that. I didn't realise how hard she was. She seemed so fragile, so vulnerable. But it was as if, never having been loved, she was incapable of loving. She wasn't able to respond to my love, she wasn't able to make a loving home. I should have realised that. I put her into a situation in which she was a total misfit. You mustn't blame her. She had other strengths; she had a very strong sense of duty."

"Oh, yes, I always realised that—"

"But you were only eight," he interrupted, surprised.

"Children sense these things. I heard what people said, what she herself said. I suppose I didn't understand a lot of it, but I did sense it even if I didn't understand."

"And do you understand now?"

She sighed and thought about it.

"Yes, I suppose I do in a way. That strong sense of duty, that strict moral code, all that condemning she used to do – when all I wanted was a cuddle . . ."

Inexplicably her eyes filled with tears. She kept her head down, so that he wouldn't see them.

"Oh, Judith, I'm sorry, so sorry. I'm sure she did her best. She believed in doing good to others. She had many of the Christian virtues—"

"But the greatest of these is love," Judith put in.

"And that, poor woman, is the one virtue that can't be constrained."

Judith, still fighting back tears, said nothing.

"But I should have foreseen it, should have realised how it would be. So in a way it was more my fault than hers."

She rubbed her cheek against his hand, thinking how like him it was to take the blame on himself. And how wrong. For hadn't he been the one who suffered? He was the one who had given up his chosen career, who had never been able to get a proper home together after that first disastrous attempt.

"No," she said firmly. "She was the one who went off and left us."

"Well, that was the outcome. But our marriage was really my fault; I was the older one, knew at least a little bit more of the world than she did. But I had so ached with compassion for her over the years, longed to help her, it just seemed wonderful to be able to do so at last. I didn't stop to think that it wasn't as simple as that."

He gazed into the fire and then turning to her again, said, "Beware of pity, Judith. Never marry for pity."

"I shan't marry for anything," she told him. "I'm going to be a career girl. And I've just decided something else. I'm going to be a barrister."

Somehow it would make it up to him for the sacrifice he'd made. She'd put the past to rights.

"I'll apply for pupillage to – what did you say he was called?"

"Michael Moorgate," he told her. "And now you've settled your career, how about having some more toast while you tell me about your walk today?"

So she told him, while the toast crinkled and browned, about walking up the dale and meeting Alice again and how awful Alice's life now seemed, how limited. She grew more indignant as she talked and ended up telling him how she, Judith, wanted one day to fight for the rights of women like Alice.

He listened, then he said gently, "It's good, darling, that you care so much about other people—"

"But?" she interrupted.

He smiled.

"But you learn as you go through life, you know, Judith, that everyone has their own way, sometimes a quite unexpected way, of dealing with their problems. People find their own way; your friend Alice may find hers in a very different way from yours. But, if she's the kind of person we think she is, she'll reach the right end just the same."

Judith nodded, but it was to be many years before she really understood what he had said.

Nine

" S ince I've stayed with you and your father that night in the Dales when we went walking," Cedric said, "my mother feels you should stay with us, by way of returned hospitality. There are very good walks where we live in Derbyshire," he added as an additional bait.

They had often walked and climbed together; in fact, it had been on a cairn on top of Sawborough that he had first proposed to her in his funny, stilted way.

It was not the last time.

"Sorry, Cedric," she would reply brusquely, "but you know how I feel, or rather don't feel."

He was all right as a companion, a reliable friend, but the idea of him as a husband was ridiculous. Besides, a husband would get in the way of her career and anyway, her experience of her parents' unhappy marriage hadn't increased the appeal of the institution to her. Her aim was still to make a home for her father, who had never had one. She reckoned she could do without matrimony.

"All right," he would say humbly. "But you don't mind being asked, do you?"

"No, but since I'm not going to change my mind, what's the point? I do sometimes think it would be better for you if we didn't see each other any more."

Then she would see fear in his eyes.

"Anything rather than that," he would say.

His parents lived in a little thatched cottage which gave straight on to the street at the front, but at the back there was a sudden rising of hills and breathtaking views. Cedric's

53

parents were very alike; they might almost have been twins. They reminded Judith of two little figures in a weather house that she had seen when she was a little girl. The woman was painted with a yellow blouse and green skirt, and came out when it was fine. The man had a yellow shirt and green trousers and came out when it was raining. It had seemed to her rather sad that such a well-matched pair never actually met.

It was not like that with Cedric's parents, of course. His mother, wearing a yellow jumper and brown tweed skirt, sat on one side of the fire and her husband, clad in a thick yellow sweater and brown corduroy trousers, sat on the other. She was busily making a patchwork quilt, which was spread across her knees. It seemed to Judith rather a pointless operation, all that cutting up of material into little bits, only to sew them all together again afterwards. But she knew better than to say so.

Cedric's father, a retired railwayman, sat reading his paper, occasionally treating them to extracts which he read aloud slowly and laboriously, pausing now and then to knock out his pipe against the chimney breast.

When the grandfather clock in the hall struck ten, Cedric's mother folded up her quilt, put away her sewing basket and said, "Father and I will go up now. You won't be later than eleven, will you, Cedric? There's a hot drink if you want one, Judith."

"Thank you," Judith said, aware that certain rules had been laid down before she arrived.

She wasn't sure if she should kiss Cedric's mother good-night, but decided against it. If she seemed too much one of the family she might give the wrong impression. So they said good-night without embraces and Cedric closed the door on his parents with evident relief.

The next hour passed quickly on the couch, but they were interrupted at eleven o'clock by an insistent banging on the ceiling.

"Coming, Mother," Cedric said, disengaging himself and going to call up to her from the bottom of the stairs. "Just ten minutes."

"Better than having her come down again," he said to Judith, as he came back into the room.

"We'd better go up," she told him, doing up her blouse. "We don't want her worrying."

"It's a terrible forecast, dear," Cedric's father said to his wife the next morning. "I don't understand anyone going out in this weather, really I don't. It's a different matter if you're a postman, of course. You've no option."

"They want to go off, Father," she told him, busy with sandwiches. "Our Cedric likes a good walk and so does Judith, seemingly."

"Picnic in January," her husband remarked, shaking his head in disbelief. He watched balefully as, later on, they donned anoraks and scarves, packed sandwiches and thermos flasks into the rucksack.

"They said on the wireless it could snow," he informed them. "There's no cause to go hiking. There's a good fire at home, isn't there, dear?"

"They can stay if they want, Father."

"But we don't want," Cedric told him, exasperated. He heaved the pack up on his back and they were out, up the lane and into the open countryside.

"I'm sorry they fuss so," he said as they set off.

Judith laughed, "It's only because they care. They don't want us to feel driven out."

The sky was bright blue, the air sharp, sometimes flecked with tiny snowflakes, brittle as slivers of glass against their faces. They walked hand in hand, heads tipped back, cheeks glowing.

"And she made such a fuss last night."

"She was only looking after me. She's not used to having a girl round the place and feels responsible."

"Can you imagine your father banging on the ceiling like that?"

It occurred to her that he was ashamed of them. That was awful. She turned to face him, "It's only because she cares," she repeated. "She's guarding me. It's jolly nice of her."

55

She was surprised at herself; she'd just realised how much she'd loved being fussed over by an older woman. She, who had never had any mothering, had often been puzzled by her friends at school who grumbled about their mothers, actually complained at their concern. It had hurt her to hear them, though she had never really understood why, just that it seemed all wrong. She realised now that she'd envied them; if she'd had a mother like that, her subconscious had been protesting, she wouldn't have been like those daughters, horrible and ungrateful.

"It isn't," Cedric was saying, "as if I had dishonourable intentions."

He spoke so solemnly that she nearly laughed. There was something unromantically pedantic about the way Cedric always reassured her that he had been brought up to respect girls and that she was safe with him, he would never go too far. The arrangement suited her; she didn't want to get too involved with him and having him around protected her from the temptation of getting involved with anybody else.

"No, I'm sure you haven't," she said quickly.

"Well, I wish *she* was as sure. Do you know they left their bedroom door open last night? And I knew damned well she was lying awake listening just in case I took one step across the landing towards your room. If I had, she'd have been out like a shot, hair curlers and all."

"I tell you she's guarding me. It's sweet of her."

"How does she think you manage when she's not there to protect you? She knows I come to see you at college."

"Ah, but it's not her worry at college. When I'm here she looks after me like a daughter. And, I tell you, I like it."

She laughed suddenly.

"Just be grateful she lets you bring in my morning tea," she said.

He grinned back at her.

"Yes, that's a joke isn't it? She lets me come down in my dressing gown, collect your tea and spend half an hour in your bedroom, sitting on your bed while you drink it."

"It's nice that she thinks like that. Cosy."

"But all the same, it's so stupid, Judith. They're both so unreasonable."

"Well, I think your parents are lovely and have been very kind to me and you're lucky to have a proper home."

"You'll have a proper home with your father soon, won't you?" he asked, helping her over a stile.

"Oh yes," she turned to him, glowing, before jumping down at the other side. "I can hardly believe it."

"It's definite, his appointment?"

"Pretty well. That's one thing about the academic life, you get a good idea where the vacancies are coming up and who's in line for them. He'll start in London a year next October. I'll be finishing my pupillage by then so I'll get lodgings and house-hunt and I'll have a house ready for him in October."

"You make it sound very simple."

"Oh, it will be," she told him airily. "It's just a question of making up one's mind to it."

Ten

J oe Dowerthwaite died on Christmas Day and made the last of his rare journeys to the village church on New Year's Eve. It was snowing and bitterly cold as his family made their way back up the lane to the farm, unaccompanied by any other mourners, for they did not follow the village custom of asking everyone back to the house after the funeral.

His widow assembled the family in the kitchen and told them their new responsibilities. It was really no more than an act of piety out of respect to the dead man, for he had been ill for so long that they had already taken over the running of the farm. But his wife had always kept up the pretence that he was in charge, knowing a farm needs its master. Now the reality could be recognised without disrespect.

Then she told them that she was expecting his posthumous child.

They stared at her in disbelief, trying hard to go on looking at her face, not let their eyes wander downwards. When, later, they did, they saw that she was bigger under those dark skirts, though it was hard to make out in that generally bulky and shapeless mass.

"One life taken away, another given," she told them.

And thus they were dismissed.

As the months passed she grew stouter, moved more slowly, let Alice take on more of the household tasks. Alice was silent now; she had lost all spirit, as she moved quietly about the house, docile, hardworking, uncomplaining. There was no more making of pretty clothes now, no talk of going down to the village. Her brothers seemed sometimes embarrassed by her presence, as if she had been the unwitting cause of their trouble.

It hadn't occurred to any of them to tell the police what had happened. It was not their way; such shameful matters were kept within the family. But Derrick did bring back the local paper which reported the case of an unemployed labourer found injured in a ditch not far from Netherby. Evidently the man had been drinking and had then been involved in a fight with person or persons unknown who had inflicted upon him injuries requiring hospital treatment. The village was agog with talk about it, unlike the Dowerthwaites who read the paper in silence before using it to light the kitchen fire.

It was a hard winter and a long one, the first heavy snow falling on New Year's Day. In the early morning, in her little bedroom in the eaves, through a window which the night had already thatched with snow, Alice observed it falling in great lazy flakes which seemed to hang together, swirling this way and that in a slow dance, as if unwilling to fall to the frozen ground.

She used to love this magical moment of waking to a world which had been silently transformed while she slept. She used to love the stillness of it and the way the rising sun, low in the sky, caught the surface and set it aglow with a light that seemed sometimes pink, sometimes orange, but always warm and sparkling as if the snow was encrusted with tiny shards of precious stones.

But this winter she felt no joy, no wonder. She stared out of her bedroom window, saw that the world was white, saw the splendour of the dawn, and felt nothing. Only a dull ache marked the absence of all feeling. Ugliness would have been easier to bear than this beauty which she observed but could no longer feel.

"Go out for a walk, child," her mother told her on the second day. "You need to get out, cold though it is."

Obediently she put on layers of extra clothes and set off across the fields and down to the beck. She stood there on the little slate bridge, lost in misery, while the sun glowed across the fields lighting up the whole countryside and the snow mantled everything in its cold and callous beauty.

She seemed to be the only dark thing in this pure white land, defiled, she felt, and unclean.

The Ewe Lamb

That night the wind got up and swept the centre of the fields and all other open spaces clear of snow, piling it up against the dry-stone walls, swirling it into drifts six or eight feet high, sculpting it into curious shapes, scooping out the centre of the drifts so that when the wind dropped they were left hanging like great frozen waves.

The drifts made life even more difficult for her brothers. Every day they set off to search for stray sheep which had taken shelter by the dry-stone walls and been buried beneath the snow. The animals could breathe for a while there, for the air found its way between the unmortared stones, but some suffocated before they could be found. The men probed the drifts with long crooks, the dogs sought them out; but many were lost, the grey wool of their dead bodies appearing only when the snow melted.

"That was the worst winter since 1947," her mother remarked when lambing started. "Thank God it's done with."

But the bad weather returned, not as relentless as it had been, but erratic with unexpected flurries of snow and thick mists which rolled unpredictably down from the high fells, obscuring the dale. They lost many lambs that year and by ill fate they always seemed to be ewe lambs, which they badly needed for breeding. Day after day her brothers brought in lambs for Alice to nurse. 'Look to this 'un,' they would say, 'its mother's dead.' And she would take the little creature, wrap it in a blanket and set it on the hearth. She would feed it with a bottle and watch it grow, the weak and buckled legs strengthening until they could support the frail body. All this Alice observed, but felt none of her accustomed joy in it.

"Don't feed this 'un," Samson said one evening, offering her a tiny orphan lamb. "Just keep it warm. I'm going to give it to a sheep that's lost her own. And she'll not take to it if she smells strange milk. It's a ewe lamb so we can do with saving it." And he went into the barn and skinned the dead lamb, as his father had taught him to do, and laid its coat over the live one so that the ewe would accept it as her own.

The deception seemed wrong to Alice at first, but when she saw how the ewe took to the lamb as if it was her own, she

61

thought her brother had done right. Besides, if it gave the baby lamb a mother and the lambless ewe a child, what did a bit of deception matter?

At last the true thaw came; the frozen waves of the snowdrifts caved in, snow slid off the roofs of outbuildings and the air was filled with the sound of dripping water. The farm track reverted to mud, the pump in the yard thawed out and water flowed freely into the horse trough. The icicles on the slate bridge dropped off into the beck and the weeds and mosses lost their glass cover. The grass that appeared on the hillsides and in the fields was green and lush from the melting snow. It was spring at last and the bleating of lambs and the answering calls of the ewes filled the countryside.

It was in the spring that Mrs Dowerthwaite told her sons that she had decided to go away to Morecambe, to a relation, to have the baby. At her age, she said, it wasn't fitting to have it at home.

A month later, large under her black bombazine skirt, she left them to take care of themselves and took Alice with her.

"It'll make a break for the lass," she said. "And be a help to me."

She had baked supplies of bread and pies for them and there were stores of cheese and everything they could need in the larder, as well as a side of bacon hanging from hooks in the kitchen ceiling. All the same, they watched the departure of their womenfolk with some dismay, not at all sure that they were going to be able to manage on their own. And that evening the house seemed even gloomier without the two women.

Eleven

When Judith had told Cedric that she'd get lodgings, house-hunt and have a house ready for her father by October, she'd only half-believed it herself. But it happened exactly as she had foretold. Here she was, eighteen months later, with the estate agent in this perfect house, standing in this empty room, which would be her father's study. It was just right, with a view over the garden. She imagined it book-lined, pictured him at his desk by the window. He didn't have many possessions but his bits and pieces would fit in here: his big leather armchair, the desk which had belonged to his father, the bookcases, one each side of the fireplace. Maybe fitted shelves on all the other walls. In the hall her grandmother's rocking chair and little table.

"You haven't seen the kitchen yet," the young man said.

"Oh, is there a kitchen as well?"

"Naturally," he said sharply.

He looked at her and she knew he was thinking she was a mere slip of a girl, not capable of buying a house. She was tempted to tell him that she was twenty-three and had been called to the Bar.

Instead she said, "I do understand that, but I mean you can always put in sinks and things, but you can't make a room feel right, can you, if it's all wrong from the start?"

He waited. She hesitated. She knew that she ought to make some formal statement about the house, but she wasn't sure of the phraseology. She realised that a year's pupillage in barristers' chambers; going with her pupilmaster, Michael Moorgate, to court; sitting in at conferences with his clients and taking notes on cases of indecent assault, breaking and entering or receiving stolen property hadn't taught her anything about how honest citizens set about buying their houses. She wished she'd read a few textbooks on conveyancing.

"We'd like to book this house, please," she said at last, able to think only in terms of theatre tickets.

"We?"

"My father and I. He's coming to London for the weekend, so he'll come and see the house with me tomorrow morning if you can arrange that. But I know he'll like it, so please could you book the house for us to buy anyway?"

It was arranged that they would meet again at ten o'clock the next morning; he was quite friendly as he locked the house up behind them, no doubt scenting a genuine sale.

There were shops nearby; she bought everything necessary for her father's comfort: *Private Eye*, *The Economist*, some biscuits and a bunch of anemones. She could hardly stop herself singing aloud on the bus going back to her lodgings.

"Who's the lucky fellow?" the bus conductor asked, helping her off the bus with more physical contact than was actually required.

She laughed and almost ran down the road. She'd done it, she'd done it! She'd found a home for them, it was like her dream house, exactly like it. After all these years. He would love it, she knew that. He had just needed her to get things moving. When she'd promised that she'd have houses ready for him to look at on Saturday she hadn't really been as confident as she sounded. But here it was, vacant posséssion too, owners packed up and gone. Quick sale.

And next week she'd be having her interview in the Middle Temple. Of course, she'd have liked to stay on at Michael's chambers when she'd finished her pupillage. They were a progressive lot of barristers there. That was why she'd chosen them, famous as they were for taking on women and anybody else who might be considered underprivileged. But her application coincided with that of a Nigerian girl, who was not only a brilliant young lawyer but also an asylum seeker. Against such credentials she didn't stand a chance.

They were kind. They were genuinely sorry that they couldn't offer her this one seat in their chambers, but said that they would find a corner for her so she could stay on as a squatter. But it seemed a negative thing, just staying on but not really belonging. She'd talked it over with her father and he agreed with her. So she had applied instead for a seat in chambers in the narrowest of little back streets, called old Wilts, in Middle Temple.

It was evidently a somewhat old-fashioned set-up, very different from her previous chambers, though its new Head of Chambers, Gerald Charlton-Pownall, was said to be intent on bringing it up to date. Anyway, she couldn't be too particular; she needed a seat somewhere. She'd just have to be very discreet when they interviewed her, she reminded herself, realising that discretion didn't come naturally, but she was working on it. She'd get her father to conduct a practice interview with her this weekend; they'd conducted these mock interviews before, though admittedly they usually got more and more absurd and ended in helpless laughter. But she mustn't think of any of that now, she must concentrate on the house they were going to buy, she told herself as she opened the garden gate.

She'd lodged with Mrs Crumb for nearly a year now. Mrs Crumb was a Yorkshire woman who had been housekeeper to a barrister in Leeds. Years ago he had moved south to chambers in the Temple, bringing his housekeeper – more than a house-keeper, most people agreed – with him. A judge when he died, he left her the house, but, possibly mindful of the feelings of his children, he didn't unfortunately leave her the money to maintain it. So Mrs Crumb took in lodgers. There was no shortage of applicants, for the house was in Morton's Fork, only a few minutes away from the Temple, so was popular with pupils and young barristers. Now, in her old age, Mrs Crumb didn't need to take in lodgers any more, for thanks to some judicious investments she was quite a wealthy old lady, but she still had one or two; not out of necessity but out of habit and the need for companionship.

The other lodger was away this weekend and had said Judith's father could have his room. Mrs Crumb was away too, but she'd left out some clean sheets. Judith made up his bed, put *The*

Economist and *Private Eye* on the table alongside it, arranged the anemones on the dresser. They glowed deep purple and blue and mauve.

They both loved anemones, partly for their colours but mainly because they were easy to recognise. Her father wasn't a country-man and, never having had a garden of his own, he hadn't been obliged to develop an interest in plants. From other men's gardens he had learned enough to instruct her, years ago: 'Most flowers are daffodils, Judith, especially if they're yellow. In the autumn, flowers tend to be hydrangeas.'

'And the birds?' she had asked, head strained back as a flock of something or other flew overhead.

'Apart from seagulls, they're all sparrows,' he had said.

She laughed as she remembered. "Idiot," she said aloud, as she stood in the doorway looking at the anemones on the dresser. "Soon we shall have a garden of our own, and walk about it in the evening, naming the flowers. And I shall get a bird table and put it on the lawn outside your study window."

Then she went back to her own room to gloat over the particulars of Number Three Colton Row. She read and re-read them, taking in all sorts of details she hadn't noticed before, like the shutters on the downstairs windows. She looked at her watch. Nearly six o'clock. He might be here any minute.

He was getting a lift with Dr Stroab and had said he would be dropped off here or else ring her from the Stroabs' house. She'd fill in the time by drawing a plan of their new home. She took a large piece of paper and, with the particulars of the house alongside, began to draw. *Roll on ten o'clock tomorrow and the appointment with Mr Whatsit.* She'd written his name down somewhere; here it was, Mr Morland-Parkes. It sounded more like a place than a person. Suitable for an estate agent maybe. She began to draw.

She'd almost finished the ground-floor plan when the doorbell rang. She dashed out, down the stairs into the hall, sure it was her father arriving. But it was a stranger who stood on the doorstep. A strange woman. In uniform.

"Are you Miss Judith Delaney?" she asked.

"Yes."

"I am WPC Jane Francis. I wonder if I could come inside for a moment?" and she held out a bit of plastic to show who she was.

Bewildered, Judith took her into a little parlour off the hall.

"I'm afraid I have some bad news for you, Miss Delaney. Your father has been involved in a car crash."

"Hurt?" her voice only just came out.

"I'm afraid so."

The other voice hesitated; WPC Jane Francis was having a struggle to get her message out.

"I'm sorry to have to tell you that he was killed," she managed to say.

"Oh, no," Judith said, her voice firm now. "That's not possible. You see, I'm expecting him at any moment, the bed's made up and everything's ready. You've made a mistake. And he wasn't driving. It was Dr Stroab who was killed."

"I'm afraid they're both dead, Miss Delaney. It was a very heavy lorry which skidded into them. It must have been instant."

"Where is he now?"

"At the hospital. I have a car and driver at the door."

"Then I'd better go and get my coat."

"Yes. I'll wait for you. Take your time. And I can't tell you how sorry I am."

"It's all right," she replied automatically. "It's not your fault."

It seemed to take her a long time to climb up the stairs to her room. At last she stood in the doorway; the drawing paper was still there with the pencil lying on it, a line half-drawn, swooping off the page when the doorbell rang. The details of the house were alongside, folded back, because she had been checking measurements. She had been doing these things. If she just went on doing them nobody need know about the ring at the doorbell. There were no witnesses. It need not have happened. She took up the pencil but her hand was shaking and she couldn't make a mark on the paper.

She crept into his room. The anemones still glowed, deep purple and blue and mauve, on the dresser. The magazines lay by the lamp at his bedside. The towel was ready for him, across the chair where she had folded it. It was all ready for him. If things are ready, you have to come and take possession of them. She would just leave everything here for him. These were real things compared to a visit from a stranger which she might have imagined.

That was it; she had imagined it all. What an awful thing to have done to him, even in her imagination.

"I'm so sorry," she said aloud.

Her own voice seemed to rouse her. She looked at her watch: ten past six. The world can't change in ten minutes. Can it?

Yet she knew it was true. She had known from the start. She put on her coat and went downstairs to drive away with WPC Jane Francis to the hospital mortuary.

All she could remember about the days that followed was being cold. She was quite frozen, physically frozen. She didn't cry. She saw to everything. She didn't forget to cancel the appointment with Mr Morland-Parkes. But she was frozen in the mortuary, frozen at the undertakers, frozen at the funeral, frozen when Cedric drove her back to her lodgings, frozen when she accepted Mrs Crumb's embarrassed condolences, frozen when she went upstairs to her room, Cedric following.

It was when she went into the bedroom, saw on the table the drawings that she had been doing when he was still alive, that the frozen centre of her being suddenly dissolved, bringing pain that made her groan aloud as she fell. Cedric took hold of her and laid her down on the bed and she lay doubled up in agony as the pain coursed through her body like blood trying to pump its way through frozen arteries. *Oh God, give me back the numbness. I understand now what it was for.*

But she could not regain that blessed numbness, the time for it was past now that she was back in the place where she had heard the doorbell ring. Cedric held her as she cried; cried until she was exhausted and there were no tears left. She felt strangely relaxed.

"What are you going to do, Judith?" Cedric asked. "I mean what are your plans?"

"If I get into chambers I'll be starting work next week."

"You're not fit. Shouldn't you wait a while?"

"No, I must work. Work saves you."

She didn't know how she knew it, but she did.

"I don't want to press you at a time like this," Cedric said, "but don't you think it might be a good idea to marry me? I don't earn a lot as a Quantity Surveyor but it's a steady job and—"

"Oh, no Cedric, please not."

"It struck me that we might go and look at the house you were going to get for your father, though I think it would be too expensive, not in my price range, if you see what I mean."

Oh, the thought of that house, the thought of replacing her father in it, with Cedric. The very idea brought back excruciating pain.

"Please, Cedric, don't."

"Well, yes, it's far too soon. I shouldn't have spoken of it, but I wondered where you'd live."

"I'll stay here, with Mrs Crumb."

Twelve

"I've nothing against women, as women," Tom Trapp said, "but there's a time and a place for everything."

Gerald Charlton-Pownall looked at his chief clerk with that puzzled sadness which such opinions always evoked in his liberal soul.

"Thomas," he began, for he always called the clerk by his full name to show respect for one who had started life as a barrow boy and yet had managed, without any of the advantages which he, Gerald, had had, to rise to be one of the most successful barristers' clerks in the business – and probably one of the richest. Years ago, when offered the choice between having a temptingly large salary or a mere ten per cent of the fees of the five members of chambers, young Tom Trapp had, with his barrow boy shrewdness, opted to take the ten per cent. So now, with thirteen members in chambers, he earned more than most of the barristers.

"But Thomas," his Head of Chambers continued, "times have changed. Women are now in all branches of the law. When you and I were new to it, a woman solicitor was a *rara avis* – I mean, well, a rare bird," he added, in case Thomas should not have understood. Then, seeing the surprise on the clerk's face, "I use the word in its ornithological sense," he added hastily.

Never at a loss for words in court, he was sometimes flustered when speaking to his own clerk in his own chambers. Ridiculous really, he knew, but he also knew that having to deal courteously with Tom's unalterable prejudices confused him.

"Nowadays," he went on more firmly, "the solicitor who brings us a brief is quite likely to be a woman."

71

"Different world, solicitors," Tom told him.

"It's a matter of principle, Thomas, it's a matter of justice—"

Tom shook his head. "It's a matter of convenience, sir. It's a matter of good business practice. You see, Mr Charlton-Pownall, I always have my progression. A brief is offered. You, sir, can't take it: too busy. Right? Right, so I offer it to Mr Preston. He's tied up in a long trial, so I go down the line until I reach the most junior of all. We never return a brief. Not since I've been with these chambers have we ever returned a brief. Because I have my progression. I've always got the next man lined up, ready to come along."

"But it wouldn't alter you progression, Thomas. The only difference would be that one of the men, or two or three, would be women."

Again Tom shook his head.

"Keen as mustard, the gentlemen are. I've known them come out of hospital half-mended if there was a brief in the offing. Look how Mr Craig keeps going with that grumbling appendix of his. And I remember when Mr Wrigley was getting married. 'Let me know if there's a brief, Tom,' he says to me. So I rung him up on his honeymoon. Second day of his honeymoon, it was, and told him there was this brief for him and he came back that very day. Didn't even wait the night. And that was in the days when a bride was a proper bride and no messing about before the knot was tied. But he came back." He nodded approvingly. "A woman would never do that," he said.

"Perhaps they're wiser," Gerald Charlton-Pownall suggested, but he sounded apologetic all the same.

"And then there's babies," the chief clerk went on remorselessly. "A woman's going to be off having them and where does that leave my progression? Where's the continuity?"

"Perhaps our practices will just have to change, Thomas. Other professions have adjusted to the changing status of women and—"

"That's as maybe. But there's something special in our case. The Bar is a rough place, it's a place for aggression. The client wants his man to be a fighter, someone who can hit back and hit hard. He doesn't want to be represented by a woman—"

"Women can fight as hard as men, Thomas, and often box cleverer," and he proceeded to list the names of several successful women barristers, silks and judges. "And don't forget that sometimes the client prefers to be defended by a woman – a man accused of rape, for example."

There was a long pause, then, "So you've made up your mind, sir?" Tom said quietly, deferentially.

Gerald Charlton-Pownall hesitated, as Tom had known he would. He didn't want to dictate. He didn't want this admirable man who had worked his way up so diligently to feel that he was being blithely overruled by his superior; made to feel that his opinion was dismissed as worthless. He wanted Thomas to see the error of his ways, not just be obliged to give in.

"We will put it to the new barristers' committee," he said at last.

Tom didn't reply, but his expression betrayed what he thought of all this newfangled nonsense of committees for this, that and the other: pupillage committees, recruitment committees, social committees, management committees, all talking for hours about things which used to be settled in no time, without consulting anybody.

"Very well, sir."

Gerald Charlton-Pownall watched him go. He sat for a moment, sadly torn; a man who on the one hand didn't want to seem to dictate to his clerk, but on the other, didn't want to seem sexist in the matter of Miss Judith Delaney.

Thirteen

T he time of the interview wasn't until eleven o'clock and the place only fifteen minutes' walk away, but Judith, restless and nervous, left the house soon after breakfast. Mrs Crumb, from her vantage point in the front drawing-room, watched her go, observing the brisk, determined walk, the straight back, the head held high.

She ached for her; she had seen her young lodger's world smashed, had seen the desolation. She knew the pain that was held tight within that resolute frame. She understood the lonely grief of it. People feel for the widowed, she thought, they feel for the parent who loses a child, but what of the child who loses its only parent, even if that child is twenty-three? Too old to be mothered but too young to know that life will one day be bearable, even enjoyable. For the old know, as the young cannot, that we all have it in us to survive. She would never have expressed such thoughts, it was not her way, but they filled her mind as she watched Judith set off for her interview.

It was a dull morning, the sky grey. A nagging wind blew autumn leaves along the streets in sudden gusts, some old and brittle, some soft, green and newly fallen. Judith made a detour along the Embankment, crossing the road to look at the barges tied up in the Thames, which lapped against them dragging its dreary burden of last night's litter. She watched for a few minutes and then re-crossed the road to walk in the gardens, remembering that last time she had come here was with her father in the spring; crocuses had brightened the freshly cut young grass which now had the unkempt look of an autumn lawn. In the unweeded beds a few plants straggled, half-dead and untrimmed.

She didn't linger but turned away towards the narrow passages and courts of the Middle Temple. Figures hurried past clutching papers and briefcases, intent on their own business. When they had walked these streets together, she and her father, she had felt at home here, sure that this was the right place for her to work. Now she felt nothing of that warmth, that confidence. She was nervous about the interview, but part of her didn't care about the outcome. It was as if she couldn't feel anything any more.

She found she was walking by the railings outside the Temple church. When they came in the summer, her father had told her that there used to be a music shop here, up against the porch, where Samuel Pepys used to come to buy songs. 'Look it up in the diary,' he'd told her. But she hadn't got round to it. "Sorry," she said now, and went in through the great, highly ornamented Norman doorway – the most beautiful part of the church, she'd thought, not greatly caring for the rest of it. But they'd strolled round together, her father and she, reading the plaques, looking at the effigies. They still lay here, the well-preserved Edmund Plowden, sixteenth-century jurist, and the rather more battered thirteenth-century knights, looking the same as they did three months ago; just as if nothing had happened.

Tears pricked her eyes and her throat began its familiar ache. It wasn't just for herself; it was for him, and not just his early death either but for his wasted life. He'd loved it here, the whole way of life, and the place too. He might have spent his days here but he'd given it up, gone for what was, for him, second best because of that foolish marriage – and perhaps also because of the needs of her, his daughter.

If only he'd known real happiness in his marriage, or in his career, his death would have been bearable. If only, she thought longingly, they'd had just a few years to live together in that house in Colton Row. If only – she mustn't think like this, she told herself. Just concentrate on the interview. Think positive. She couldn't alter the past but perhaps she could redeem it by having the career at the Bar that he had not allowed himself to have. She mustn't let anything stand in the way of *that*. Certainly *she* wouldn't make a foolish marriage when the time came. And

76

now she mustn't spoil her chances at the interview by hanging about in this cheerless building grieving for her father in front of effigies which would outlast them all. Determinedly, she set off for Old Wilts Buildings.

It was in one of the narrowest streets of all, and the house surely one of the most rambling. The ground and first floors were occupied by other lawyers; familiar names were inscribed on their doors, listing their celebrated occupants in elegant script. She read them as she went up the stairs. On the second floor she found the door she was seeking and went in to be met by a scruffy youth with a lot of black hair, a pale face and dark circles under his eyes who introduced himself as Charlie and led her to the chief clerk's room.

"Mr Trapp," he said. "Here's Miss Delaney."

She saw a grey-haired, avuncular looking man, pink-cheeked and with the clean look of the elderly fair-skinned. He looked at her benignly as he shook her hand, explained that the Head of Chambers would be free in about ten minutes and offered her coffee.

He saw a presentable looking young lady, who was, with her short tidy hair and neat dark suit, as like a man as any woman could hope to be. Besides, he had withdrawn his opposition to her appointment when he had discovered that the other candidate was a young, left-wing West Indian.

Fourteen

T he Dowerthwaites called the baby Joanna, that being the nearest they could get to her father's name of Joe.

She was a perfect baby, the midwife said. She had none of that crinkled, dried prune look of most babies, nor was she one of the podgy variety. Her skin was smooth and shell-pink, her little limbs rounded but not fat, her eyes deep blue, big and solemn. She was, from the start, a beauty.

Her brothers were instantly besotted. They had never spoiled or fussed over Alice, who was too near them in age. She had been there to tend their needs, as their mother did. She was a worker like themselves, though of the female species.

Little Joanna, however, was a different matter altogether. They gazed in awe at her, they worried about her, fetched and carried for her. They were astonished that, tiny as she was, she knew how to sneeze and cough and yawn. They were far too fearful to offer to hold her, they scarcely dared touch her at first. But as she grew stronger, her little body firmer and able to hold itself upright, they took to carrying her round the farm, putting her up on their shoulders or letting her ride on one brother as he crawled on all fours round the kitchen floor, while another steadied her on his back.

When she began to walk and become conscious of herself as a little person, they found her, if possible, even more irresistible. She would toddle towards some forbidden object on a table and tentatively reach out a hand for it, at the same time looking up at her brothers, challenging them with her eye, already aware, knowingly mischievous. And these dour men, who had been impervious to the charms of farm kittens, or soft and downy ducklings or dewy-eyed calves with long lashes and white stars on their foreheads, were utterly captivated.

She would have been spoiled beyond bearing if it had been left to her brothers. But feminine wiles didn't stand much of a chance when Hilda Dowerthwaite was around. Yet even on her face, there was a softness of expression when she looked at her latest born, which had not been there when she had regarded her older children.

But the biggest change was in Alice herself. Into her shattered life, Joanna brought peace and security and unquestioning love. Busy all day with her baby sister, she no longer spent hours brooding, re-living that hideous night. She was too much in the here and now. Gradually her confidence returned, for this tiny being depended on her, had been entrusted to her by her mother.

For from the start there was no doubt that she was to be in charge of her baby sister.

"I'll have the farm to mind," her mother had told her, the day after they returned from Morecambe. "You'll have to see to the baby."

"But I don't know how, Mam," she had said, terrified. "I might drop her."

"You'll learn. Babies soon teach you what's what. You'll learn more from her in a week that you'd have done on that nursery course in a year."

And so it proved; in no time at all she was feeding the baby, changing nappies and handling her with casual assurance. She talked to her constantly, she who had moved in silence for so long.

"In the very cold winter before you were born," she told Joanna one evening as they all sat round the kitchen fire, "the tap and the pump were frozen and our Derrick had to go to the beck and break the ice to get water for us."

"I doubt she'll make much sense of that," Derrick said, looking down at the baby on his sister's knee.

"And your brothers were out all day feeding sheep with hay and nuts," Alice went on regardless, "for there was no grass for the poor things to eat."

"She's a mite young to understand about nut supplements," Derrick continued to mock.

"Nay," their mother cut in, "you can see the little lass likes to hear Alice talk. She's not taken her eyes off her sister's face this ten minutes."

"And some of them huddled against the walls and were covered in snow," Alice carried on. "And your brothers and Old Spot used to seek them out."

"He was the best sheepdog we ever had," Edmund explained, addressing the baby. "Old though he was, he could track a lost sheep better than any younger dog. By, but we were glad of him that winter."

"Tell her about the sheep that lasted, Alice," her mother said. "The ones that ate the moss and lichen off the walls."

"Well, Joanna, when the thaw came we found four of them huddled against the wall under a snowdrift and they'd been there for five weeks, your brothers reckoned. They were as thin as thin and had lost all their wool, but they'd lived."

"It goes to show they can survive in snowdrifts," Edmund put in, as if Joanna had denied the possibility.

"And, do you know, Joanna," Alice told her little sister. "They got better and grew new coats."

"Mind you, they were crossed with Scottish Blackface," Samson explained. "I don't know if Swaledales would've survived."

"Tell her I'm going to Lanark next week to buy Scottish Blackface," Derrick said.

"Tell her yourself," Alice told him.

So her eldest brother took the little girl on his knee and explained about the crossbreeding of sheep.

"She wants to know what they look like," Alice said.

"They've got black faces and big noses, so they look like your brothers," Mrs Dowerthwaite put in.

To Alice's surprise, the men all laughed and Joanna, catching the festive atmosphere, hesitated for a moment at this unaccustomed sound and then, to their delight, joined in, looking round at each of them in turn as she spluttered and giggled and bounced up and down to show her appreciation.

Thus Joanna transformed life at Sloughbottom Farm, filling it with talk and laughter. When she was christened the Dowerthwaites invited the congregation back to the farm for tea; at Christmas her brothers bought Alice an automatic washing machine and in the spring the two eldest boys went courting.

Fifteen

"So how are you enjoying life in chambers after all these months, Judith?" Tim asked. "Funny lot, aren't we?"

She was sitting with Tim and Freddy, the two other junior barristers, in the Wig and Whistle, where they occasionally met for a snack lunch. It was a dark, unappealing little pub, the decor neither ancient nor modern, just brown and boring, but it was cheap and the dour Scottish couple who ran it, Duncan and Flora McScabbe, did a good line in soup and sandwiches. The great and the good of the legal world were never seen there, but it suited the leaner pockets of the younger barristers, still complementing their meagre earnings by marking A-level exam papers.

Tim and Freddy never seemed to have any money; Freddy because he was buying what he described as a hugely expensive flat and Tim because, as he would say with a shrug of his shoulders, he just seemed to be in a permanent state of bankruptcy. He was engaged to the daughter of a baronet but said he would never be able to afford to marry and her father didn't hold with paupers. Freddy had a partner called Fiona but they lived apart, each of them too fond of their own flat to bear the thought of moving in with the other.

They were a contrasting pair, Tim and Freddy, Judith observed in the detached way she viewed people nowadays, seeing them but not quite relating to them. Tim was slight, dark and sharp-featured. Physically, you'd have expected him to be quick-moving, very active, but he was as slow-moving as a much bigger man, whereas Freddy, big and fair, was the restless one, much sharper in speech and manner than laid-back Tim with his languid drawl and bemused expression. Tim had come to the Bar via Eton and Cambridge, Freddy via grammar school and scholarships.

"Enjoy?" she repeated now in answer to Tim's question.

It seemed such a strange word to describe her life at the moment. She did everything she should, she tried to make herself be interested in all that was going on about her. But *enjoy*? She didn't seem able to relish anything any more; she observed the life in chambers, the bustle and camaraderie of this little community, the sense of sharing though they all went about their own individual business, but somehow she wasn't part of it. She could put her mind to her work, but her heart was not in it. Nothing seemed to matter as it would once have done.

Sometimes she indulged – or was it tormented? – herself by imagining that she was telling her father everything that had happened during the day. She would lie in bed relating funny things that had been said in court, hear his answers, imagine their laughter. On and on she would talk to him until she wept. Then she either fell into an exhausted sleep or lay awake wondering how on earth she would cope with work the next day.

Tim was looking at her, waiting for an answer. She pulled herself together.

"What I like the most," she said briskly, "is going into court with one of the senior barristers. You know, taking notes for them, listening to their cross examinations, going into the cells with them."

"And the rest? How do you find all the poring over law books? It's pretty boring stuff, isn't it?"

She shrugged.

"It has to be done," she said.

That was how life felt at the moment: something that had to be done.

"It strikes me," Freddy said, "that you don't get your fair share of work from our Tom."

She had noticed that herself, suspected that it had a lot to do with her being a woman. But it didn't enrage her as it would once have done. The old Judith would have waded in, demanded an explanation, complained to the Head of Chambers. Sometimes she despised herself for not having the guts to do anything about it. She resented Freddy's drawing attention to it; she didn't want to face it.

"Maybe, but I do have a plea in mitigation tomorrow and should go and read it up now," Judith said, looking at her watch, for all the world as if she hadn't done more than enough work on her plea already.

She got up quickly before either of them could point out that a miserable little plea of mitigation was a pretty poor offering from Tom after all these months.

"I must go too," Tim said. "I've a conference at half-past two."

"She's a bit subdued for a barrister," he remarked later to Freddy as they parted on the stairs.

"I think she's sad," Freddy told him.

Back in her room, Judith looked at the one piece of work Tom Trapp had given her, apart from a few applications for bail, since she arrived. It was a plea in mitigation for a client with the unlovely name of Darren Grunt.

This Darren Grunt was a member of one of the many gangs which flourished in his area. One night, pursuing a member of a rival gang down an alleyway and finding his quarry had eluded him, he vented his rage instead upon an innocent thirteen-year-old who was unfortunate enough to be in the vicinity. He beat the youth about the head with a broken billiard cue which he happened to be carrying until the boy, covered in blood, slumped to the ground unconscious. He had already pleaded guilty; all Judith could do was to find as many mitigating circumstances as possible.

Next day in court she spoke at length of her client's miserable childhood, abandoned by his parents, shuttled between foster homes and institutions. She spoke movingly of his jobless poverty and of his remorse for his crime.

The judge sentenced him to two years in prison; it might have been much worse, she thought as she went to see her client in the cells afterwards. But Darren Grunt neither thanked nor blamed her. He was resigned, as if prison was just one more event in his short and gruesome life.

She did not stay long with him; when she came upstairs she was surprised to see Freddy waiting for her in the corridor.

"Come and have a cuppa," he said, steering her towards the cafeteria.

"I didn't know you were here."

"I was watching you. Up there at the back of the visitors' gallery."

"I never saw you. Did I do all right?"

"No, you were awful."

"*Freddy!*"

She stared at him.

"I said everything in his favour that I could think of," she protested.

"Oh, that's nothing," he told her.

"Of course, it was a pity I forgot about the Probation Report until the judge had started his address—"

"That wasn't too good; judges don't like to be interrupted. But you did something much worse."

"What?"

"You called the judge '*sir*'. Over and over again."

"I didn't, did I?"

"You did. Sometimes 'my Lord', sometimes 'your Honour' and sometimes 'sir'. It's not a mistake any self-respecting criminal would make, Judith. Learn from them."

She followed him to the counter, watched as he put the steaming cups on to a tray, then sat down with him at one of the not-very-clean formica-topped tables, automatically pushing aside a dirty plate and dropping a crumpled paper napkin into an ashtray.

"Well, thanks, Freddy," she said. "It looks as if I'm a hopeless case."

"Oh, no, you'll be all right," he told her cheerfully. "We all make mistakes and need someone to tell us the truth. That's what friends are for."

* * *

Mrs Crumb was more encouraging.

"Two years for grievous bodily harm?" she repeated, nodding her head judiciously. "Not bad. You did well by your client. Look, I've got the sherry ready. Your father would have been proud of you. Oh, there's a message for you. It's to ring this number."

It was Cedric.

She had noticed something in the newspaper about a fire, just a short paragraph, but she hadn't read beyond the headline, hadn't seen the names beneath.

"Oh, Cedric, I'm so sorry."

"Can I come and see you?"

"Saturday?"

"Yes."

A farmer, burning straw in a nearby field, had let the flames get out of control. Sparks had landed on the thatched roof. Cedric's parents, sitting downstairs by the fire in the evening, were unaware until a neighbour beat on the door and shouted that there were flames coming out of the bedroom window.

"Oh, Judith," Cedric said, breaking down when he told her. "It was so stupid and unnecessary. They were safely out. They were out of the house, people saw them in the doorway. Then he said something about his post office book and ran back. Before they'd realised what she was doing, she'd run in after him. She found him. The stairs had fallen on him. She didn't go back for help. Just stood there tugging and suffocating."

He paused, then went on more calmly. "The firemen were marvellous. They tried again and again and they did get them out alive, but they were past saving."

"I wish I'd known. You should have told me straight away—"

"No, you've had enough to bear. I wasn't going to involve you until it was all over. Not so soon after – well, you know."

She realised that he had kept going, as she had done, numb with the horror of it, seeing to everything mechanically.

"I've got to go up there next weekend. Insurance men are coming."

"I'll come with you."

*   *   *

87

Although he had described it, although she had thought she could imagine it, the reality was different from anything she had envisaged. There, where once she had stood and admired the thatched cottage, was now a black husk, a burnt-out shell with a gaunt and ragged chimney rising out of the ruins of what had been a home. Bits of twisted timber, blackened beams, hung down from the rafters; piles of burnt thatch lay strewn about in the mud. Fire and water had reduced that neat little cottage to this filthy carcass and the smell of smoke still hung over everything.

She thought of the rooms, lovingly swept and polished; she thought of the trim little couple in it, of all their treasures; she thought of the quilt that had lain across the green skirt. She stood and looked at the ruin of their home with disbelief.

"We'll go for a walk, Cedric," she told him after the men had gone, and she took his hand and led him away from the blackened ruin of his home and up into the fields behind.

"It's the pointlessness that I can't get over, Judith," he said. "I mean, it was so *stupid*. For a post office book! And it wouldn't have mattered anyway. They have records. Oh, I know, he didn't stop to think, just ran back on an impulse. I suppose we all do stupid things in a crisis, when we're shocked. But it cost him his life. And hers."

She didn't interrupt. He needed to talk. Just talk. She realised that in the two weeks since the fire, he hadn't talked like this to anyone. He needed her now.

"And you see I was the one who persuaded them to go there a few years ago. They were in a terrace house before, but I thought this place was better. I liked to think of my parents in a cottage like that. Snobbery, probably."

"No, you just thought it was a better home for them when he retired."

"The terrace house had a slate roof."

They walked in silence for a while.

"And – I didn't tell you this – I was going to go home that weekend and I went hiking instead. Stayed that night, that very night, in a hut in the Lake District. If I'd been there, like I'd promised, I'd have heard the fire start, smelled smoke. And I wouldn't have let the old man go back for that damned book."

"Ssh, don't be so hard on yourself."

"And he was a simple man. He probably did really believe in that moment of panic that all their savings were lost if his book got burnt. I should have seen to these things, seen that he understood."

They walked and talked all day. And in the weeks that followed he wrote to her every day and rang every evening. She listened, she consoled, she let him back into her life. She ached with pity for him. She longed to help him until one day she heard herself say, "Do you still want to marry me?"

"Of course."

"Then we could, couldn't we? Get married, I mean."

Afterwards she thought it must have been one of the least romantic proposals ever made. And it wasn't even a leap year.

Sixteen

A lice sat on the bus in the market square in Pendlebury, Joanna alongside. The bus always waited here for a few minutes on market days, allowing extra time for all the passengers, mostly women laden with shopping, to climb on board; the driver noisily revving the engine now and then to hurry them up. They were just about to set off when Clara came running up to the bus-stop, waving at the driver and calling out to him to wait.

Red-faced and strung about with parcels, her bleached and frizzy hair escaping from a crocheted yellow hat which almost matched it in colour, she managed to heave herself aboard, handing up some of her bulkier shopping to the conductor before she clambered up the steep step.

"Thank you, Nathan. Yes, up on the rack if you don't mind. I can manage the rest. By, but I've never seen a queue like the one in the bread shop today. I thought I'd never get served and the time ticking over. Oh, Alice. Thank you, love."

Alice had lifted Joanna on to her knee and Clara now flopped down on the seat beside her, spreading her legs wide so that she could accommodate her parcels in her lap, her ample thighs spilling over the sides of the seat.

"My, but it's good to sit down," she said, sighing deeply. "Oh, what a rush! I seem to have bought half the town. And I only came in for a prescription for Aunt Ella. But there it is, the sales are on and I never could resist a bargain," she added, shaking her head in disapproval of her own weakness, while at the same time smiling in toleration of it.

"Now then, Alice. We don't often see you in Pendlebury. What's brought you in this morning?" she asked as the bus pulled out and made its slow way along the narrow main street out of the town, up the hill, past the church and out into the open countryside.

"We came to get some shoes at Baxter's for Joanna."

Joanna, who hadn't taken her eyes off Clara's face, obligingly thrust forward her feet for inspection.

"Ooh, aren't they lovely?" Clara cooed at her. "Aren't you a lucky girl. I bet they cost a pretty penny."

"She wanted to wear them," Alice explained, "so I let her keep them on and Tom put her old ones in the box."

"He fancies you, Alice, does Tom Baxter."

"Oh, no, Clara," Alice exclaimed, blushing.

"Oh yes, he does," Clara insisted, her mouth pursed in teasing mode, her eyes knowing. "A little bird told me."

"He's just being very helpful, that's all," Alice told her, wishing Clara didn't have such a loud voice. "We've always got our lads' boots there and taken them back for repair. Tell Clara what colour your shoes are, Joanna," she told her sister, to change the conversation.

"Red."

"Clever girl. And what colour's your jumper?"

"Pink."

"That's right."

"And what colour's my coat?" Clara joined in.

"Blue."

"Well, I'd have said more turquoise myself. But that's as may be. How old is she now, Alice?"

"Two and half next month."

"Yes, I remember your mam was expecting when your dad died. We were all surprised. We wouldn't have thought that he'd have—" she was going to say, 'had it in him', but changed it to "—been quite well enough," out of respect for the dead.

Alice nodded, gazing out of the window as her cousin chattered. She didn't often come into Pendlebury: it was a treat for her to watch the countryside go by as the bus wound its way between gently sloping fields. On a bright windy day such as this, cloud shadows ran along the hillsides as if racing the bus.

The Ewe Lamb

"They say they're going to get rid of the conductors, to save money," Clara was saying. "Just have drivers. It's a sin and a shame, having to find your purse when you get on and all your shopping to carry. I don't think they'd sack Nathan, though. He's grand. He once stopped the bus just here and got out. We all thought he'd been taken short. Well, it must be difficult for them sometimes, mustn't it? But it was just that he'd seen some mushrooms and hopped out to gather them. Mind you, he did apologise for the delay caused, but we all just clapped. What's a bit of delay matter? It isn't as if the Queen's coming to tea."

Alice wondered what Joanna made of all this, as she sat, evidently fascinated, not taking her eyes off the rubbery contortions of Clara's hard-working mouth.

"She's quiet, isn't she?" Clara remarked as they left the main highway and turned off into the winding road that led to the village. "Her speech is all right, is it? She's not backward or anything?"

"She speaks very well," Alice said indignantly. Then she added with uncharacteristic asperity, "When she gets the chance."

She regretted it instantly, but Clara didn't seem to notice.

"And how'll you get up to the farm? You'll never carry her all that way, will you?"

"I've got the pushchair. The conductor's kept it for me by the door. He'll hand it down for me."

"There you see, they don't think of pushchairs, do they, when they talk about getting rid of conductors? That's the house where that lawyer and his daughter used to live," she went on as, coming into the village, they passed a drive end. "You know, the one whose mother ran off and left the child on her own. Only eight, she was. I forget her name."

"Judith," Alice told her. "I was at school with her."

"Well, you would be, wouldn't you? You're of an age."

"She was a few years older. She used to come back here, after they'd left, for holidays with her father. They used to rent the cottage on the green but I haven't seen them for a while."

"Oh, she stopped coming when her father died."

93

"He *died?*" It was too shocking to believe. "Are you sure?"

"Quite. I had it off Peggy Mitchell and she had it off Florrie Whittaker who used to rent the cottage to them. She'd know if anybody would."

"Oh, *poor* Judith," Alice said, her eyes filling with tears.

"Yes, both parents gone, it's very sad. Gone in different ways, mind. Not that that makes it any better. Mind you, I expect she had connections in the town. They never quite belonged here, in a way."

"Oh yes, Judith did. She loved it here. She'll miss coming. I know she will."

"They say she's following in her father's footsteps. Going to be a lawyer." She laughed. "Well, I suppose we all do, follow in our parents' footsteps, I mean. Your brothers are following in Joe's footsteps and you're following in your mam's and I expect little Joanna here will do the same when she's grown-up."

"No, she won't. I want better for her."

She was tetchy about her younger sister, Clara thought. More defensive of her than she'd ever been of herself.

"Well, she's good with her colours, I'll say that for her," she said as the bus shuddered to a halt by the green. "What colour's my hat, darling?"

Joanna looked at it thoughtfully.

"Banana," she said at last.

Joanna slept soundly as Alice pushed her up the long winding lane to the farm. Watching her, she thought there was nothing more relaxed than a sleeping child. Other small animals weren't like that; they jerked into wakefulness at the slightest disturbance, whereas Joanna's little body, securely strapped in as it was, jolted in rhythm with the ridges and hollows of the ground and her head lolled, sometimes forward, sometimes from side to side, as she slept, floppy as a rag doll, all the way home.

As she pushed, Alice thought of what Clara had told her about Judith; news which she had put to the back of her mind to think about when she was alone. She knew how close they had been, Judith and her father. She herself had hardly known him but

94

what she did remember most was how Judith had once said he had read to her at night and how she had thought it was a very odd thing for anyone's dad to do, used as she was to the silent presence of her own father.

Now that she had the care of Joanna, she understood it all better. There was no way she was going to have Joanna worried about not being able to read, the way she herself had been. She read to her every night when she was tucked up in the little bed next to her own big one in the bedroom in the eaves. And she bought her books. One day she was going to get a bookcase for her; for the moment the Ladybirds and Beatrix Potters rested on the shelf of the kitchen dresser.

"*Peter Rabbit*!" Samson had objected. "What are you thinking of, stuffing her head with that nonsense?"

"It's not nonsense and she loves that story. She can't abide Mr McGregor."

"Worse than rats they are. Whoever wrote them tales knew nowt about farming."

"Oh, yes she did. Beatrix Potter married a farmer and was one herself. And she was so good at it and so happy that she stopped writing her stories."

"Of course she stopped. She'd found out the truth about rabbits."

Samson came in early that evening and she was late making the tea.

"I'm all behind with going into Pendlebury this morning," she told him. "Could you take Joanna up and read to her tonight?"

"Nay, I'm not much of a one for reading."

"Go on, Samson. She's no dad to read to her."

Puzzled, Samson was about to refuse, but Joanna had already climbed up to reach one of her books and, still holding it, held up her arms to be lifted. Never able to resist such an appeal, Samson picked her up and carried her to bed.

In a few minutes Alice went to the foot of the stairs to make sure all was well.

" 'The tale of Johnny Town-mouse' " she heard the gruff voice begin. Slow of speech as he was of thought, Samson read the words very deliberately. " 'Johnny Town-mouse was born in a cupboard. Timmy Willie was born in a garden.' "

She smiled as she went back to preparing the tea.

"Samson not in yet?" her mother enquired, coming in to the kitchen.

"He was early, Mam. He's upstairs reading a story to Joanna."

"Our Samson reading! By, but she can wrap him round her little finger."

She shook her head, but Alice could see that she was not displeased.

"He's being long enough," her mother said later. "Go and see if she's playing him up."

So Alice went as quietly as she could up the uncarpeted stairs and stood in the doorway. It was almost dark now; Samson had moved over to sit by the window to catch the last of the fading light. He was reading steadily on, the little book looking smaller than usual in his great hands.

Joanna was sound asleep.

Samson, intent on the book, didn't notice Alice standing there. " 'One place suits one person, another place suits another person'," he read, having reached the last page. " 'For my part I prefer to live in the country, like Timmy Willie. The End'."

He sat still and thoughtful even though he had finished. Alice left him and went quietly downstairs.

"Goodness, is it that late?" he exclaimed, looking at the kitchen clock when, eventually, he followed her.

"You didn't need to go on reading once she was asleep," Alice told him. "Didn't you notice she'd gone off?"

"Yes. But I wanted to see how the story ended," he said simply.

He stood for a moment by the fire, thoughtful, not his usual self, as if the simple tale had unsettled him.

"It's like you and that Judith," he said at last. "Town and country."

"I've told you, Samson, she's a country person at heart. When we were little she was my best friend and I *know*."

"Well, she's not your best friend now."

In his confused way he lumped them all together: townspeople, governments, writers of books in favour of rabbits. They all seemed to present some indefinible threat to his way of life.

"Oh, Samson, you're so, so – I don't know, *obstinate*."

"Will you stop your argufying, you two, and come and have tea?"

"Sorry, Mam," Alice said, going over to the table. Samson followed.

As she sat down she thought of Judith, who had neither parents nor brother to sit at table with. It was lucky she was so clever; she hoped that by now Judith had a good job and was successful in a world far away from Sloughbottom Farm.

Seventeen

J udith watched as yet again Tom Trapp handed sets of papers
to everybody except herself. It seemed to her a bit like dealing
out a pack of cards. The picture cards went to the senior
barristers: the king (a murder trial at the Old Bailey) to Mr
Charlton-Pownall, the queen (armed robbery at Snaresbrook) to
Eddie Paston, the knave (unlawful wounding somewhere in the
West Country) to Charles Wrigley. The medium cards, the sixes
and sevens, had already gone to colleagues busy with breaking
and entering, drug-pushing and unlawful wounding. The lowest
denominations were being handed out to the younger members:
dangerous and careless to Tim, indecent assault to Freddy.

Finally, he turned to Charlie. "Now, you're to take this
envelope to the Bailey and give it to Mr Fescue. Wait and see
if he needs to send anything back with you. Here's the money for
the taxi," he said, counting out some notes and coins. "And get
yourself a haircut with the change."

Watching him, Judith thought that perhaps one of the reasons
she hadn't objected to Tom's treatment of her was that she
couldn't help liking him. She appreciated his good qualities: the
fatherly way he trained the junior clerks; the way he looked after
everyone, the paterfamilias of chambers. So, when the two of
them were left alone, she said as much as she turned to leave. He
smiled and offered coffee; evidently he was in an expansive
mood.

"I see myself as a carer, a butler to the barristers," he said,
offering her the sugar.

"A kind of legal Jeeves?"

"Exactly. I like the phrase. I shall use it; thank you for that.

99

You see, barristers aren't fit to see to their own lives, Miss Delaney. They have to have the everyday things seen to for them. *They* have to see to their work. They have minds especially adapted to it which don't fit them for much else."

"Perhaps that will change when there are more women barristers?" Judith suggested innocently. "Women do seem awfully good at juggling several lives at once. I mean, I have women friends who manage their careers and their families—"

"I've little experience of such matters," he interrupted coldly. "But George Gimbal, who clerks for Number Four, has had many women barristers in his set. Now, George is fond of ladies, a happily married man, but he tells me it doesn't do."

"Why doesn't it do?"

"It leads to trouble and distraction in chambers. Trouble and distraction, George Gimbal says. Of course, as I have already said, I have no experience of it myself. Until you joined us. And I'm sure I hope you'll be very happy here. I expect an attractive young lady like yourself will soon marry and settle down. And leave the fighting at the Bar to the menfolk. I always say, ladies aren't fighters, God bless 'em. Where should we all be if they were, eh? And now, if you'll excuse me, Miss Delaney, I must answer that telephone."

As he spoke, Judith felt a sudden upsurge of rage, something she hadn't felt for a long time.

"Blatant sexist twaddle," she muttered to herself as she went back to her room. "He talks about caring, but how much does he care for women barristers?"

Would it make it worse or better when she got round to telling him she was getting married? she wondered as she settled down to read a thick tome on the law of negligence, in the hope that one day her knowledge of it might prove useful. One day, surely one day, she would be given some work of her own.

But she wouldn't get work unless she was prepared to fight for it, she realised now. She pushed the book away and gave herself a silent lecture. *You must snap out of this,*" she told herself. *Enough of apathy, enough of smothering your resentment and pretending Tom Trapp is a likeable chap who is probably doing his best for you. You've known all along what's going on. Fight back, Judith Delaney.*

These thoughts were interrupted by a knock at the door. Tom was standing outside in the corridor.

"That telephone call, Miss Delaney," he said, "was from Mr Craig. Or rather, from his wife."

"Oh, yes?"

"He was troubled again with his appendix during the night and had to be taken to hospital. This time they have kept him in and will operate today."

"Oh, poor Geoffrey. But it's as well to get it over. That grumbling appendix has been bothering him for ages."

"Indeed, yes, and I shall of course inform our Head of Chambers and no doubt he will arrange for our good wishes to be expressed in floral form."

He paused, coughed and then went on, "But the matter I wish to see *you* about, Miss Delaney, is this brief. A shoplifting case of Mr Craig's, which clearly he will have to return. Nobody here will be available to take it, I know, apart from yourself. The client has insisted upon a jury trial, though she would have been better off before the lay beaks. Fortunately, all the papers are here."

He indicated the papers he was holding.

She could hardly believe it.

"For me?" she said, and her voice came out in a whisper.

"I am offering it to you, Miss Delaney. And I must tell you that he has arranged a conference with his client for tomorrow at eleven o'clock. You may wish to postpone it. The case is not due to be heard for two weeks."

"Tell them to come for the conference just the same."

"Thank you, Miss Delaney."

After he had gone, she stood motionless for a moment in the corridor, the brief in her hands. Her first jury trial, she thought as she gazed at it. It was only a little roll of paper with a tatty piece of red tape round it, but she carried it back into her room as if it were written in precious stones on pure gold.

*　　*　　*

Her room had once been the end of a corridor with a cupboard on either side and a window at the end. By means of removing the cupboards and knocking out the walls on each side of them and fixing a door, a tiny room with a disproportionately large window had been carved out. It could contain a table and chair but not much else. For this, her first conference with her own client and solicitor, Judith managed to squeeze in two more chairs. She put the papers on the table and went to await her visitors down in the clerks' room.

Her first thought on seeing her client was that it wouldn't be possible to squeeze her into the room. For Rosie Playbell was enormous. She was so fat that she seemed to have to row herself along the corridor, pushing the air back behind her with arms like tree-trunks. As she paddled herself along her body rolled gently from side to side.

It was hard to judge her age. Her brown face was unlined and cheerful, with big, lively eyes and a full mouth whose natural contours seemed to be set in a huge and permanent smile.

At first, when she met her in the clerks' room, Judith didn't see the tiny solicitor hidden behind the massive body of his client.

"I'm Brutall," he told Judith, peering round Mrs Playbell, his pale little face appearing from under her armpit. "Managing clerk of Dodgson, Caper and Burnstone."

Somehow they all contrived to shake hands.

Judith had sat in on many such conferences, so she knew that although she had read all the papers several times and knew the facts of the case, she must get Mrs Playbell to tell her story in her own words, so that she could get an idea of what sort of impression she would make in court.

"Tell me, Mrs Playbell," she began, "what happened on the morning of March thirteenth when you went into Boyson's store?"

"I went to de counter where all dem stockings is," she began and her voice was deep and lilting. "And den out of me bag I takes me own pair."

"And why did you do that?"

"To match dem up with dem other stockings," Mrs Playbell told her. "You see, I never can abide dem tights. Dem tights is all right for you skinny folks but day's no good for us fat ladies."

She smiled and it was a smile which filled her face and seemed to overflow on to her vast bosom which heaved with silent mirth.

"De trouble wid dem tights, day never reach de tops of de legs. All right, you buy a big, big pair and what happens? Dey runkles up round dem ankles but still dey don' reach de top. Dey stretches across somewhere above dem knees like as if dey was a webbed foot on a duck."

And now it was a real laugh; head thrown back, mouth wide open, white teeth brilliant against pink tongue, her stomach heaving with mirth, she radiated pure joy.

It occurred to Judith that in the dock she might seem rather too cheerful for a woman accused of shoplifting.

"So," she interrupted, "you wanted to buy stockings, not tights. But why did you need to take those others with you?"

"Look, dat's simple. You ladders tights, dey finish, thrown out. But you ladder stocking, you got one left. It's no good on its own. You need matching ones. So I always gets de same den it don' matter if one laddered. But, man, deese counters have so many different kinds. And you need to match *exactly*. It must be de same size, de same denier, de same amount support, same thickness, same shade, same every damn thing."

"Yes, I see that."

"So I don' write it all down, I just takes me last pair and compares what is written on de box with what is written on de ones on de shelf. Otherwise you gets home and you got de wrong thickness or you gets Champagne instead of Burgundy so when you puts dem on you got odd legs."

She thrust her legs forward as far as she could in the confined space and truly, Judith observed, the stockings matched. She also observed that Rosie Playbell had the remarkably trim ankles often seen on stout ladies.

"No trouble at all wid stockings and a good corset," Rosie remarked.

"So you took out the box containing your last pair of stockings and walked along the display shelves comparing it until you matched it up?"

"Exactly. An' when I match it, I pick up four pairs of stockings from de shelf."

"And then?" Judith prompted.

"Den I put me box back in me handbag and I took de four other packets over to de checkout."

"Then?"

"I wait in a queue. Dere was dis ol' lady asking about a reclaim and humbugging the assistant and holding us all up. But in de end she goes away, grumbling. And I put down me four boxes and pays for dem. Den I leave de store."

"You were out in the street when you were stopped?"

"Dat's it. I was through de swing door and out on de pavement. Den suddenly dis lady comes from nowhere and she taps me on de shoulder and she says, 'Will you show me the content of your plastic carrier bag?' I'm surprised but I shows she and she looks at dem and de receipt which was in wid dem. Den she says, 'Now show me de pair you put in your handbag.' So I showed she and she ask me, 'Where's the receipt for *that* pair?'

"And what did you say to that?"

"I tell her de truth. I throwed it away weeks ago." She laughed again. "And still I didn't guess what it was all about. I thought she's one of dem ladies with de clipboard and questionnaire who stop you in de street and ask silly questions.

"But den," she went on, more solemnly now, "she say, 'Accompany me back into de store to de manager's office', and I begin to be nervous. It was a big, grand sort of place, about ten times bigger dan dis room and I feeling uncomfortable." She paused, then went on, "And day told me I stolen me own box of stockings."

By now she was looking thoroughly woebegone. The light seemed to have been turned off in that big expressive face, the brown eyes had lost their sparkle, the mouth turned down at the corners as she relived the scene.

"I was disgusted! I got up an' said I was going an' wouldn't shop in dis store *ever again*. Den day say it's a police matter now and I'll be prosecuted for shoplifting because dat is company policy."

"And what did you reply?"

The answer surprised her.

"I said I'm ringin' me husband's solicitor."

"Mr Brutall? Your husband rang Mr Brutall for you when you got home?"

"No, me husband's not at home right now."

"He works away?"

"Oh, you might call it dat. I ring de solicitor meself."

"My firm has had the honour of acting for the Playbell family in the past," the solicitor confirmed.

"I see," Judith said. But she didn't. She'd mistaken the situation. This must be quite a well-off family if it regularly instructed solicitors. She needed time to think.

"I think you've told me all I need to know for the present," she said. "Mr Brutall and I will consult and be in touch with you again."

"An' I must go to me work," Mrs Playbell said, getting up with surprising agility for one of her bulk.

"What is your work?" Judith asked, following her out of the door.

"I'm a lollipop lady," she replied. "Day all likes me, de mums and de kids. Day say dat with me between a bus and de kids, de kids is real safe," and, shaking with laughter, she made her way, with that curious paddling movement of her stumpy arms, down the corridor, towards the stairs.

Her solicitor stayed behind, his pale little face looking anxious.

"Miss Delaney," he said. "About the husband in this case—"

"Ah yes, he who works away from home?"

"Not exactly. I think I should tell you that Mr Playbell is, as you might say, one of her Majesty's guests."

"He's in prison?"

He nodded. "Brixton," he said. "Eighteen months for receiving stolen goods."

"Oh." She sat down, dismayed by this turn of events.

"And yes, we have acted, as I said, for the family. Her brother-in-law, Buster Playbell, is inside too for conspiracy to fraud and recently her father-in-law got ten months for breaking and entering."

"But *she* hasn't a record?"

"Oh, no, nothing against Rosie. But this afternoon I'm seeing her husband's uncle at Snaresbrook, awaiting trial on a taking and driving away charge."

She led him down the corridor feeling much less optimistic now. She would have liked to ask if he had ever known any of the Playbells to be successfully defended, but thought it might be tactless.

As she stood at the top of the stairs, Freddy and Tim came up.

"Hi there, Judith, you look worried," Tim said, waving a bottle in her direction. "Come and join us for a sherry. Freddy and I are celebrating his win. Against all the odds, he got away with breaking and entering."

His room wasn't a great deal bigger than her own, but at least there was room for the three of them to sit comfortably as Tim poured out the wine.

"So how's Judith's first case going?" he asked, handing her a glass.

"They've just left, my shoplifting lady and her solicitor."

"Was that your two I saw going up the stairs earlier on? A huge black lady and a tiny little white man?"

"It sounds like it: Mrs Rosie Playbell and her solicitor."

"Her solicitor? I thought it was her lunch," Freddy remarked.

"Playbell," Tim repeated slowly. "She's one of *the* Playbells?"

"What do you mean?" Judith asked, trying to forget what the solicitor had said.

"They're a famous family of villains, Judith," Tim told her. You'll never get her off."

"Of course she will. Don't be so depressing, Tim," Freddy put in. "It's Judith's first case."

"And it's not poor Rosie's fault if she happens to have married into a crooked bunch like that," Judith said indignantly. "Since men are the criminal sex, there's bound to be a lot of innocent women married to criminals."

106

"Good for you, Judith," Freddy said. "I've never seen you so full of fight."

She looked at him, surprised. It was true; today was the first time she'd felt truly alive since – since the awful event which she could not bring herself to put into words, even in her head. But now she really did feel strongly about something else, care about it. It was as if a mist had been lifted, so that the edges of things were once more clear and sharp. Of course, she reminded herself, the mist could descend again, but at least she knew that its lifting was possible.

"And furthermore," she went on, belligerent in her newfound confidence, "nobody will know about her relations."

Tim shrugged.

"Not officially, no. But it's one of those names known to the police, the magistrates, prosecuting counsel, everyone. It just doesn't help to be called Playbell if you want to be found not guilty. I reckon old Tom's landed you with a loser for your first brief."

"The point is, what is Judith going to do about it," Freddy said. "How old is this woman?" he asked suddenly.

"Hard to say exactly. Middle-aged."

The two men looked at each other.

"That's your defence then," Tim told her. "Women *d'un certain âge* do these absentminded things like picking up an extra pair of stockings and popping them into their handbags. It's a well-known psychological fact. Plead Guilty but Menopausal."

"She isn't guilty," Judith told him firmly. "And that sort of nonsense does the cause of women no good at all. How can we say on the one hand that we can do jobs as efficiently as men and then use an emotional excuse like premenstrual tension or the menopause to get us off a crime?"

"Your job isn't to have theories about women's rights, it's to do the best for your client, Judith," Tim reprimanded.

"But I *am* doing the best for her, I tell you. She says she's innocent and there's no way she should plead guilty."

"Use the menopausal plea, get a doctor as a witness," Tim

went on, ignoring her, "and the judge will give her a suspended sentence and a course of HRT."

"Don't listen to him, Judith," Freddy told her. "If she insists she's innocent, you'll find a way of getting her off."

"I'm going to," Judith pronounced, getting up. "I'm going to Boyson's hosiery department right now."

"It's a waste of time," Tim told her. "And anyway, there's no rush. Do sit down. You're suddenly so restless. I don't know what's got into you. Stay here and have another glass of sherry."

"No. I'm off to find out all I can about the stocking trade."

"Let her handle it in her own way, Tim," Freddy put in. "And anyway," he went on to divert the conversation, "Rosie'll stand a better chance than the old lady who collapsed from hypothermia outside the supermarket."

"What happened to her?"

"They found a frozen chicken under her hat."

Eighteen

R osie Playbell's case was to be heard in one of the older courts, run down and with too many stone stairs and dusty corridors. A recent attempt at refurbishment, mainly by the application of beige and green paint to its walls, had succeeded only in garishly highlighting its decrepitude, like thick make-up on an old woman's face.

As Judith climbed up the stairs, after spending half an hour talking to Mr Brutall and their client in the corridor, the burden of responsibility, like a physical thing, weighed heavily on her shoulders. Rosie had been so cheerfully confident, so sure of being found innocent by twelve fellow human beings who would be bound to understand how she chose and bought her outsize stockings. It would be awful if she let her down – and you can never be sure with juries, everyone kept saying. *Be detached, Judith*, they said. *You win some, you lose some. Don't get involved.* All right in theory. In practice, it was the cheerful face of Rosie Playbell with its huge and trusting smile. She looked across at her now; Rosie almost filled the dock with her ample form, the female prison officer dwarfed beside her.

There were seven women and five men on the jury; that was hopeful, she thought. Or was it? She decided she liked the look of the middle-aged lady with a velour hat and anxious eyes. The younger one next to her had a kindly look too. She didn't much care for the expression on the face of the man at the end, a right old misogynist he looked. But her perusal of the jury was interrupted by the clerk of the court telling them to be upstanding for the judge.

Counsel for the prosecution opened the case. Victor Randall was a very young man, his hair thick and dark under the new white wig. He was nervous and his high-pitched voice somehow contrived to make the charge seem silly, as he recounted in detail the events that had taken place in Boyson's on March thirteenth. For the first time she understood how some people might think it was rather a lot of fuss over a pair of stockings.

"Mrs Tracker," Victor Randall addressed the store detective in the witness-box," is the defendant the same person you saw at the stocking department in Boyson's store on March thirteenth this year?"

"Yes, I recognise her."

"And could you tell us what happened on that occasion?"

"I observed the defendant walking along the shelves looking at the different packs of stockings. She picked up four and put them into the wire basket which the store provides for customers. I then observed her put another packet into her own bag."

"This is Exhibit One, your Honour," the clerk of the court said, taking it and showing it to the judge, before handing it to the witness.

"You recognise this as the packet in question?"

"Yes, sir."

"And what did you do then?"

"I followed her to the checkout and watched her pay for the four boxes. I then followed her out of the store and asked her to show me the packet that was in her bag, which she did. I asked her to show me the receipt for it. She didn't have one. So I asked her to accompany me back into the store."

"And could you tell us what happened within the store?"

"I took her to the manager's office."

The store detective made a good witness, presentable to look at and precise in what she said. Judith, who had been hoping for a gauleiter who would offend the jury, was disappointed.

Rosie's face was beginning to get that woebegone look and every now and then she turned sad brown eyes towards Judith as if she was the only friend she had in the whole world. None of the Playbell family was in the public gallery; perhaps, in view of what Tim and Freddy had said, it was just as well. Maybe they were all in prison.

"Did she offer any explanation for the fact that she hadn't paid for these goods?" Victor Randall was asking.

"She said she had brought them in with her. It seemed an unlikely tale so we decided to prosecute. That is the company policy on shoplifting. If shoplifters get away with it, our honest customers are the ones who ultimately pay the price."

There was a nod or two from some of the women on the jury.

"And how did the defendant react to this accusation?"

"She showed no repentance. At first she was inclined to laugh and then she became angry."

"Thank you, Mrs Tracker. Those are all the questions I have to ask."

His witness having made a good impression on the jury, Victor Randall sat down with a look that showed he felt himself well named.

Judith rose to conduct her first cross-examination. Her hands were shaking and something curious seemed to have happened to her knees, but she had her questions ready and well rehearsed. She had practised her words to the bedroom mirror many times.

"Mrs Tracker," she began, with a confidence that surprised herself. "You say that you saw the accused holding this package. But did you see her take it off the shelf?"

The store detective hesitated.

"No," she said. "I don't think I actually saw her take it off the shelf."

"You don't *think* you saw her take it off the shelf? You realise, I'm sure, the importance of this question and you realise too the importance of being fair to this defendant?"

"Yes."

"I wonder then if you could please try to be a little more specific?"

Again the hesitation. Then the witness said slowly, "No, I didn't see her take it off the shelf. I assumed that since she had it in her hand and was standing by the shelves that she must have picked it up before I saw her."

"You *assumed* but you didn't *see*?"

Judith managed to inject a note of astonishment into her voice

111

that the detective could have been so remiss, and was gratified to observe signs of disapproval manifesting themselves on the faces of the jury in slight pursing of lips and almost imperceptible shaking of heads.

"I have no more questions," she said.

She was surprised to find she had quite enjoyed cross-examining. She listened carefully to what the next prosecution witness, Police Constable Blogton, had to say in evidence. He added nothing new; he had been called to the store by the manager, cautioned Mrs Playbell that anything she said might be used in evidence and charged her with the theft of goods belonging to Boyson's Superstore.

At first she thought she wouldn't put any questions, but then something about the youthful cockiness of the young policeman made her change her mind.

"Constable Blogton," she began in the friendliest possible way. "We have heard how you charged Mrs Playbell with shoplifting. Can you tell the court something of her manner when you did this? Was she aggressive in any way?"

"Can't say as she was, miss. Upset a bit, maybe. But not difficult, not like some of her kind who tell you you're a racist if you suggest they're not abiding by the law of the land."

Judith was quiet for a moment to let his words sink in. Then, "When you say 'some of her kind', Constable, who exactly do you have in mind?"

"Well, people who come from where she comes from."

"She comes from Hackney. She was born there. Are you suggesting that people from Hackney feel that the police are prejudiced against them?"

"Oh, no, miss. Come from Hackney myself."

"I see." She paused again and then enquired, "And had Mrs Playbell ever been in trouble with the police before?"

"No, miss. We've nothing on our files against her."

"So she is, as far as you know, a lady of good character who has a clean record?"

"Yes, miss.

"Thank you, Constable. I have no more questions."

112

So far, so good, Judith thought as she prepared to call her first witness for the defence, Rosie Playbell herself.

With careful questions she prompted Rosie to tell the tale she herself had heard two weeks before. The jury listened attentively. It was hard to tell what they made of it.

Next, she called the headmistress of St Swithen's Junior School.

"Thank you for sparing the time to come to court, Mrs Summerfield," she said.

Mrs Summerfield was a big, motherly woman with a strong Scottish accent.

"Och, I'd do anything to help Rosie," she said. "We all love Rosie."

"By 'all', you mean you and your staff?"

"And the children, and the parents. We tried to keep it from the children, but news of the case got out, as these things do. They've all been sending messages and gifts to cheer her up."

"You would describe her as an honest person?"

"Oh yes. She doesn't, of course, handle money for the school, but the parents have been known to entrust sums to her to bring in to school if the children have forgotten it. She's utterly reliable. If there had been any doubt about that over the past ten years, she wouldn't have been kept on in a position of such trust."

"Thank you, Mrs Summerfield, you have been most helpful."

The next witness she called for the defence was one Laurence Bachelor.

"You are the sales manager of Merrihose & Company, of Leicester, Mr Bachelor?"

"Precisely so. That is correct."

He was a dapper little man, sharp-featured with a small spike of a nose propped up by a ginger moustache. His hair was carefully brushed sideways across his balding scalp which glowed pink and shiny through its inadequate thatch. He articulated very emphatically, his lips noticeably mobile. They were pink and moist and somehow lent him a rabbity look; an impression increased by his little pink hands which he waved about in front of him like paws.

113

But he came across as a man who knew his job and the jury, Judith told herself as she continued her questioning, were being asked to believe him as a witness, not accept him as a lover.

"You are responsible, Mr Bachelor, for sending your goods to the shops?"

"That is correct. For three years and two months I have been in charge of despatching hosiery to our retail outlets."

"And you supply packets of stockings such as these, to stores such as Boyson's?"

She held up one of the four packets which Rosie had bought.

"Exhibit Two, my lord," the clerk said, taking it and showing it to the judge before passing it to the witness.

The sales manager of Merrihose & Company looked at the packet in his hand as carefully as if he had never seen such a thing before, and then gave it as his opinion that it did indeed contain the product made by his firm.

"And can you tell the court if you have any system to control the despatch of these products?"

"Indeed we have. It would be impossible to carry on our business without one. Every batch of stockings which is made has its serial number printed on the packaging. There, you can see it on the box."

With his tiny right paw he pointed to a row of figures imprinted on the cardboard.

"Thank you, Mr Bachelor. Could that be shown to the jury?"

The clerk did his job; the members of the jury passed the package round as if playing a game of pass-the-parcel, examining the tiny indentations as it passed from hand to hand.

"It is done in rather the same manner as sell-by dates are imprinted on groceries," the chirpy little voice continued. Mr Bachelor then permitted himself a little joke, "Not, of course," he said, "that ladies need fear that our hosiery should go *bad*, but this enables us to trace to which batch any pair of stockings belong, in the unlikely event of there being a complaint. Thus, it guarantees that we can keep track of our stock and also maintain quality control, which is a very important consideration for

Merrihose & Company, who have been in business for nearly one hundred years."

"How often, Mr Bachelor, do you change these numbers?"

"Frequently. Approximately every two months. It does, however, depend to some extent on sales. It would be less frequent in the summer, when sales fall off because the ladies tend not to be wearing hosiery as much as they would in the winter and therefore buy fewer pairs."

Clearly Mr Bachelor didn't believe in answering questions in three or four words if he could possibly answer them in thirty or forty. Some of the jury were fidgeting; she tried to bring him to the point.

"So if you had the batch number you would be able to know the approximate date when each packet was sent out?"

"Between certain limits, yes."

"Mr Bachelor," Judith went on quickly to prevent him rambling on. "I would like you to look at these four packets of stockings and tell me when you think they were despatched to Boyson's. You have, of course, the necessary papers to refer to."

Once again Exhibit Two was handed to the witness. He studied the number and then looked at a list in a file.

"These were sent out at the end of February," he said. "There could be some pairs in the shops still."

"Thank you. Now please will you look at this packet and identify the date it was despatched to Boyson's from the number printed on it?"

"Exhibit One, my Lord," the clerk told the judge.

Again the witness looked carefully at the number and then checked it against his list.

"This pair is much earlier. It must have been despatched in the late summer of last year."

"So in your view it must have been bought earlier than the other four pairs?" Judith asked and promptly regretted it, for Victor Randall was immediately on his feet pointing out that the witness might know when the goods were despatched but could not possibly know when they were sold; an opinion backed by the judge.

Judith had no option but to resolve that next time she wouldn't push her luck and meanwhile, say, "I have no more questions, Mr Bachelor. Thank you, you have been most helpful," and move swiftly on to her next witness, the manager of the lingerie department.

"Miss Foulds, you have been the manager of Boyson's Lingerie department for some time?"

"Ten years."

"Could you describe the system by which goods reach the shelves of your store – you call it, I think, a 'superstore'?"

"Yes. The goods are delivered by the supplier to our warehouse area. They are then removed, as required, from the warehouse and placed on the shelves by our shelf-fillers."

"Members of the jury will have seen the shelf-fillers hard at work when doing their shopping?"

"Yes."

"The number of times shelves are filled would, of course, depend on the rapidity with which the goods in question are taken from the shelves by customers?"

"Yes."

"You must help me with this – but perhaps it is a matter of common sense – that when shelves are filled, the older goods at the back are brought forward and the newer goods are placed towards the back of the shelf? Perhaps this is a matter about which instructions are given to the shelf-fillers?"

"Yes. That is the system which the shelf-fillers are trained to carry out. It ensures an even turnaround of stock."

"Obviously, one doesn't want older stock hanging about, if I may use that phrase?"

"Absolutely right."

"How many times a day or week would the shelf where stockings of this type," Judith went on, holding up one of the boxes, "are displayed have to be filled?"

"I cannot give a categorical answer."

"Can you help the jury by giving an estimate. Let me suggest at least once a week?"

"To an extent that would depend on the season, but I would think that once a week is a fair estimate."

116

"And your answer would cover the period with which the jury are concerned in this case?"

"Yes."

"I am grateful to you. Does it not follow from your answers that it is highly unlikely that stockings delivered to your warehouse in August were still on the shelves and available to customers in the following February?"

"Highly unlikely. Impossible, I should say."

"Miss Foulds," Judith went on in order to forestall queries from the prosecution, "is it possible that sometimes, despite all instructions, stockings might linger on the shelf, odd packets getting pushed to the back and lying there for months?"

The manager was incensed.

"Indeed not," she said, sounding affronted by the very idea. "Even if the shelf-fillers ignored instructions, the stock is checked and cleared each month and the shelves regularly wiped down."

In the face of such indignation, Victor Randall decided against cross-examining. Clearly the store manager was one who wasn't going to admit the possibility of any lapse in her system – even to secure a conviction. In his final speech, he spoke rather vaguely about the need to protect society from shoplifters. When her turn came, Judith turned with confidence to the jury and fixed her eyes on the woman with the velour hat and anxious expression.

"Members of the jury," she began. "It struck me today that some of you might think that the charge of stealing a pair of stockings is a trifling thing, something undeserving of the full protection of the British legal system. But what is at stake here is not a pair of stockings worth two pounds, it is the good name of a British citizen who has been wrongly accused. You have heard, not from the defence but from a prosecution witness, that she has a clean record, a reputation unbesmirched. The defendant has much to lose if she is wrongly found guilty; she holds a position of trust; she guards the children in her community; she is loved by them and trusted by their parents."

She paused; they were looking at her intently. The anxious eyes of the behatted lady were upon her, the kindly faced one was radiating good will. Even the old misogynist was looking as if he might once have been human.

"The defendant has already suffered dreadfully from this false accusation. She has been sustained by gifts and good wishes from the many families who know and love her and who see her every day as she does her duty of ensuring the safety of their children. But doubt has been cast upon her honesty. Her good name has been tainted. You – and only you – can take away that stain. I call upon you to go now and do your duty by this innocent woman; release her back into her community without that stain upon her character."

She sat down, surprised to find that the paper in her hand was trembling. She looked across at the dock and was rewarded by a smile that seemed to split Rosie Playbell's face in two. The court adjourned while the jury withdrew and she ran down the stairs to join Rosie in the cells.

They had hardly time to speak before they were recalled for the verdict. *That's a good sign*, she thought. They'd have taken much longer if there'd been any argument.

There had been no argument. A unanimous verdict of Not Guilty was returned. She was so overjoyed that she nearly jumped up and asked for costs, forgetting that it was a legal aid case.

"Oh, you was lovely, you was perfect," Rosie said yet again, as they sat drinking tea with Mr Brutall in the coffee bar afterwards.

"Well, really it was Mr Bachelor's evidence that convinced the jury, you know, and the manager's."

"Ah, yes but it was you thought of de whole idea of de numbers and gettin' Mr Bachelor in de first place. He was just de rabbit you pulled out of de hat," Rosie said.

Judith laughed; so Rosie had thought of rabbits too.

"And I'm grateful to you, Mr Brutall," Rosie went on, as he rose to leave them, "for finding me dis lovely lady to defend me. I must be honest and say at first I rather it'd been a man, a proper lawyer, but not now I doesn't. Dis lady did me very nicely."

After he had gone, Rosie looked at her watch, a tiny little gold thing embedded in the flesh of her massive wrist, and said, "I must be goin' along now meself. He's a nice little bit of a man, isn't he? No pretentions."

"You've known him a while, I believe?"

"No. Never sets me eyes on him till we came to you."

"Oh, I'm sorry. I thought he'd worked for your husband and his relations . . . ?"

"Oh, yes but I never had nothin' to do wid dat. I don' believe in women interferin' in men's work. Women don' understand dat kind of a thing. All dis women's lib nonsense, I've no use for it at all."

"Oh," was all Judith could say, deflated.

"A woman shouldn't go interferin' and questionin' about her husband's work. My mudder always used to say, 'A woman's place is in de home'. All right a little bit of job like lollipop lady, when de childers growed up but not de serious work. Anyone who knowed me'd say, 'Rosie'd never have taken dem stockings, Rosie knows her place'. I'd no more go thievin' than my man would go washin' up de dishes. Crime's man's work," she concluded emphatically, with a conviction in her voice that would have done credit to Tom Trapp.

Man's work, woman's work indeed! Judith thought indignantly as she hailed a taxi to take her back to chambers. It was awful that people, especially women, could still talk like that. She remembered telling her father years ago how she would fight for the Alices of this world. He'd made some cautionary reply which she couldn't quite remember for the moment, but she did remember the scene as they sat by the cottage fire in peaceful Netherby.

As she was driven through the noisy, crowded streets of rush-hour London, she lay back, suddenly tired after all the nervous tension of the day, and thought of the village with its tranquil lanes and meadows and never-changing hills. And Alice still there; no doubt married now and doing her woman's work while her husband got on with his because that was the way of their world. There was something strangely reassuring about it and, weary as she was, she wasn't sure whether the thought made her sorry or glad.

Nineteen

"He's asked me out to the pictures, Peter has," Alice told her mother as she put Samson's newly soled-and-heeled boots down in the scullery and came into the kitchen. "He says it's very good and did tell me the name, but I can't remember it."

"I thought he might be asking you," Hilda said. "From something he said to me a while back. You could do worse. He's a good steady lad."

"Who's steady?" Samson asked, coming in holding the boots which he had picked up in the scullery and was now critically examining.

"Peter from the shoe-shop."

"Well, he's made a good job of my boots."

"He doesn't do that himself," Alice told him impatiently. "It's done out the back somewhere. His dad owns the shop so he helps with the management."

"I know that. I was just saying."

"I remember it in his grandfather's day," Hilda said. "He was a very big man, like Peter. Good strong stock, the Baxters. A good family business too. And it'll be Peter's one day."

She was sitting by the fire making a rag mat, the sacking spread across her knees, a pile of clippings alongside. For as long as she could remember, Alice had watched these mats being made, first by her grandmother, then by her mother. She loved to watch the speed with which those practised fingers worked, jabbing with the prodder to make a hole, pushing one end of the clipping through while the other hand caught it on the other side, then swiftly jabbing another hole nearby to push through the other end. Then jab again, push and jab, hole after hole,

121

almost as quickly as a sewing machine. Her mother used the same prodder as her grandmother had done; made out of deerhorn it was, filed down, smooth and polished with use.

She didn't make the mats herself; she did the finer sewing for which her mother said her own fingers were now too clumsy. But she had always helped with cutting up the rags for clippings. They had to be from strong material that didn't fray and would withstand heavy wear, so they came from suits and coats, from her mother's heavy skirts or her father's thick pyjamas, familiar from washing and ironing over the years. So when the mats were finished and lying on the stone kitchen floor she would look at them and remember when they had been whole garments, and it seemed as if the family's intimate history had been stitched into these rugs.

The one that her mother was making now was a small one for Joanna's bedside, so she had tried to find bright colours for it. Mostly the rag mats were dull, with much grey and black, leavened now and then with a bright centre piece made out clippings of gran's red flannel petticoats. But this one was going to be really colourful: Clara had donated an old yellow tweed skirt and her mother had sacrificed some deep red curtains which might otherwise have been good for another two years hanging at the parlour window.

"So, it's all right if I go?" Alice asked now.

"How'll you get back?"

"He'll walk me up from the bus. Then he'll stay the night with his cousins in the village so he'll be handy for the bus in the morning. He likes to be in the shop early, before the staff come in."

"So you've got it all worked out between you, then?" her mother enquired in a voice which was, for her, positively arch.

"If he fancies our Alice, he'll maybe mend the boots for nowt?" Samson suggested, suddenly perceiving an advantage in the situation.

"Don't be so soft," Alice told him, blushing. "And I've not made up my mind to go anyway."

But she did go.

It seemed to Alice that he treated her like a queen, this tall young man with his nice manners. He took her out for supper at The Crown where he ordered half a pint of cider for her and had a pint of beer himself. She had never had cider before and felt slightly light-headed as they walked across the market square to the cinema, but it passed. Once there he bought her a box of chocolates and paid for the best seats.

It was the first time she'd been taken out like this and been made so much of. She felt really special, a new sensation for her. Afterwards they had coffee and talked. She chatted much more than she usually did, telling him about the farm and about Joanna and all the funny things she was saying nowadays. He, who was usually shy, found himself telling her about his plans to expand the shop, even start another one in Bestwick, ten miles away. Maybe, even, he would one day own a whole chain of shoe-shops. Go right up to the Lake District perhaps; there was a lot of walking done there too.

They were still chattering as they caught the last bus back to Netherby, but fell silent as they got off and walked through the village and up the lane to the farm, suddenly aware of being alone together under the sky.

It was a clear, moonlit night and the lane wound ahead of them, silvery, ribbon-like. He wanted to say something more than chat, but couldn't find the words. He'd only had one girlfriend, Gloria, a schoolfriend of his sister. He'd liked her but hadn't dared do anything about it because he didn't know if she liked him enough for that, and he didn't want to offend her. So she'd given up on him and gone with somebody else. His sister had said it was all his own fault for being so feeble and how could poor Gloria know if she liked him or not if he didn't *do* anything?

He didn't want to make the same mistake with Alice, who was much nicer anyway. But still, he had the same fear of offending her; there was something quite refined and gentle about her. After much thought, he said, as he opened the little gate into the copse, "I've really enjoyed this evening, Alice, and I hope you have too?"

"Oh, yes. It was really good, was the picture. And all the rest too, the meal and everything, was lovely."

"We might go again?" he suggested, taking her hand to help her over a little ditch and then across an uneven patch of ground. This autumn's leaves were lying thick on top of last year's and there were branches and sticks among them, so she needed a hand anyway, he thought.

He felt her tense herself, but she didn't take her hand away so he held on to it as they walked between the trees, not talking now. He knew that soon they would be out of the copse, in the open, and in no time back at the farm. He must act boldly now, he knew that. So he let go of her hand and put it round her waist instead, his arm resting across her shoulder.

Alice felt the weight of his arm, heavy on her back. Four years ago the attack had been, four years since she had suddenly felt the weight of that other man's arm, but it might have been yesterday. It might be now. All the pent-up fear, kept sealed within her for years, erupted. The same terror and horror seized her again. Helpless in the grip of panic, she pushed him away, shouting, "No, no, *no!*"

He stood, this gentle giant, aghast, not knowing what he had done wrong, while Alice ran, stumbling and sobbing across the field to the safety of the farm.

Twenty

E ven on their honeymoon, Judith began to suspect that all that she and Cedric had in common was a love of walking. And even that, she soon came to realise, was not the same kind of love.

She loved to be part of the Dales countryside: to be at one with the sights and sounds and smells of it; to stand and feel the wind in her hair and hear the faraway bleating of sheep and the sad, desolate cry of the curlew. She loved to watch the shadows race across the hillsides under the windswept clouds. She loved to lean against an old dry-stone wall and feel, beneath her fingers, the roughness of the lichen that encrusted it. It was as if the sights and sounds of her childhood were part of her being, engrained in her so that when she came back among them, she felt that she had returned home and something deep within her was anchored and at peace.

It was different for Cedric; he enjoyed passing briskly through the countryside, he delighted in the healthy exercise it afforded him, the good it did his muscles. He was keen on calculating their mileage and how fast they had walked. "Come along," he would sometimes say when she stopped to gaze about her or searched idly in the warm grass for a chirruping cricket. "Come along, or you'll reduce our average."

She tried to laugh him out of it.

"Oh, just come and listen to the skylark," she said on their last day, as he stood, pack on back and eager to be off again after their picnic lunch, and she lay on the springy sheep-cropped turf watching the lark fly higher and higher, straining to hear the last of its song as it spiralled away into nothingness, and then

125

plummeted down, only to climb again and again, still singing as if its heart would break, as if its tiny body and feathers were nothing but pure sound.

Grudgingly, he sat beside her and listened for a while.

"Very nice," he said, "but a bit repetitive, don't you think? That was a skylark we heard yesterday, wasn't it?"

And he glanced at his watch as if to say: Really, when you've heard one skylark, you've heard them all.

"We must keep up the hiking," he said, as he unpacked his boots when they got back to the little basement flat she had found for them in Fleet Street.

"What, hiking in the back roads of London?"

He laughed. "No, there are organisations which take you to suitable places by train. I'll enquire, if you like."

She didn't particularly like, but he enquired all the same. "It's a club run by a Major Tennant," he reported that night. "Ex-army man. Retired now. Sounds very friendly, very jovial. He suggests we start with an easy walk, just twelve miles. What happens is that we all meet up at Hayes. On the station."

Judith, slicing chicken into thin slivers, only half-listened to this talk of majors and leaders. They had agreed to take it in turns to cook the evening meal. Since she had no knowledge of traditional cooking, she had decided to get herself a wok and do what the accompanying book told her to do with it. So here she was, slicing chicken, carrots, courgettes, onion and a misshapen root of ginger all very carefully and with the concentrated deliberation of the unpractised.

"It so happens," Cedric was saying, "that the Major is the leader on this walk, so really it's ideal for us to start on this one."

"Once I've stir-fried all this," she told him, adding nuts, "we've got to eat it straight away, otherwise it'll go all gooey and horrible. Are you ready?"

"Yes, I jogged around the office a few times before coming home, so I'm ravenous. What exactly is this?"

"It's a Chinese recipe. Do you like it?"

"Well, it's different," he said, chewing judiciously.

"That means no," she said, smiling.

"No, really, it's very good. It's just that my mother used to make us English meals and so I suppose I'd rather expected something more, well, more—"

"Familiar?" she suggested.

Then she laughed and leaned across to take his hand. "It's your turn tomorrow, so you can cook us meat and two veg, followed by apple pie and custard."

"Oh, I thought I'd just get us something ready-cooked from Sainsbury's."

"Cheat," she said and kissed him.

He was looking so much better now, she thought; that shocked look which had dwelt behind his eyes and clenched his mouth had gone. He was getting back to his normal self, she thought, and then realised that she didn't really know what his normal self was like.

It was a mixed little group that assembled on Hayes station in a cold drizzle that was more like January than October. There were several muscular old men, some middle-aged women, grey of hair, stout of calf and determined of expression; all kind and friendly to the newcomers. Among the latter, apart from themselves, were two schoolboys who had been sponsored to raise money for a new scout hut and a very earnest Asian girl who said she was researching into the leisure habits of the English. "This must be a typical English way of spending Saturday," she pronounced as they set off into a wet and cutting wind.

As they plodded through suburbia, the jammed Saturday traffic pouring forth noxious fumes, the leader's wife said cheerfully, "It's good to be out in the fresh air after London, isn't it?" and Judith nodded and wondered if she was quite sane.

Not very sane herself either, she thought; if she'd had any sense she wouldn't be here at all but at home studying her new brief. Things were looking up at work; since Rosie Playbell's case she'd had two more shopliftings, a grievous bodily harm and a mugging. She suspected they had come her way despite Tom rather than because of him, but was thankful all the same.

127

Once out of the town, the rain began in earnest, driving horizontally. But, anorak hoods up, faces down, her companions kept up a spanking pace along muddy lanes and waterlogged paths. Then, for a moment, the sky brightened and the rain ceased as they crossed a field of stubble. A sudden shaft of sunlight lit up the countryside with a pearly light, that curiously threatening sheen that suddenly illuminates stormy weather, presaging worse to come. She stood gazing about her. A rainbow appeared as she watched, arching right across the field, its colours disappearing into the gold of the stubble.

"All right, are we?"

It was the leader coming back to round up the last of his troops. She hadn't realised she was so far behind.

Embarrassed, she apologised. "I just stopped to look at that," she said, nodding towards the rainbow, which chose that moment to vanish as quickly as it had arrived. Swirling black clouds appeared from nowhere to darken the sky where it had been.

"That's all right, my dear. I always gallop up and down the line, you know, to cheer on the stragglers. There are always one or two that need a bit of encouraging. Amazing what the odd merry quip will do."

She accelerated and after that kept well up with the others, fearful of occasioning a merry quip.

At midday they reached the pub, where, over their lasagne and mixed grills, they discussed their average speed on various other walks, remedies for blistered feet and hiker's cramp. The thunderstorm was well underway now: forked lightning lit the windows, sheet lightning opened up the sky, followed by deluges of rain.

"Wouldn't it be sensible to catch a train back from Haybury?" she suggested. "It's only half a mile away."

They looked at her with disbelief at such a crass suggestion. "We have to do our twelve miles," they told her.

Cedric, embarrassed for her, said, "Easy isn't the point, dear." He sounded just like his father.

*   *   *

128

The Ewe Lamb

On Monday it was Cedric's turn to cook.

"I'll take these papers home with me," she told Tom. "My husband's making the dinner tonight."

"Oh, you've got one of those modern marriages have you?"

"That's right."

"Wouldn't do for me. I like my creature comforts."

"And what about your wife and her creature comforts?"

"Oh, Mrs Trapp wouldn't want me in her kitchen."

Cedric, it turned out, had forgotten to do the shopping.

"You could easily have done it," she said. "You leave work so much earlier that I do."

"Well, I had to go jogging and—"

"Had to?"

"And then I thought you'd probably have something in. My mother always had stocks in her store cupboard."

"Your mother didn't have a job."

"Well, I suppose she always thought it was a job, looking after my father and I."

"Me," she corrected automatically.

"You?"

"Oh, never mind. That was how things were then, but we're supposed to share the chores and you just forget all about it and go off jogging. Look," she went on more calmly, "why don't you go and get something at the takeaway while I get some work done?"

She tried not to feel resentful; she didn't want her marriage to go wrong on such trivialities; sometimes she had an awful feeling that it was going wrong anyway of its own accord.

They had been married nearly a year when he asked, as he finished his press-ups and prepared to join her in bed, "Would you mind very much if I was away for four days? I'd take two days off work and tag them on to the weekend."

Four days without Cedric: *what bliss!* was her immediate reaction. Then, shocked at herself, she said quickly, "Of course I don't mind. Where are you going?"

"We're going to walk to Birmingham."

"Wouldn't it be quicker to go by train?"

He looked at her, puzzled. Sometimes he couldn't make her out at all.

"The point *is* the walking, dear," he explained. "We'll come back by train, of course."

He yawned.

"Must set the alarm," he said, reaching for it. "I must be swimming by seven. You should join me one morning."

"No, thank you. I don't fancy arriving at chambers all damp."

"It's very good for you. I read in the 'Benefits of Natation' booklet that breaststroke strengthens the pectorals more than any other form of exercise. And for women, it firms the breasts."

"My breasts are firm enough already, thank you."

"In that case you could concentrate on the crawl. It's excellent for the thigh muscles and strengthens the back."

It wasn't that she had anything against exercise, she just felt he was obsessional about it, so ended up taking less of it than she would otherwise have done.

"One must keep fit, you know," he told her now.

"Why?"

He laughed.

"You're a funny old thing," he said, kissed her briefly and was soon asleep.

His interest in sex, so enthusiastic at first, if a bit rushed, had quickly diminished. On weekends when they had once lain in bed making love for half the morning, he now had to be off for a training session. His lovemaking became a cursory affair; a bit of business he had to get through before setting off for the sports centre. She felt increasingly frustrated.

When, at breakfast the next morning, he said, "How about an exercise bike for your birthday? We could share it. It's very good for the leg muscles, especially for the calves and quadriceps", she pointed out that sex was good exercise too.

He looked puzzled, as if pondering which set of muscles that particular activity might possibly improve.

She had lunch that day with Freddy and Tim. The Wig and Whistle, still their favourite eating place at lunchtime, was crowded as always with the young and impecunious; while Tim ordered drinks at the bar, Freddy and Judith battled their way across the crowded little room to a table in a gloomy corner by a wilting rubber plant.

"There's a new system," Tim said when he joined them with the drinks. "The McScabbes have contrived to find a suitably surly waitress who will come in her own good time to take our order."

She was a short, thick-set woman of indeterminate age whose swarthy face bore an expression of deep resentment. She appeared to speak no English; in silence she glowered at them through the curtain of dark hair which almost hid her face as she stood by their table holding a pad and pencil, ostensibly waiting for their order but looking as if homicide was more what she had in mind.

"Three rounds of cheese and ham, please," Freddy requested. "And I'd like mine toasted."

She showed not a flicker of interest and walked away. They looked at each other.

"Do you think she understood?" Judith asked.

Tim shrugged.

"Time will tell," he said.

"I wonder where they found her?"

"There's an agency that specialises in them. It's called something like the Surly Waitress Bureau. This one is a fine specimen, the archetypal, incomprehensible, uncomprehending foreign waitress. No pub should be without one. Cheers. Here's to the rest of 1981."

"I don't know why we should drink to it," Tim objected. "It's been a pretty foul year so far, what with the riots and the ghastly Ripper trial. I was deep in the Law Reports about it just before we came out."

Judith shuddered.

"I couldn't bring myself to read the details," she said.

"You should," Freddy reprimanded. "If you're going to make a success of the Bar, you've got to face human nature even at its most revolting."

"I know. You're right. Otherwise Tom will have an excuse to say women are too squeamish to do what he chooses to call man's work."

"Well, at least the Ripper's confessed and his four-year reign of terror's over."

"And there was the Royal Wedding to gladden our days," Judith pointed out.

Tim groaned.

"Don't mention weddings," he said. "One of the reasons I can't afford to get married is that I'm always buying wedding presents for everyone else. Poor Ethne, she does so want to marry me, but Daddy will fuss on about the dangers of poverty."

"She does quite well out of her business of arranging exhibitions, doesn't she?" Freddy asked.

"Would that she did! It's kind of you to think I might be a kept man and there is nothing I should like better, but alas, no. Although she's awfully good at organising, she doesn't seem able to organise *and* make money at the same time."

Judith didn't join in the conversation; she was wary of talk of marriages nowadays with her own in such a parlous state. Whether by some instinct of tact or just by chance, Tim and Freddy rarely asked about Cedric, for which she was truly grateful.

The waitress was approaching with a tray.

"Thank you so much," Tim said, "that's really most kind. Let me help you. I'm sure Freddy will overlook the fact that his sandwich comes untoasted."

She ignored him, dumped the plates down on the table and walked away.

For a while they concentrated on eating. Then Tim said, "Does anyone else think we ought to do something about Tom?"

"What sort of a something?" Judith asked.

"Early retirement preferably."

"How old is he?"

"It's a state secret, Judith, but whatever his age he doesn't look it."

"Certainly he's very well preserved."

"Fossilised might be the better word," Tim told her.

He looked at his watch.

"I've got to be off," he said. "In court this afternoon. But you two stay on."

"No, I've got to get back. How about you, Judith?"

"My man pleaded guilty so the case folded. I've nothing now until the middle of next week."

"Why don't you have a break?" Freddy suggested. "You're looking a bit peaky."

"Really, Freddy, that's not a very chivalrous remark," Tim rebuked him. "Our Judith is looking her usual radiant self, hers is the light that brightens our chambers."

Judith laughed, but she realised that she was showing the strain of the past months and that Freddy had observed it. He was right; she ought to get away for a few days. It occurred to her that if she left the flat after Cedric set off on his march to Birmingham tomorrow, she could fit in three days in Netherby. She hadn't been back since her father died; suddenly she longed to be there again, to be home once more among those hills. There, if anywhere, surely she'd be able to think clearly and sort out the mess she'd got herself into.

Back in chambers she called in on Tom.

"Two days off," he repeated dolefully. "Well, if you don't mind risking missing a brief. I hope you won't need cover while you're away."

"No, everything's under control."

At first they said there was no room at The Curlew, but then offered her a little room under the eaves, if she didn't mind having to go down two flights of stairs to the bathroom and lavatory. She didn't mind; she took the room and began looking up train times.

There was always a point on the train journey north at which she felt a tug of recognition; it wasn't just the way that towns and suburbs were replaced by scattered villages and hamlets, or even the way that hedgerows gave way to dry-stone walls; it was something friendly and welcoming in the way the landscape opened out, in the way the light fell on the hills and fields; the way the shadows, cast by low and puffy clouds, moved swiftly across the countryside, as if racing the train. There was something in the very air of the place that spoke of homecoming.

She loved it in all weathers, but particularly a day like this, she thought as, having settled in at The Curlew, she set off to walk to the head of the dale. It was one of those fresh days of early autumn which feels more like spring, when the ruffling wind lifts the grey coat of the sheep as they graze, exposing the paler wool beneath, and the birds swoop and soar catching every breeze that blows across the fells. One of those days when the sun comes and goes, but the air is always warm and the wind soft against the face. On such a day she had always loved to walk and feel glad to be alive.

On such a day she walked now, determined to use the strength it gave her to sort out the muddle of her marriage without meanness or self-deceit. She paused at the brow of the first long hill and climbed up on to a stile to rest and look about her, her eyes lifting to the nearby hills and then to Sawborough towering in the distance. Suddenly she heard voices and, glancing down, saw in a hollow in the field, just a few yards away, a young woman playing with a child, a little girl of about four or five. The mother was throwing a big woollen ball at the child who flung her arms out wide so that it bounced against her stomach and fell at her feet.

"No, Joanna, clap your hands together like this and catch it," the young woman called, demonstrating with her own hands how it should be done.

Joanna clapped enthusiastically but missed the ball and fell over. The woman scooped her up, held her for a moment in the air, laughing. It was then that, head flung back, she caught sight of Judith on the stile.

Judith jumped down and walked the few yards to meet her.

"It's Alice, isn't it?" she said. "And this must be your little girl?"

How lovely to think of Alice happily married and with a daughter. How unlike the mess of her own marriage.

134

"Nay, it's my little sister, Joanna. Our Mam's latest."

"She's lovely."

"She's all right," said Alice, which Judith rightly interpreted as Dalespeak for she's absolutely perfect and let no one gainsay it.

"Say hello to Miss Delaney," Alice instructed her sister.

"Oh, please let her call me Judith," she said, partly to avoid mentioning that she was married, as she and the little girl smiled at each other.

"You're staying in the village?" Alice asked.

"Yes, I got the last room at The Curlew."

'They say it's difficult to get anywhere to stay, now that her at the shop doesn't take in lodgers any more."

"You'll have to start doing bed and breakfast at the farm," Judith told her and instantly regretted it because Alice looked so shocked.

It was a terrible suggestion to make to a member of the Dowerthwaite clan, recluses that they all were. "I didn't really mean that," she said, embarrassed. "I know you wouldn't think of such a thing."

But Alice was looking thoughtful.

"There's them as do," she said.

She was quiet for a moment, considering it. Something else was also on her mind.

"I'm sorry," she said hesitantly, "very sorry about you losing your father, Judith. I mean to say it must be very hard to be on your own, worse than it was for me when *my* dad died.'

Judith thanked her, knowing that expressing condolences would not come easily to Alice, and they were the more heartfelt for that reason. She couldn't bring herself to explain that she was not, in fact, any longer on her own. It might embarrass Alice if she mentioned it now, she told herself, feeling guilty all the same about deceiving someone who was, after all, her childhood friend.

Joanna was offering her the ball, so Judith took it and began to play with her, glad of the distraction.

She stayed for a while, throwing and catching, and it seemed idyllic to be here in this field playing this innocent game after all the complications of London; a feeling that stayed with her after they had parted, they to go back to the farm and she to walk on up to the head of the dale. It had always been a favourite haunt of hers, this place where the beck emerged from the rocks and began its slow journey down to the village, past farms, under slate bridges, sometimes hurrying down tiny waterfalls, sometimes meandering in great loops that would, in later years, turn themselves into bow-shaped pools as the stream found a shorter way.

Mostly it flowed through open fields, but now and then it was shaded by an overhanging tree, not the lush weeping willow of gentler climes, just some tough little thorn bush which had rooted itself into the bank and withstood the winds by bending with them so that its rough and spiky branches were blown back like unkempt hair. Sometimes it was joined by other little streams, flowing down from the surrounding hills, so that by the time it reached the village it was a wider beck, where the dark shadows of trout could be seen in the evening gliding between great mossy stones or sheltering under packhorse bridges.

She loved to lie up here on the short grass by the rocks where the beck first saw the light of day and listen to its ceaseless chatter. Or she would sit up and watch it, mesmerised by its endless flowing. It seemed to gather itself together after emerging from the crag and pause for a moment as if revelling in the sunlight after its long sojourn underground. Then it widened and moved slowly towards a little ridge of rocks, where it hesitated for a moment on the brink, before sliding down a mossy waterfall into the pool below.

She must make herself face this thing honestly, she told herself, up here, in solitude, she had no excuse not to. She had been wrong to let Alice think that she was on her own; she wasn't on her own. She had Cedric, didn't she? But the truth was she didn't want him, felt more on her own with him than she would without him. It was time to admit that she had made a mistake. She had married the wrong man. What would she say to a friend who had done that? 'Leave him,' she would say. 'You've no children to worry about. If you're not happy, get out of it.' But it was not so

136

simple. It was not Cedric's fault; why should he have to suffer?
She had known what he was like and had refused to marry him
once. But the awful thing which had happened to his parents had
made her desperately sorry for him. Who wouldn't have been?
But she needn't have married him. Hadn't her own father warned
her once, '*Never marry for pity, Judith*'? She could hear him quite
clearly now, after all these years.

Of course that was what her father had done and she had easily
seen what a mistake he had made. It's so much easier to see other
people's mistakes, she thought. And then, God help us, re-enact
them. No, it wasn't a re-enactment: her father's marriage had been
wretched, hers merely ridiculous. Tragedy repeating itself as farce.

All these ideas, these arguments with herself, occupied her
mind for the next three days, whether she was walking among the
hills or banging her head on the sloping roof of the little bedroom
in the eaves. But by the time she caught the train back to London
she had resolved that she would tell her husband she must leave
him. And she would do it immediately she got back to the flat.

She got home to find Cedric, clearly exhausted after his four-
day hike, in bed and already sound asleep. She couldn't possibly
wake him to impart such awful news. Poor Cedric, who had done
nothing wrong except to be what he was. Instead she fell into a
fitful sleep and dreamed, as she sometimes did nowadays, that
she was in court.

It was Cedric who was being arraigned.

'*You are accused of being criminally boring,*' Judge Paxton-
Martin was saying. '*How do you plead?*'

'*Not guilty, my Lord,*' she heard herself reply. She was there in
her robes, defending him but, for some reason dictated by the
dreamworld, she was in the dock beside him.

'*On what grounds does he plead not guilty?*' the judge demanded, peering down at her. He had grown a beard and looked
alarmingly like a mountain goat.

'*He did not know that there was such an offence as being
criminally boring, my Lord,*' she heard herself reply.

'*Ignorance of the law is no excuse,*' the judge said, putting on a
little black cap. '*You should know that, my friend.*'

They're going to hang him and it's all my fault, she thought in a panic, and woke up wet with sweat.

Two days passed and still she couldn't break the news to Cedric. On the third evening he came in late, having done two hours jogging instead of his usual forty minutes.

She was sitting at the table working on her next case, when he came in. He kissed her on the top of her head and then went and stood in front of the mirror.

"I think I have a problem," he told her.

"Oh yes?"

"I'm afraid I have developed Jogger's Nipple," he said solemnly.

Odd that one remark should have settled what days of thought had not enabled her to do; she had to get away from him or go mad.

Odder still that he seemed less put out by her news than she had expected.

"Well, if you really feel that you'd rather we parted, Judith," he said matter-of-factly, "I wouldn't do anything to try to prevent it."

"Thank you. You're being very understanding."

"I should be able to stay here, though, wouldn't I? It's so very convenient for the sports centre."

"Yes, we can make arrangements about the mortgage and so on. I'm sure it would be possible," she told him, surprised that he didn't want to get away from their flat with all its associations.

'I think I may go back to Mrs Crumb,' she told him.

But he didn't seem very interested in what she was going to do.

"May I keep the exercise bike?" was all he asked. "I mean you've never really taken to it, have you?"

Twenty-one

"**B**ed and breakfast? Bed and breakfast? On Sloughbottom Farm?"

Samson Dowerthwaite repeated the words in thunderous disbelief. With his wide-shouldered stocky frame, his big head thrust forward, his eyes angry and glaring, he looked like his own Friesian bull when it was shut up in the paddock away from the soothing influence of the females of the herd.

Alice did not flinch in the face of this onslaught; she stood, all five feet two inches of her, in front of him, unafraid. Perhaps the fact that the daisy chain, which Joanna had made for him that morning, still dangled, limp and forgotten, about his swarthy neck, did something to make his rage appear less awful.

"Wherever did you get such an idea? Never from our mam, I'll be bound. More like that Clara—"

"No. It was something Judith Delaney said last year when she was—"

"I might have guessed. One of them interfering townfolk," he said with the satisfaction of one who had never underestimated the malign influence of all who visited the Dales from foreign parts.

"Just lightly she said it," Alice went on, unabashed, "but it set me thinking ever since. The farm's smaller now and—"

"And there's smaller numbers to work it," her brother pointed out. "And our mam's getting no younger—"

"I'm as strong as ever I was," his mother said, opportunely coming in from the scullery carrying, as if to prove her words, two laden coal scuttles which must have weighed half a hundredweight between them.

She put them down and looked at her children.

"You'd never go along with this daft scheme of our Alice, would you, Mam?"

"She's spoken of it," she said, sitting in the rocking chair and stirring the fire. "And I've given it thought. You'd do better to do the same, Samson, instead of railing."

She spoke slowly. They both waited.

"With your brothers away and married, each with the portion we agreed, the acreage here's enough for you to manage, Samson, with a wife when the time comes. Now we have to think of Alice."

"Alice'll be wed and off when she finds her man."

"I don't want a man," Alice said with a sudden ferocity that silenced him.

"Bring in the log basket from the scullery, will you, Alice?" her mother asked.

When she had gone, her mother said, "It's only right and proper to make provision for her, Samson. We've to make up to her for what happened."

He looked blankly at her, confused by the turn the conversation had taken, as a bull is confused when its quarry alters course.

"It would be a nice little business she could manage," his mother told him, as Alice returned with the log basket. "Set it down there, love."

"And I'd see to the housework and the hens and that, just as I do now," his sister reassured him, as she put down the basket, brushed her hands on her apron and went and sat down near her mother.

"And what about the extra cooking?"

Alice shrugged and smiled up at him. "I've done the breakfasts for years and it's never bothered you," she said. "It'd just be a matter of laying little tables in the dining-room and cooking a bit extra."

She could picture it all: the neatly set tables, laden with porridge and plates of fried bacon and eggs, just like her brothers had always had. It would only be a matter of introducing a few refinements in the way of butter knives and toast racks.

"She'll manage, don't you worry, lad. She's a capable lass is our Alice," their mother said, getting the words out slowly, unused as she was to giving praise.

He looked from one to the other, then he shook his great head and moved his feet about, as if needing to paw the ground.

"Others do it—" Alice began.

"Let others do what they fancies," he burst out. "We've never been bothered about what others did, have we, at Sloughbottom? It's a farm, not a, not a . . ."

He wasn't a man who easily found the right word, but it seemed as if 'brothel' might have been the one he sought.

"Café?" his sister suggested.

"That's it. I'll not stay and see our farm turned into some kind of wayside café like they have on the roads for lorries. It's a farm, I tell you, a decent working farm."

"And still would be, son," his mother said, speaking more gently than usual, because she understood what he felt, wrong-headed though he might be. "We make money out of an empty field, so why not money out of an empty bedroom? There's your gran and grandad's old room and the big one your brothers shared—"

"And there's the box room," Alice put in. "I could make that really pretty with bright curtains and bedspread to match. They expect basins in bedrooms nowadays and—"

"Basins in bedrooms?" her brother interrupted, enraged once more. "And what about plumbing? Did you think of that? It's not long since we had nobbut pump in t'yard and not even a tap inside and—"

"But we do now," she told him, "and have had for a long while, so it wouldn't be difficult to fit in basins. And they like kettles in their bedrooms too for making tea and coffee."

Samson looked at the kettle on the hob.

"You'll have fires in the bedroom? And be carrying buckets of coal upstairs?"

"Nay, lad. Electric kettles is what she means."

Plumbing. Electrics. He was silenced by the enormity of it. For this frippery, his mother was prepared to loosen purse strings

141

which she'd kept tightly drawn against the buying of tractors and modernising of milking sheds.

He tried a different line of attack.

"Who'd want to stay here anyway?" he demanded. "There's nowt for 'em to do. And they'd not want to damage their cars coming down our track."

"It's high time we did something about the track," said his mother, who had for years refused to spend money on levelling its bumps and potholes. "It's not a big job to fill in the ruts and put gravel down. In time, our Alice will need a car to get provisions and take Joanna to the big school."

"Our Alice have a car?" he repeated outraged. "Her as can't even drive?"

"She'll learn."

"We went to school in t'cart till we were old enough to walk on us own."

But he spoke without conviction, not really believing that what had been good enough for them would be good enough for Joanna.

"I think hikers would come," Alice said, answering his earlier question. "Ramblers and those students who come for the rocks."

"Geographers," he said in disgust, "tapping t'millstone grit and limestone wi' their hammers. Backpackers. I tell you, we can do wi'out any of that sort in our house."

"You'd hardly know they're here," Alice foretold. "We'll use the back stairs and all the far end of the house. And it'll only be in the summer, when you're out in the fields all day."

"The best thing," their mother said with finality, "is for me and Alice to work out what's needed. We'll set it all down, get plumber and electrician up from the village to give us a price and then we'll know where we stand. And don't you fret," she added, giving her son a shrewd look. "I'll not spend a brass farthing until we've got it all sorted."

And so it was; for weeks his mother and sister pored over lists and figures, talked in undertones of lights and basins and pipes; held rather louder discussions with the village plumber and

electrician, who then moved in and made themselves at home,
banging and sawing and drinking tea. Alice bought yards of
material to cut and sew; in the kitchen the treadle sewing machine
whirred constantly under her foot, while even Joanna was
conscripted to help with tacking and unpicking.

"Children will come to stay," she told her brother. "And I
shall play with them."

So all three of his womenfolk were against him now. He ceased
to argue, just withdrew into lowering silence and endured the
presence of the village workmen in his home by vacating it in
favour of the fields and outhouses.

"Come and have a look at the room we've finished, Samson,"
Alice said one morning when he came in from the milking. "I'll
doubt you'll recognise it."

He knew the bedroom well: after his grandfather had died,
his bedridden grandmother had occupied it for years. He had
spent hours there when he was little, playing on the wide-
boarded polished floor. His mother, too busy to mind him
herself, said grandma liked the company. They didn't bother
with each other much; his grandmother sat up in bed knitting
socks or sewing a rag mat while he got on with playing farms
on the floor.

He remembered that room as he followed his sister upstairs
now; recalling the darkness of it, with its brown paintwork and
heavy mauve curtains which blocked the light from the window.
He remembered the chest of drawers with the pock-marked
mirror unsteady on top, the marble washstand with its jug
and basin and dish for the soap, and the cupboard by the bed
for the chamber-pot. He remembered the sheet which hung
across one corner of the room, hiding the clothes which hung
on a rail behind it.

Above all he remembered the big iron bedstead, with its dark
purple counterpane, where his grandmother's body had lain
when he had been sent upstairs to take his leave of her. He
remembered how he had opened the door and the sheet, which
hung in the corner hiding the clothes' rail, had billowed out in the

143

draught like a ghost so that, terrified, he had rushed out again with hardly a glance at the waxen figure on the bed.

Alice opened the door now on a room he truly did not recognise. It was a bright room with cream walls and white paintwork. New curtains, drawn well back from the window, blew gently in the breeze, framing a view of Sawborough, so that it looked like a picture on the wall. Alice showed him how she had fitted a kidney-shaped piece of plywood, then glass to match, on top of the chest of drawers, and hung curtains from a rail, so that it looked like a very elegant dressing table. In the same material she had made a padded window seat in the deep recess under the window. In the corner where the sheet had once billowed was now a fitted cupboard and next to it the new basin. Above the basin was a little glass shelf and a china splashboard decorated with roses, while below it all the pipes had been boxed in, so that altogether it looked like something you might see in a picture magazine.

"Well, then," Alice asked. "What do you think of it, our Samson?"

He nodded.

"It's different," he conceded. "It's not the sort of place a man would want to sleep in."

Twenty-two

"In my day," Mrs Crumb said, "if you made a mistake you had to take the consequences and that went for marriage too."

"And you think that was better?"

"No, it was daft. Better to scrap it and start again."

"Well, I don't intend to start again."

It was two years since her divorce and already it seemed as if the marriage had never been. Sometimes she wondered where it had all gone; there had been passion at first, real enough at the time, but there was no trace now even of remembered feeling.

Blessedly there was no guilt either, since Cedric had remarried with surprising speed: a placid, undemanding girl called Patsy, who worked part-time at the gym and had taken pity on this skinny young man whose wife had left him; volunteering to cook a meal for him now and then – an arrangement which became permanent when she became pregnant. She gave up work in favour of full-time domesticity, moved into the flat and Cedric exchanged the exercise bike for a tandem.

All this they had told her when she called on them, at Cedric's invitation, to sign some papers concerning their previous joint ownership of the flat. She had observed that he had put on weight, seemed less obsessive about exercise and was altogether more relaxed. *I was bad for him*, she had realised. He sensed that he exasperated me and it made him defensive. Keeping fit was the barrier he hid behind. Patsy doesn't do that to him; she brings out the best in him in her undemanding way. Soon they will begin to look alike, just as his parents did.

"On the other hand," Mrs Crumb was saying, "it made you

145

think twice before you got married, if you knew you wouldn't be able to get out of it."

"I remember when I came back and told you I was getting married, you said, 'Marry in haste and repent at leisure'. You were proved right."

"I'd rather have been proved wrong."

They were sitting in Mrs Crumb's crowded drawing-room. To say that the room was overfurnished would be an understatement. Hardly any carpet could be seen between the sofas, desks, chairs, stools, cake-stands, sewing-boxes and assorted tables that made crossing the room a kind of obstacle course. When Judith negotiated it she always held her skirt close to her body in case she inadvertently swept something breakable off one of the many little tables, for every available square inch of surface was covered with photographs and ornaments.

Mrs Crumb was a magpie of a collector. Fine Meissen figures jostled for space on the mantelpiece with souvenirs from Morecambe. The judge's collection of minor Impressionist paintings hung on the wall, interspaced with souvenir plates and watercolours given by Mrs Crumb's not very talented friends. A beautiful Sèvres urn graced a delicate Queen Anne table next to a lumpen piece of earthenware brought back from a trip on the Rhine. The big mahogany china-cabinet was crammed with pieces of eighteenth-century silver and various artefacts marked EPNS or made of chrome which Mrs Crumb had acquired on her travels. 'I always like to bring something back,' she would say as she unwrapped yet another vase or ashtray.

Mrs Crumb herself was the same sort of mixture, Judith often thought, as she listened to her talk, which was a mixture of wisdom and dottiness. She seemed to have had little formal education beyond having the three R's drilled into her at her elementary school, but had read widely and haphazardly; learned a lot from various acquaintances of the judge, especially about the law, but hadn't somehow fitted it together. She uttered the wildest *non sequiturs*, had fearsome prejudices about most things and then showed sudden and unexpected perception. She had only the vaguest notion of what order things came in historically, so simply lumped them all together in a time she referred to as 'the olden days', a period which covered everything from the ancient Greeks to her own childhood. She was shrewd and sharp, prided herself on being a Yorkshirewoman who called a spade a spade, spoke of sensitivity as a weakness and was kinder than she cared to admit.

"I think I've been very lucky," Judith said, answering her last remark. "These last two years have been better than I deserved, particularly your letting me come back here."

Mrs Crumb shrugged.

"Oh, you'll want to be having a flat of your own again soon."

"Do you want me out?"

"It's up to you," said Mrs Crumb, who wouldn't for the world have admitted how much she wanted Judith to stay.

"I'm very happy here. I don't think I want the worry of my own place just now. And I certainly don't want to marry again."

"And what about having children?"

Judith shook her head.

"I don't want them. I realised that when I was married to Cedric."

"Are you sure it wasn't just *his* children you didn't want?"

She tried to think honestly.

"No, I think it was children as such. Anyone's children. I mean, they are so much more of an encumbrance for a woman than they are for a man. They take over her body, stop her working properly," she shuddered at the thought of it, "No, that sort of family life is not for me. I'm definitely married to the Bar."

"You've had plenty of work recently, haven't you?" Mrs Crumb said approvingly. "Well, judging by the amount you bring back with you."

"Yes. It seemed to start with the Rosie Playbell case; all her criminal connections got wind of it. All right, I know that criminal law doesn't pay well, but I really do love it and the money doesn't matter the way it would if I had a mortgage and a family to keep."

"I suppose they're nearly all legal aid cases, aren't they?"

Judith nodded. "Yes, and I know people grumble about it, but on the whole it's a good system. At least it does try to give the poor a chance of justice which they didn't have before legal aid came in."

"Oh, there was always the Poor Persons' Defence," Mrs Crumb contradicted her. "It cost three pounds, five shillings and six pence. Three guineas went to the barrister and half a crown to his clerk."

"I didn't know that. So the clerk did quite well?"

"He'd get more today if he got Tom's ten per cent," said Mrs Crumb, who seemed to know the ways of every set of chambers in the Temple.

"I'm afraid my maths isn't up to it. I'm not even sure what half a crown was – or a guinea, come to that."

"Three guineas is three pounds and three shillings, which was sixty-three shillings. So if he got ten per cent of that he'd get six and a bit shillings, which is much more than a measly half-crown, which was only two and a half shillings," Mrs Crumb told her with the rapidity of one brought up on mental arithmetic.

"I'm impressed," Judith said.

"If I didn't have a good head for figures, I wouldn't be as well off as I am," Mrs Crumb told her. "I'd probably have got into the clutches of one of those financial advisers and lost the lot. Mind you, I did have a good bit of advice at the start from a friend of the judge's but I've managed it all myself since. If ever you want any help, you just tell me."

"You were born before your time; you'd have made a wonderful barristers' clerk," Judith told her, getting up.

Mrs Crumb gave one of her unexpected cackles of laughter.

"I'd really have liked that," she said, "though Tom Trapp wouldn't care to hear you say it. I'd have got you rich in no time."

In bed that night, Judith thought about what they had said. It was true, she didn't want to marry again. She felt she'd done the marriage bit. She revelled in managing her own life; doing what she wanted when she wanted, working late without having to worry about letting somebody know and thinking about their plans as well as her own, being able to make decisions without having to consult anyone else.

Looking back on it all, she was grateful to Cedric for providing her with a marriage which had been absurd enough for there to be no possible regret at its ending. I've got all the advantages of widowhood, she thought as she settled down to sleep, and none of the grief.

Twenty-three

T he bed and breakfast business turned out to be less dreadful than Samson had expected; he was surprised at how little he saw of the visitors. He ate his breakfast undisturbed in the kitchen as he had always done and was out in the field before they were out of their beds. They seemed to know their place; sometimes, if they saw him outside, they would enquire about walks and footpaths and other foolishness, but Alice had printed a little notice to put in each room explaining about the dangers of farm machinery, so they kept out of his way in the yard. And when he saw families come with children of Joanna's age, who played with her in the home meadow, he almost forgot his objection to the scheme.

Alice's life was transformed. She still did all her tasks about the farm and cared for Joanna, taking her to school by car – for she had passed her driving test first time, unlike her brother who had failed his, due to driving through red lights, unaware that he was colour-blind. She went to evening classes on bookkeeping and ran her little business like a professional.

"You'd hardly know her for the poor little mousy bit of a thing she was when she came down to that whist drive," Clara said, shaking her head in amazement. "Goes and sees her bank manager, bold as brass. Her, who couldn't say boo to a goose."

"She's not proud with it, though," her friend replied. "Not like that Maisie Preston. Maisie's like a cock that thinks the sun rises because he's crowing at it, she is."

"Nay, our Alice isn't that sort. By, but she's good with her needle."

All her free time, Alice spent adding new touches to the rooms,

149

here a silk lampshade, there a new bedspread. Tasks which would have seemed a chore to other women were a delight to her. At school it had always been the academic girls who were thought successful, who were esteemed and confident, fulfilling themselves by going to university and having careers. But Alice's skills had not been thought much of, so she had though little of them – or of herself. It was only now that she had scope to use them that she came into her own. Like a plant that has been moved into the right soil, she flourished and blossomed.

"Three years since she had her first booking," her mother said to Samson. "And she's never had a complaint. And she's paid off the loan for the car. I'm right proud of her. And so should you be too," she added when her son stayed silent.

"She's done all right," he said and they both knew that no higher praise could be expected.

"We've been thinking about the stables," his mother went on.

"Stables?" he repeated, as if the word was foreign to him.

"They're not used for owt but storing tackle that should've been thrown out years ago. And the roof's all but gone."

"Nay, I fixed the gap with corrugated last winter."

"They'd make four grand rooms, our Alice reckons."

So Alice was called in and they both got at him.

"You see, our Samson," Alice explained. "What a lot of folk want nowadays is a bathroom of their own. *En suite*, they call it. We'd charge more, of course. The one at the end could be a big family room for parents with young children."

He didn't raise the objections he'd done before; let them get on with it, 'on sweet' bathrooms and all.

"It'd be best to start at the end of summer," Alice went on, "then we can get the the roof slated and all made watertight before the winter, so we can get on with indoor work in good time to open for the new season."

She'd taken to referring to the time when the visitors arrived as 'the season', as if they were some kind of crop, he noticed. Or migrating birds.

He shook his head, said, "I don't see what's wrong wi'

corrugated," but they both knew it was only because he had to say something, not because he expected it to be heeded.

So in the autumn the scaffolders and roofers moved in, removing what was left of the old stone tiles, laying felt, hammering in the new timbers. One day Samson counted seven men and groaned at the thought of the cost.

"It puts up the value of the farm," his sister said, reading his thoughts. "That's two coffees, one with two spoonfuls of sugar, one without, and five teas, two with plenty of sugar, one with not much and one without."

"She spoils them men," Samson grumbled to cousin Clara, who had come up to the farm to help. "They could bring their own."

"Well, why not give them fresh, if it keeps the lads happy? And they're held up now waiting for the slates. They were promised for noon and it's gone two o'clock."

Even as she spoke they saw it, the big lorry climbing slowly up the lane, laboriously rounding the corner into what used to be the farm track but which was now a macadamised road. Squinting into the sunlight, for it was an unseasonably hot and brilliant day, they watched it manoeuvre its awkward way into the farmyard, the crane it carried only just sliding under the lower branches of the tall pine tree.

In deference to the weather, the crane driver was scantily clad in the briefest of shorts and skimpy T-shirt. He was a very fat man; his stomach fell over the top of his shorts like a sack of potatoes and when he bent to secure the crates of slate to the hook of the crane the gap between his buttocks made a dark valley.

"By gum," Clara exclaimed, "but he's got a cleavage like the Grand Canyon."

Twenty-Four

J udith gazed at her reflection in the mirror with disbelief. How could her face and neck be covered in this rash on the morning of Tim's wedding day? Tears of frustration and disappointment filled her eyes as she looked at the pink, flat spots and then at the invitation on her dressing table in which Sir Albert and Lady Bullroyd requested her presence at the marriage of their daughter Ethne on Saturday 10th October 1987.

She felt awful; her throat was sore and her neck swollen and tender. Overcome by weakness she climbed back into bed, illogically relieved that she didn't have to travel to Doncaster after all.

It was still only six o'clock. She waited until seven before ringing Freddy from Mrs Crumb's telephone in the hall.

He was sympathetic but brief.

"Oh, poor Judith, I am sorry, but look I have to dash, duties of best man to attend to up there, you know. I'd have gone up last night but the case went on and on."

"You will explain, won't you, to Tim and Ethne?"

"Of course. And I promise I'll give you a blow by blow account of the wedding the first day you get back to work."

"Thanks, Freddy. Enjoy yourself."

Mrs Crumb insisted on calling the doctor.

"Spots can be anything from measles to smallpox," she pronounced.

"It's been eliminated," Judith told her wearily.

The doctor felt the glands in the back of her neck and diagnosed German measles.

"When I was young everyone tried to give little girls German measles to protect them against getting it in pregnancy," Mrs

153

Crumb told her as she came up with a hot lemon drink. "They used to have a tea-party for any child who got it and invited all the little girls in the neighbourhood in the hope they'd catch it. So you'll be all right now."

"Except that I don't ever intend to get pregnant."

Mrs Crumb sighed.

"It seems a waste of the German measles," she said.

Freddy kept his word; on her first day back in chambers he took her out for lunch at the Wig and Whistle and described the wedding service in detail.

"But the amazing bit was the reception," he told her, as he put two glasses of red wine down on the table between them. "Ethne's dad is the archetypal self-made man. He's one of those wartime businessmen who made a fortune out of armaments. It was easy money. The contracts were all on a cost plus basis, so it was impossible to lose. Anyway it set him up and earned him his title. After the war he bought up the local squire's estate which was going cheap."

"Who told you all this?"

"Well, Tim had told me quite a bit and I moved about among the locals and they were full of it. I think they like the old boy, find him a bit of a card. He bought up everything, you see, from the tenanted farms on the estate to the portraits of ancestors hanging on the walls of the ballroom. He's put in a lift lined with pretend books."

"Oh, to think that I missed all this!"

"You also missed the longest speech ever made by a bride's father."

"Ah, so he's proud of his daughter? That's nice."

"Well, she's his only one, the child of his old age. He married late, you know, so he's old enough to be her grandfather. I suppose he was too busy making money to get round to procreating. So, yes, quite a bit of the speech was about her, but much more was about himself and how well he'd done. He explained that he'd spared himself no expense over this wedding and gave us a rough breakdown of what it had cost—"

154

"Freddy, you're exaggerating!"

"I swear I'm not. And it was true. The meal was superb and after the dancing at night there was a supper that was almost as great as the wedding breakfast and between times the champagne flowed and caviare lay around in huge dollops and everyone enjoyed themselves hugely – and noisily too, it must be said."

"How did Tim take all this?"

It was somehow hard to imagine the languid Tim in this rather brash festivity.

"Oh, he was very laid back, was our Tim. So were most of his old Etonian friends and relations. One or two of them seemed to own a county or two up there and said how old Bullroyd had improved the estate, mended fences, all that sort of thing, apart from making the house much more habitable. Apparently it used to be a pretty draughty castle of a place before he set about it."

"But to think how they were engaged all those years because they couldn't afford to get married."

"Oh, Tim's always exaggerated the poverty bit. He's been doing very well at the Bar for years."

"You too?"

"Well, all of us. These have been good years for all lawyers, especially civil barristers and solicitors in the City. Millions of tax payers' money has gone in legal fees for privatisation. No tendering, no limits set, money for jam."

"I'd rather have our criminal work, any day."

"Me too," he said, nodding and briefly taking her hand.

"But how about you, Judith?" he asked, looking closely at her. "Are you really better? You look spotless."

She laughed.

"That's not much of a compliment. I don't think Tim would approve. Do you remember when he rebuked you for calling me peaky?"

"You *were* looking peaky. And you know our Tim. He charms people by telling them what he thinks they want to hear."

"And you tell what you think they *ought* to hear?"

"Only if I care about them."

Before she could reply a young man dressed in black leather

155

bedecked with much clanking metal and bits of what appeared to be Nazi insignia crashed his way towards them on aggressively heavy boots. He was the latest in a series of young men who had replaced the original surly waitress at the Wig and Whistle but he seemed to have kitted himself out for kicking his way into a football crowd rather than waiting at tables.

The gentle smile with which he put down the tray and the care with which he arranged their bowls of soup and plates of sandwiches therefore came as something of a surprise.

"You can't judge by appearances," Freddy remarked when he had gone. "I suppose some of them just dress like that because they think it's fashionable and not because they mean to terrify old ladies."

They were silent for a while relishing their carrot and Stilton soup.

"I'd forgotten how good Mother McScabbe's soup is," Freddy said, helping himself to more garlic bread. "But you still haven't told me if you're quite better."

"I'm fine, thanks, since you ask. And the spots faded in a few days. Actually, I think I was in the right place, curled up in bed during the hurricane, listening to it raging and thinking how lucky I was not to have to go out in it the next day. How did you get on in the great storm?"

"Well, it was a bit embarrassing," he said shamefacedly, as he stirred his soup. "I seem to be the only one who didn't realise what was happening. I slept through it all and when I got up in the morning and there was no electricity, I just thought it was a power cut."

"Slept through it! How could you? It was a tremendous racket. We didn't even try to sleep. Mrs Crumb brought her transistor radio into my room and we listened to the reports by candlelight."

"Even when I set off for work I didn't realise what had happened. I noticed that there weren't many people about and there was nobody else at the bus-stop—"

"But there weren't any buses, were there?"

"No. Everyone knew that except me. So after a bit I decided to walk."

"But didn't you notice all the debris?"

"Well, it did strike me that the council had been uprooting rather a lot of trees, lifting some of the pavements in the process. Of course there were lots of branches lying about, but I just put it down to autumn. I remember having to do a few detours but I was thinking about work and didn't really pay much attention."

"What happened when you got to chambers? Was anybody there?"

"Only Tom."

"You have to hand it to him. Tom can be relied upon in times like that."

"Well, he lives pretty near. The only other one to get in was young Peterson and Tom had sent him packing, like he did me. He'd heard on the radio that people shouldn't go to work and was very upset that he couldn't ring everyone up but of course the telephone lines were down. But since nobody else had tried to get in, it didn't really matter."

"So you went home, leaving Tom alone at his post?"

"No, I went walking round London. There were some amazing sights, you know. I saw a boat up a tree. It had blown off the Serpentine. And there was scaffolding in Thomas More Street that had been tossed about by the wind as if it was made of matchsticks. I didn't stay there long, I can tell you."

He shook his head, remembering.

"And what was the damage like round you?" he asked.

"Our little park was devastated and quite a few of the trees in the road were blown over. They seemed to have hardly any roots. Mrs Crumb says they were badly planted in the first place. She's written to the council telling them to prepare the ground better next time."

Freddy laughed.

"You have a very knowledgeable landlady. You're always starting sentences with, 'Mrs Crumb says'."

"Oh, not much escapes her beady eye. You know how they tie the trees to stakes with leather thongs?"

"Yes, I've seen them."

"As the tree grows, they get too tight and nobody comes back to check. So Mrs Crumb goes along the roads slackening the ties herself and cursing the council for cruelty to dumb vegetation."

They were quiet for a minute as the Hitler Youth waiter brought their coffee.

"And of course you missed the other disaster by being ill," Freddy said, heaping in sugar. "Black Monday. I can't tell you what a doom laden day it was in chambers. All our wealthier colleagues looked ready to leap out of the window. They were traumatised; they really had believed that this crazy boom could last for ever; it was to be the bubble that would never burst."

"It's the end of yuppiedom, isn't it?"

"Well, that's one good thing to come out of it. But it's the others I'm sorry for, because the fallout will affect everyone."

"But not Mrs Crumb. You'll hardly believe it, but she sold most of her shares before Black Monday, literally just a few days before the crash. Put it all into her building society."

"She's a wizard, that landlady of yours! Oh, it's good to have you back at work, Judith," he said suddenly. Then he added, just as suddenly, "Time we were off," and got up.

"It's as well we came early. There wouldn't be a hope of a table now," Judith said, glancing round the crowded room. "I don't know how we'll push our way through this lot."

There seemed to be a solid block of people crammed into the Wig and Whistle, all talking, drinking, smoking. Freddy went ahead, forcing a way between the jostling bodies, making a path down which she gratefully followed.

"Phew, it's good to get out into the fresh air," she said as they stood in the narrow alleyway outside the pub.

"Yes, it's pretty rough in there. Look, why don't we celebrate your return to health somewhere a bit less scruffy? How about going to Pedro's one evening this week? I'm fearfully tied up with this fraud case at the moment. Then I've a burglary, but how about Friday?"

"That's fine by me. I should have got through my indecent assault and dangerous driving by then and there's always the weekend to work on my rape case."

*   *   *

Pedro's Restaurant, just off the Strand, was convenient for the
Temple and they often had a meal there if they'd been working
late. Judith's interest in cooking hadn't survived her marriage. If
she did try to cook in the kitchen she supposedly shared with Mrs
Crumb, her landlady invariably took over and ended up doing all
the work, which made her feel guilty so she preferred to eat out as
often as possible.

"It was amazing," Freddy said, shaking his head, as they sat at
the corner table he'd reserved for them. "Absolutely amazing,
whenever I think of it I start laughing," and he giggled as if to
prove his point.

"Is it something you've remembered about the wedding?"

"No, it was in court this morning . . ." and he broke off to
laugh again.

"Would you please just *tell* me," Judith begged. "You've been
shaking your head and spluttering ever since we arrived."

"I was waiting until we'd got the ordering done and settled in."

"Well, we're ready now," she told him, picking up her soup
spoon.

"I won't bore you with all the details of the case—"

"Details of cases *never* bore me. You should know that by
now."

"Well, briefly, my client was charged with burglary and the
prosecution case turned on the evidence of one man, a witness
who said he had heard this van drive up the back lane of his
house and stop. He said he had looked out of the kitchen window
and seen it parked by the backyard of the next-door neighbour's
house and two man get out. The defendant was accused of being
one of them."

"By the way, who was the judge?"

"I was coming to that. It was Hanshaw."

"Commonly known as Old Hacksaw because of his brutal way
with defendants," Judith remarked, pulling a face.

"The same. Did you know that he fancies himself as a wine
buff?" Freddy asked, and when she shook her head, went on,
"Well, he does. People who've dined with him say he's the sort
who fusses endlessly over the wine, takes its temperature, sniffs

159

it, swirls it round his glass for minutes on end and generally makes such a fuss that you feel guilty about drinking it. You feel you should just dab a little of the precious stuff behind your ears."

"So?"

"The timing was crucial. My client had an alibi from quarter-past seven. Frankly, I didn't think we'd a chance when I heard the prosecution witness being examined in chief. He was such a precise little chap, somewhat Pooterish; very polite, very clear that he'd heard the van at half-past six."

"I suppose you tried to throw doubt on that?"

"Oh, yes. In my cross-examination I pointed out that most of us don't spend our time looking at our watches so it's very easy to be an hour wrong about the time of a little incident like hearing a van, you know the sort of thing."

He paused for a drink of wine.

"Hacksaw, who had seemed to be dozing up till then, cut in and said, 'Really, Mr Blake, is this necessary? This seems a very reliable witness and he has twice said that he heard and saw the lorry at half-past six'."

Freddy was a good mimic and exactly caught the tone of Judge Hansaw's harsh, dry voice.

"I ignored that interruption and asked the witness how he could be so sure of the time. 'Well', says the little man, 'We were having a small dinner party, Mavis and me, for a very nice couple we owed. Dinner was to be at eight o'clock sharp. Mavis likes the meal on the table at the right time, not hanging about losing flavour in the oven. I'd bought a very nice bottle of claret' – the judge nodded approvingly at that – 'and I thought an hour and a half would be the right length of time to prepare it, so I went into the kitchen at half-past six to put the claret into the refrigerator—' "

Freddy was doing a perfect imitation of the Pooterish voice but couldn't go on for laughing. It was infectious; Judith found herself joining in, but managed to say, "So what happened?"

"There was an explosion from the bench. 'You did *what*?' screamed old Hacksaw. 'I put the claret into the refrigerator, my

The Ewe Lamb

Lord,' says the little man. 'You should be ashamed of yourself,'
Hacksaw tells him. And from then on we were home and dry."

He drank some more wine and went on, "In his summing up he
said to the jury, 'You may *possibly* believe the evidence of this
man, or you may think him a wholly unreliable witness,' and
looked at the poor little wine-abuser with the contempt other
men might reserve for paedophiles. The jury drew the right
conclusion and found my chap not guilty. I think he was as
surprised as I was."

"And that's why you've ordered this special claret this evening?"

"Yes, my treat. And besides, I've got a favour to ask."

"Go on."

"I need an alibi for Thursday week. Fiona wants me to go to
yet another outdoor production of Shakespeare."

"What's the play?"

"*The Tempest,*" he said with disgust. "I loathe that play. I
can't stand that pompous git Prospero lording it over everybody,
revelling in power like some ghastly politician and then being
pious about giving it up when he's sick of it at the end. Like those
old men who decide to be chaste after a lifetime of womanising. It
doesn't fool us, does it? we know they've no option. Where was
I?"

"You were talking about *The Tempest* – not your favourite
play, I gather."

"Well, Caliban's okay. I've got time for Caliban. But that
doesn't make up for the awful Trinculo and Stephano assing
about while the audience tries dutifully to giggle. You can tell
real laughter, Judith, in the theatre; a genuine outburst of
surprise and joy and it's shared and it's a cleansing thing somehow. Not like that with Trinculo, my God."

"Why don't you just tell Fiona you don't want to go?"

"I can't. I don't want to hurt her feelings. So I thought it would
be simpler to tell her I'd promised to take you somewhere. Some
Bar function or other. Then we could go to the pictures."

"*We* needn't go anywhere. You could just stay on your own in
your flat."

161

"She might come round and check. She's getting a bit jumpy. She wants to get married. And it isn't as if we even live together."

Freddy's love life had always struck Judith as strange, the two of them living in separate flats. But who was she to talk? she'd remind herself.

"She's got this thing about settling down. I reckon she's broody. But I'm quite happy as I am."

"But, Freddy, if she wants children, she'd bound to want to settle down. It's all right for you men – women have a deadline."

"She's not old, for goodness' sake. Only thirty-two."

"I think she's being perfectly reasonable. Not everyone conceives easily. She can see herself postponing and postponing because of you, and then maybe finding she can't have kids and that's a thought that terrifies her."

"I suppose so." He sighed. "But *you're* not far off it and you don't fuss about babies."

She laughed. "It's all right for me. I don't happen to want them. But I can understand how some women feel about it. Are you really being fair? If you don't want marriage and children, maybe you should let her go. Let her find someone else who does, I mean?"

"But I've got used to her. We've known each other since we were kids and then we met again and found we lived fairly close in London. It just sort of evolved."

"It's not you I'm worried about; it's her."

He smiled, said, "You're a nice person, Judith," and, to her surprise, took her hand and kissed it. "I'll think about it," he said.

Twenty-five

" I can see you're upset, Miss Delaney," Tom Trapp said. "As my friend George Gimbal always says, one of the problems with lady barristers is that they do tend to get emotional."

Too angry to answer, she walked out of his office and straight to her room. She was standing at the window, fists clenched, when Freddy came in.

"Something wrong?" he asked.

"Sorry, Freddy. Please go away. I'm not fit for company just now."

"All right. I'll come back in half an hour to take you out for a drink."

Later he found a quiet corner in the bar for her, brought her a brandy and said, "What's it all about?"

"I can't talk about it here. Really I can't."

"Well, you need to talk about it somewhere, whatever it is. Drink that up and we'll get a taxi round to my flat. It's a disgusting night."

"Is it? I hadn't noticed."

Sitting by the gasfire in his flat, another drink in her hand, she began to feel better. It was a comfortable room, full of books and papers, the shutters closed against the gloom and fog outside.

"You know I was prosecuting," she began, "in the rape case, *R v. Howard?*"

"Yes. Your first rape, wasn't it?"

"Yes. We presented our case and today the defence was cross-examining, which is a polite way of saying they were crucifying the victim. You'd have thought *she* was on trial, not the rapist."

"The judge didn't intervene?"

163

"No, he just let it go on and on. I tried, but was disallowed. Then the defence started trying to prove that she hadn't been raped so that he'd get his man off with indecent assault."

"And did he?"

"No. They found him guilty."

"Well then, that's all right. You won. Congratulations."

"Oh, Freddy, how can you? It isn't 'all right'. Why should she endure that trial, surrounded by all those men and having to describe – ugh! I understand now why a lot of rapes don't come to trial." She looked miserably at him and added, "I don't think I could cope with another rape trial."

She meant it. There were times when she longed to get away from the criminality of London, to escape to Netherby where such things didn't happen, where the Alices of this world played innocent games with their little sisters. She knew of course that it was a false vision, but she did find the idyll comforting sometimes.

"Oh, yes you could cope," Freddy said, getting up and coming over to put his hands on her shoulders. "And will."

She looked at him uncertainly, but she knew he was right. She had chosen her way of life and it was not Alice's way and she must stick with it, accept the bad times for the challenges that they were. That was the thing about Freddy; he always expected her to accept challenges.

"Your mixture of intelligence and compassion's just what's needed," he told her. "There, that's enough of praise."

He let go of her and strode towards the kitchen.

"I used that half-hour you needed in your room," he called back over his shoulder, "to go shopping. I've bought a meal for us. Just a few minutes in the microwave and it's ready. We can talk afterwards. Have another glass of wine while I see to it."

So they sat one each side of the gas fire, nursing trays of processed nourishment. She felt soothed and, as they ate and drank, talked of other things.

"Did Fiona enjoy *The Tempest* last week?" she asked.

"Yes." He paused. "We've split up."

"Oh," Judith said putting down a forkful of modified starch, hydrogenated vegetables, stabilisers, preservative and gelling agent. "I'm sorry. Did you have to do it so abruptly?"

"I didn't do it. She did. She ditched me. She said pretty well what you'd said. She wanted a family and since I didn't want to settle down, she was off."

Good for her, Judith thought but didn't say so.

"I'm sorry," she said again. "It's always sad when people part."

"Well, I was a bit surprised, I must say," he conceded.

"There's one thing," Judith said, always one for looking for consolations. "Since she did the ditching, you're spared feeling any guilt about it. I mean, obviously you feel hurt, but that's better than feeling guilty."

"Oh, I wouldn't have felt guilty," he assured her. "And I don't really feel hurt. Well, hurt pride maybe."

"But you've been together a long time, Freddy."

"Well, not exactly together. A sort of semi-detached couple we were. But all the same . . ."

"And I've done nothing except talk about my worries."

"That's all right. Look, there's yoghurt or yoghourt for puds."

He reached over to a side table and offered her a selection of cartons.

"Help yourself. They're different colours but all taste the same. By the way, what was the trouble with Tom?"

She looked at him hopelessly, "Oh Freddy, I was so stupid. As I came back this evening, pretty upset by the trial, Tom called me to tell me about something or other. He was in one of his genial moods, you know, asked how I was doing and I said, 'Frankly, I'm pretty angry at the moment, since you ask', and then I briefly told him why. And he looked benign and patronising as if I was an awkward child who couldn't cope with its homework and said that women barristers had a problem because they were too emotional."

"So you stamped off down the corridor?"

"I didn't stamp."

"Oh, yes you did. I heard you. That's why I came along. Something's upset our Judith, I thought."

165

"Thanks." She smiled across at him. "You've been a good friend to me since I joined our chambers."

"Really? I seem to remember you didn't appreciate various criticisms—"

"Such as?"

"The plea in mitigation for a start."

"You were right. I was very bad. I needed a friend to tell me so."

"And I seem to remember you weren't too pleased when I told you you'd risked over-egging in the Playbell case."

"But you were right again. I got away with it that time, but since then I've always been careful not to ask that one question too many."

"It seems a long time ago now."

"Yes. It's funny how I used to think of you as very much my senior, my mentor. But you can only have been a couple of years older than I was."

"It was unfair really. It was just that I'd had much more experience in court from the start. Thanks to Tom feeding me briefs. He didn't do the same for you. Hard to prove, but I think our Tom had his prejudices."

She nodded.

"And you were so trusting, Judith, always saying what a nice fatherly chap he was. I didn't seem able to disillusion you. And of course he *is* a nice chap."

"A lot of people with fearful prejudices can be nice in other ways. I was a bit low at the time, hadn't much fight in me. I'd no idea you were watching over my interests."

He laughed.

"Well, you're certainly doing all right at the moment. If solicitors ask for you, Tom can't stand in your way."

"And now I'm unmarried perhaps he won't want to?"

He looked at her thoughtfully, began to say something, stopped and filled up her glass instead.

Twenty-six

F rom being tiny Joanna had been fascinated by flowers.
When she was scarcely more than a toddler she would go
and play in the croft, where Alice or her mother could keep an
eye on her from the kitchen window, and stagger back to the
farm clutching straggly bunches of bluebells and sweet cicely,
meadow buttercups and celandines, so that in the summer the
house was always full of jam jars of wilting flowers.

When she started school, Alice would sometimes meet her on
sunny days so that they could walk back up to the farm together
and give the child a bit of fresh air, which she reckoned was good
for her after being stuck indoors all day. In the summer the wide
banks on each side of the lane were alive with grasshoppers and
bright with cow parsley and foxgloves. There were more delicate
flowers too and these were the ones Joanna would love to seek
out. She would find wild thyme and marjoram, not so heavily
scented as the ones which grew in Alice's herb garden, but
spreading and plentiful in the warm shelter of the wall.

At first Alice used to try to hurry her along, but then, seeing
the pleasure she got from looking for the flowers, let her dawdle,
picking harebells and cranesbill, meadowsweet and clover from
the bank.

"We could have a picnic on the way home," Joanna suggested
one hot afternoon in early July. "We could sit and have a picnic
every day, we could."

"Nay, love, we've not time to be having picnics," Alice began,
laughing at the very idea. Then, seeing the child's face fall, she
paused and thought about it – it was, after all, the easiest time of
the day for her; the men's dinner was done and it was still too

soon to think about tea. Why shouldn't the time be given to Joanna to play, the way the village children did after school?

"But we'll ask our mam all the same, love," she said.

She braved her mother that evening, sure that she would say that farming families couldn't afford to fritter time away on frivolities such as picnics the way some folks did. But her mother only nodded, said that she herself would do Alice's afternoon tasks – everything from feeding the hens to doing the ironing.

"It'll be good for the little lass," she said. "It's not like she gets much spoiling."

So the next day Alice packed up a basket with cakes and biscuits, a flask of tea and a bottle of orange juice.

"You shall choose a place to picnic," she said to Joanna, who danced ahead of her looking for just the right place, afraid of spoiling everything by making the wrong choice.

"Don't leave it too long," Alice warned. "Or we'll be home before you've made up your mind."

In the end she chose the spot where the stream, which gushed down Boar's Back, met the lane, going under it so that for a moment the lane became a bridge. When it emerged in the field on the other side, the water seemed to have been tamed; it flowed more gently, widening and slowing into a pool, then narrowing again to go under a little slate bridge before meandering off to join the beck.

This was the side they chose, climbing the stile and settling themselves against the south-facing wall so the sun was hot on their faces as they sat eating their picnic. Afterwards, Joanna ran down to play by the water and Alice drank her second cup of tea, leaning back against the wall, enjoying the warm roughness of the lichen-encrusted stone as her mind tried to adjust itself to this unaccustomed idleness.

Through half-closed eyes she watched Joanna, who was crouched by the stream, her long hair shading her face from the sun, observing everything that grew here. Water mint abounded in the shallows and the banks were carpeted with the big glossy leaves of marsh marigolds. There were water avens too with their bell-shaped flowers, deep red, but paler pink inside. There was a patch of something which looked, with its great coarse leaves and long, thick stems, like rhubarb.

She picked a stem and offered it, as something she might cook, to Alice, who rejected it with, "Now don't you go eating that stuff. It's butterbur and probably poisonous. They call it wild rhubarb, but they shouldn't."

Joanna looked at it carefully.

"No," she said, "you can see it isn't rhubarb. Look, it's all hairy. It would do for a parasol, though," and she held it over her sister's head.

Alice took it, glad of its shade. Afterwards, whenever they came to picnic here, Joanna always picked her a leaf of butterbur, which Alice, knowing how children relish such small rituals, accepted gratefully and used as a parasol.

Soon Alice came to look forward to this hour as the best part of her day as well as of Joanna's, who, summer after summer, never tired of exploring the stream, utterly absorbed in the life that she saw down there in the water. For it wasn't just the flowers that abounded; there were water skaters skimming the surface, minnows darting under stones and pond boatmen who really did seem to row their little bodies across the stream. And down below among the stones and weeds, she could see caddisworms crawling along in the cases they had made for themselves out of grains of sand or little pieces of stick, invisible until they moved because they were so well camouflaged.

Joanna watched them, her dark eyes intent, and could hardly believe that one day they would turn into flies that would swarm over the stream in the evening. It was even more amazing that other little grubs would climb up out of the mud and turn into dragonflies that would dip and dart over the water, their brilliant colours gleaming and flashing in the bright sunshine.

It was an idyllic time; it felt to Joanna like a world of its own, quite apart from the everyday life on the farm or at school, a world which only Alice shared and even she was a little apart up there by the wall, quiet and somehow different from her usual bustling self. And when she said, "Time to be going now, Joanna," she sounded subdued, as if she too didn't want to

169

break the spell – not that they were really sad because there was always tomorrow.

They would walk up the lane together, sometimes chatting, sometimes not, according to how hot it was and how they felt, and if there was much to tell about the day at school. Her face was glowing and prickling with the sun and fresh air, her brown sandals were grey with the dust from the lane, the stems of willow-herb and water avens, kingcups and red campion were sticky in her hands. Years later she could remember the feel of it all.

It couldn't last for ever: Alice knew that, even if Joanna didn't. The time came for Joanna to start at the big school in Pendlebury; there was homework to be done and a bagful of books to be carried. Alice now met her off the school bus in the village and drove her straight back to the farm. She, too, was busier now with summer visitors to see to, so neither of them had time to dawdle in lanes or picnic by streams.

Twenty-seven

I t was nearly two years since the great storm, but the park still looked woebegone and bedraggled, Judith thought, as she sat on the bench and surveyed the bare scrubbiness of it, with the newly planted trees struggling to establish themselves among so much devastation.

She was feeling woebegone herself; she wasn't quite sure why, except that she didn't seem to be getting to grips with the murder case she was working on. *I need a break*, she told herself; one of the snags of being on your own is that you don't organise yourself a holiday, at least I don't.

It came to her suddenly that she must get herself to Netherby; just the thought of a few days up there, back to the place she felt most truly at home, made her feel better. She got up, left the depressing park and walked quickly back to telephone.

"I'm afraid we're fully booked at The Curlew," the new owner said. "I'm unable to help you. No, I don't know that there is anywhere else in the village. There's Sloughbottom Farm, of course, but that's a long way out. But they do a very nice bed and breakfast, I'm told."

"*Sloughbottom*?" Judith repeated, astonished. "You mean where the Dowerthwaites used to live?"

"And still do. It's Miss Dowerthwaite as runs the business. I can give you their number."

So she took the number and rang the farm. A crisply efficient young woman answered, the firmness of tone so unlike Alice's hesitant speech that for a moment she thought it must be someone else.

"Yes, we can put you up next week," Alice said. "There's the

171

little room in the house, no bathroom, just a fitted basin or there's a chalet room with *en suite* bathroom and all facilities. It costs six pounds more."

She opted to pay the extra six pounds. But she spoke absently, for the words rang strangely in her head: *chalet*, en suite *bathroom, fitted basin, facilities*. It didn't sound at all like Sloughbottom Farm.

It bewildered her, too, to look upon it when she arrived. It was still a farm, of course, but it was as if the life of the place had moved from the dairy to the parlour. It reminded her of the feeling she'd had when a little Cornish fishing village, which she and her father used to know, had turned itself into a tourist resort, so that when they went back there after an absence of five years they found its butcher's converted to a souvenir shop, its old ironmonger's purveying goodies to the summer visitors, selling T-shirts and hiring out wetsuits. Her father had explained the economics of the thing and how times must change, but she had felt uneasy with it all the same.

So now it seemed to her that this old farmstead had changed. She had known other farms where sheep were kept mainly so that townspeople could watch their lambing, and where hens and ducks were kept as much for the atmosphere they provided as for the eggs they laid. Sloughbottom Farm was not like that, but it was certainly prettified. It was as if the old farmhouse had lost some of its dignity in the process of keeping up with the times. Then she told herself that this was sentimental nonsense and that, if she hadn't happened to know the farm before, she would never even have thought it. And anyway, she had always thought it was a dreary looking place.

But Alice, little downtrodden Alice, what a confident businesswoman she had become! Was this really the girl who had thought it such a treat to be allowed to go to a village whist drive? She was so busy over the weekend that Judith scarcely had a chance to talk to her, but on her last night she invited her out to dinner at The Curlew. The once-shy Alice accepted readily.

"It'll be grand," she said, "to get away for an evening."

During the meal she asked about Judith's work, showing a surprising interest in what was going on in the law.

"We had a judge staying last year," she said, when Judith mentioned the case of the Guildford Four, "and he explained a lot about it. I reckon they'll win their appeal, don't you? And in the end they'll have to let the Birmingham Six appeal too."

They went on discussing various topics that had been in the news recently and, whether it was the Hillsborough disaster or the Salman Rushdie affair, Judith realised how well-informed Alice was. It was as if, although she had never gone out into the world, the world now came to her. Furthermore, Judith observed, she had firm and commonsensical opinions about everything. At first Alice's new found confidence amazed her, but the more she listened the more she realised that she shouldn't have been so surprised: Alice had always been thoughtful and capable. It was she, Judith, who had been wrong about her, mistaking diffidence for weakness.

All these thoughts went through her mind as the two of them sat over their meal, putting the world to rights.

They talked of old times, too.

"You were the one who got me reading," Alice reminded her.

"Impossible!"

"No, honestly. It all came together somehow, that afternoon at your house. I can still remember the feeling."

"It's the sums I remember most."

Alice laughed.

"Oh, they were always a struggle," she admitted. "I never could manage maths. But, do you know, when I took a short course in how to do accounts two years ago, I really loved it? I suppose it seemed to have a reason to it now, a purpose. They call it *motivation* nowadays but it just means having a reason really, doesn't it? It's thanks to you I began the business, you know," she added.

"Me?"

"Yes. You suggested it when you came up nine years ago."

She remembered that moment of embarrassment when she thought she'd said quite the wrong thing and must have horrified Alice with the idea of bed and breakfast on Sloughbottom Farm.

"I started in a very small way and it just grew," Alice was saying, "but it was you put the idea into my head in the first place."

How strange, Judith thought, that lives so far apart, as different as hers and mine, can touch at a certain point, a certain critical point, and influence each other, though unwittingly.

"Well, I'm glad it's all worked out so well," she said. "I can see you really enjoy it."

"Oh, we get quite a bit of fun out of the guests," Alice told her. "Some of them are really odd. You know Mam's old rag mats? I mean they were what people used to make because they couldn't afford to buy carpets or rugs, and anyway they never wasted anything in those days."

Judith nodded.

"Well, we've twice had ladies come and ask if she'd make them one! Can you imagine? People who can afford holidays wanting to put a rag mat in their homes. 'They're all the thing nowadays,' one of them told Mam. 'Very expensive to buy.' Another one asked her where she bought the rags!"

They both laughed, then she went on, "And we had a university man and his wife, keen horticulturalists they said they were, and they saw Samson turning the compost for me for the vegetable garden and he had this funny sort of far-back voice and he said, 'Splendid, splendid, my man, ecologically very sound. I see you are up-to-date in your gardening methods.' Up to date! That compost heap's in the same place, next the dung pile, that it was in Grandad's time. Then he said, 'All that wasteful business of throwing vegetable matter into the dustbin is out of favour now, you know.' I had to laugh, I mean, since when did they send the dustcart up to Sloughbottom Farm? For days afterwards, our Samson, who isn't very good with his words, kept muttering, 'Them haughty culturalists, they don't know owt about nowt.' "

"I can just hear him!" Judith said, laughing. "But, seriously, he doesn't mind your doing bed and breakfast, does he?"

"Nay, he kicked up a bit at first, but he's got used to it now. Any changes I make, I'll make slowly."

"Are you thinking of making some?" Judith asked, wondering what new enterprise Alice had in mind.

"I think I might do dinners," Alice told her. "I could make a better summer pudding than this," she added, looking critically at her dessert. "And that soup was no better than it ought to be. Out of a tin, if you ask me, with a bit of something added to perk it up. Not that I haven't enjoyed coming out, don't think that."

"No, I know what you mean. And I agree with you about the soup."

"So, what do you think, about doing dinners, I mean? Would people like to have an evening meal at the farm, or would they rather go out of an evening?"

"I couldn't say. *I* don't mind driving down, but I suppose people with families might rather stay in."

"It'd be cheaper for them."

"Do you get a lot of families?"

"Some. In the school holidays. But mostly it's couples. You can always tell the ones who aren't married."

Judith smiled.

"How?" she asked.

"Well, for a start, they often arrive in separate cars. Then they talk to each other too much at mealtimes. Married people don't bother. And sometimes she'll ask him if he takes sugar in his coffee. Little things like that. We had one man used to ring up his wife every evening. I could hear him in the hall telling her about this conference he was at. But it's none of my business, so long as they pay the bills and behave proper like. Times have changed."

"And so have you," Judith told her.

"Like as not," was all Alice said.

"I somehow imagined you'd marry young and be a farmer's wife—"

"No, I'll not marry," Alice said with, it seemed to Judith, uncalled-for ferocity.

Afraid she'd touched some raw nerve, she asked after Joanna. Alice's face lit up with pride.

"She's doing right well. They think highly of her at school."

"Does she have any idea what she wants to do eventually?"

"It's a problem choosing. She's a good all-rounder, her teachers say. They even talk of university but she seems to like art best and she's forever out looking for plants and flowers. I don't see as they'd mix really, book-learning and flowers and painting and suchlike."

"Maybe she could be a botanist? That's something she could study at university as well as enjoy at home."

"Could she? They haven't suggested that. They have these evenings for parents, you know, and Mam goes to them but she doesn't make much of it. I mean, she left school when she was thirteen, Mam did, so it's not so easy for her to talk to teachers as it is for some."

She looked thoughtful as she stirred her coffee.

"It's hard to know what to say about it," she said. "But one thing I do know. I'm not having our Joanna brought up as I was. I want better for her."

Determination was in her eye and the set of her jaw as she spoke. She was old Hilda's daughter all right, Judith thought.

176

Twenty-eight

C ompassion wasn't an emotion she'd ever expected to have
for His Honour Judge Hanshaw, but Judith found herself
feeling sorry for him today.

It was a day of misunderstandings in court, which started with
the judge apparently recognising the defendant and saying,
"Have you been up before me?" and the defendant replying
in a puzzled kind of way,

"I don't know what time your Worship gets out of bed."

Everyone should know that defendants and lawyers speak in
different tongues, Judith reflected, but it didn't stop the jury
from tittering.

The defendant, an untidy-looking young woman with badly
dyed hair, was accused of stabbing her husband to death with his
own knife. Judith's leader, Sir Timothy Fosdyke, QC, was
defending and Judith was his Junior Counsel. It was Friday;
the case having been postponed for three days owing to the non-
appearance of the key witness, now in the witness box.

"You were due here on Tuesday," Judge Hanshaw told him
severely. "It is now Friday. Why were you not in court three days
ago?"

"My mum got burnt on Tuesday," the witness told him.

The judge's stern countenance softened and he said with
unaccustomed concern, "I am sorry to hear that. She was not
badly burnt, I hope?"

"Oh, yes," the witness told him. "They do a thorough job at
Woodgreen Crematorium."

Judith made a mental note to tell Freddy at the weekend. He
was away on a case in Yorkshire today, but on Sunday they

177

planned to walk on Hampstead Heath, go to the pictures at the Everyman and have a pub supper at the Smugglers' Arms.

It was a good relationship, hers and Freddy's, she reflected as she ate pizza and drank coffee in the canteen at lunchtime. In the last two years they had become close friends, without emotional involvement; they neither of them wanted to marry or have children, they loved the Bar, shared jokes, helped each other with work, always had time for each other. It was a very equal, balanced friendship, sometimes one giving, sometimes the other. He'd enjoy that remark about Woodgreen Crematorium, she thought as she went back in to court.

The afternoon progressed as badly as the morning. The dead man's mother tearfully described in the witness stand what a virtuous son he had been to her, what a considerate husband to two consecutive wives, what an ideal father. The judge allowed her to sit as she described this paragon of virtue, whose character fitted rather oddly with the evidence that he had two convictions for affray, had been in prison for unlawful wounding and that the police had been called three times in the last year to his house to deal with domestic violence.

Witnesses were called and it was a depressing picture they built up of family fights and jealousies, rows and heavy drinking. Her leading counsel was leaving the questioning of the last witness to her, saving himself for more important matters.

"You were in the Spotted Dog on the night of September twenty-fifth?" she asked this friend of the murdered man.

"That's right."

"And can you tell the court who was with you at the beginning of the evening?"

"Me and George and Terry."

"But," Judge Hanshaw interrupted, "in your deposition you stated that George's wife was there."

"Terry *is* George's wife, my Lord."

The judge nodded, discomfited. It just isn't his day, Judith thought.

"And later the defendant and her husband joined you?" Judith resumed.

"That's right."

"And you all drank?"

"I didn't. I was driving," the witness told her virtuously. "But the others did. Beer."

"And how much beer would you say the defendant's husband drank that night?"

"Oh, the usual," the witness shrugged. "About nine or ten pints."

There was a gasp from the bench.

"Nine or ten pints?" the judge shrilled. "That is more than a *gallon* of beer."

"That's right," the witness agreed, obviously not sure what all the fuss was about.

"And when did you leave the Spotted Dog?" Judith asked.

"About four o'clock."

"Four o'clock in the *morning*?" came the outraged cry from the bench.

"That's right, your Honour."

"I hope the landlord wasn't serving alcohol at that illegal hour?"

"Well, he must of, or we wouldn't of bin there, would we?"

"I think," Judge Hansaw said, resting his brow momentarily on his hand, "that we will adjourn this case until Monday at ten o'clock."

"I knew Jack Hanshaw when he was a young barrister," Mrs Crumb said that evening, after Judith had recounted the day's events. "Not that he was ever what you'd call exactly young. You know how some people are born middle-aged? Well, Jack was born elderly. He always had that dried-up look and that high-pitched, harsh voice. It was odd in a young man, but he seems to have grown into himself now. Much happier for him."

"Well, he didn't seem a very happy little judge today," Judith told her.

"Do you like my pebbles?" Mrs Crumb asked in one of her swift changes of conversation. "Brought them back from Brighton. I've put some in a bowl on your dressing table for you."

Judith thanked her, though she didn't really relish Mrs Crumb's habit of putting leftover souvenirs into her bedroom. All the same, she thought, as she got undressed that night, they were very pretty, those blue and green sea-smoothed pebbles.

Years ago, when she was quite small, she had gone with her father to the seaside – she couldn't remember where – and had collected pebbles like this on the shore. They were a deep blue when they were wet but turned almost grey when she kept them at home. Some eyes are like that, she reflected now; Freddy's eyes, when he was amused were that lively blue, but when he was worried or sad about something they could look quite grey, she thought turning Mrs Crumb's pebbles over in her hand. Then she asked herself what in the world she was doing, thinking about the colour of Freddy's eyes, for goodness' sake! She put the pebbles down and concentrated on flossing her teeth.

Twenty-nine

It was misty when they met at Hampstead tube station and there was a smell of rain in the air.

"Oh, it's good to see you," Freddy said, hugging her.

"And you."

"And great to be out in the fresh air after a week in that stuffy court. Lord, but my case was dreary. How was yours?"

As they walked up the hill to the Heath, she told him, with suitable exaggerations, about the various misunderstandings in yesterday's cross-examination.

"I can't match those," Freddy said, "but I did have one bit of misinterpretation."

"Which was?"

"My leading counsel asked the defendant what she was wearing and she said, 'My skirt and blouse and a jacket and kickers.' And he said, 'And what were you wearing on your feet?' and she looked surprised and said, 'Well, I've just told you – my kickers.' Apparently 'kickers' are what the young call their trainers nowadays."

"I'd have thought it was rhyming slang for knickers. Like Mary Jane which used to be marijuana, is now rhyming slang for cocaine. Somebody ought to write a phrase book for lawyers to use in court to translate the language of their clients and witnesses."

"They have. There's a *Lags' Lexicon* and Partridge's *Dictionary of the Underworld*. Then there's a judge writes pieces in *The Magistrate* on the jargon of the underworld. I've learned quite a few from him recently. I didn't know that a month in the slammer is called 'a moon', six months 'a carpet', twelve 'a stretch' and five years 'a handful', did you?"

181

"No, the only familiar one is a stretch."

As they walked and talked, the mist grew thicker until the bare branches of the trees were scarcely distinguishable from the grey November sky. There were very few people about on the heath now and, when they did appear, they seemed to loom suddenly up out of nowhere. The drizzle turned to steady rain.

"Bloody weather," Freddy said, pulling her under a tree. "Let's shelter here for a moment. I mean it's been glorious all week and now this. Sod's law."

"Never mind. It's still refreshing. I don't care about getting wet."

"Well, I do – care about your getting wet, I mean. You know," he went on, looking at her in his puzzled kind of way. "I feel quite protective about you. I don't know why. And I know you'd hate the thought."

She didn't actually, she found to her surprise. But knew better than to say so.

"What sort of tree is this?" he asked suddenly.

"I don't know. Some sort of an evergreen."

"Jolly considerate of it to keep its leaves on."

She laughed; it was the sort of absurd thing her father used to say.

"I think we can forget the cinema, don't you?" he said. "We can't sit in wet clothes for a couple of hours."

As he spoke, the rain, which had already penetrated the thick upper branches of the tree and gathered in pools on the foliage, began to fall on them in fat heavy drops.

"Let's make for a dash for it," he said. "You'll get cold here and it can't be any wetter out there."

Holding hands, they ran all the way back to the tube station and were drenched by the time they got on the train.

"My flat's nearer than your place," he said, "so we'll get off there."

She nodded. Water was dripping from her hair and running down her cheeks. He took out a large handkerchief and wiped her face, then his own.

As they left the station, rainwater was gushing down the side of the road, gurgling in gratings, flooding over the pavement. Passing cars sprayed them with great waves of water. The rain came at them from above and below and all sides.

"It's like being under the shower," Judith gasped, when at last they reached the door of Freddy's flat and fell into the dryness of the hall. It was suddenly quiet; they could hear the water dripping from their clothes and on to the floor.

"You get straight into the bath," Freddy said, leading the way, "while I get into some dry clothes. You can borrow my dressing gown while your things dry. Meanwhile, I'll get some tea ready. You just lie in the bath and relax. There's some oily stuff to soak in."

This was Freddy in organising mode; she didn't argue.

As she lay in the bath she could hear him moving between kitchen and drawing-room. There were sounds of china being arranged, of a kettle being filled, cupboards being opened and shut. They were comforting little sounds, she thought, proving that somebody else was in charge.

She remembered how she used to lie in bed when she was small, listening to similar sounds, but then there had always been a sense of dread that soon the day would begin, another day on which she wouldn't be able to do anything right, however hard she' tried. In fact, the harder she tried the more her mother seemed to have found fault, as if she was irritated by her daughter's hopeless attempts to please.

It wasn't like that now; where there had been dread there was just pleasurable anticipation of tea and friendship. Oh, yes, it was very pleasant to lie here in the warm and silky water and hear Freddy organising things.

Freddy was nearly a foot taller than she was and weighed fourteen stone. His thick winter dressing gown enveloped her in its navy-blue folds. She tied the belt tightly round her middle to keep it all together and spread her clothes on the radiator.

"Splendid," Freddy said, as she came into the drawing room. "You look like a bishop. Tea's nearly ready. I've made some sandwiches. I haven't any crumpets but we can make toast by the fire."

"I do envy you your bookshelves," Judith said, wandering round the room while he closed the shutters. "I still have books in boxes in Mrs Crumb's loft."

"Don't you ever think of getting a place of your own?"

She shrugged.

"Sometimes," she admitted, "but on the whole the *pied-à-terre* with Mrs Crumb suits me. I don't have any domestic worries."

"Do you have furniture stored as well as books?"

"No, I left it all for my husband in the flat."

For a moment he looked quite stricken.

"Husband?" he repeated, as if disliking the word. Then he laughed. "Sorry, but it sounds so odd. You know, I just can't think of you as ever having been married."

"That's all right. I can't either."

They stood for moment, silent, then she said, "It was a somewhat semi-detached affair, a bit like you and Fiona."

"She's getting married, by the way," Freddy remarked, leading her across to the gasfire and beginning to pour out the tea.

"Oh, good."

"Yes, I'm pleased too."

"Funny how one's always glad to hear of other people getting married, even though one doesn't want it for oneself?"

"Mmm. Not very logical. Those are egg sandwiches and those are ham. I'm starving. How about you?"

She nodded, helping herself. She always felt at ease with Freddy, she thought, sitting comfortably back in the armchair. There weren't many men you could sit with like this, in a dressing gown, guzzling tea by a gasfire and just feel happily companionable.

"The barrister I had dinner with last night was saying just that, having recently been divorced," Freddy remarked.

"He was prosecuting, was he?"

"*She* actually. Yes, she was prosecuting, but we got on well and had dinner together most evenings."

Judith felt a sudden twinge of something she couldn't quite define. If it hadn't been old Freddy she might have mistaken it for jealousy.

"Yes, she was a nice person," he went on. "You'd have liked her. Very quick in court, lovely to look at, very good voice. She should do well."

"Especially now she's got rid of her husband," Judith put in sharply.

Freddy laughed.

"You're probably right," he said. "More tea? Or would you rather have alcohol?"

"Goodness, no. It's only just gone five o'clock."

"Is that all? I thought it was later, it's so dark. There's the tea and now I'll make some toast."

"Do you know what I envy, Freddy, apart from your great book-lined drawing-room?" she asked leaning comfortably back in her chair.

"What's that?"

"Your magnificent gasfire."

It was one of those wide, old-fashioned gasfires with curved funnels which glowed orange in the flames and made a soothing, hissing sound.

"It's as old as the house," Freddy told her. "They don't allow them to be installed now. And if I break any of the flutes I can't replace them."

"Flutes?"

"That's what we knowledgeable ones call those funnels. They're made of the most fragile material. I suppose it's the live flame that makes them so attractive. It's the nearest you can get to the real thing."

"I do love a proper fire. One of my earliest memories is of lying in bed in a room with an open fire. I suppose I must have been ill. I remember my father sitting by the bedside and stroking my head. When he thought I was asleep he got up and crept out very quietly and took ages shutting the door without making a sound. But I wasn't asleep at all. I just lay there watching the patterns the flames made on the walls and ceiling. I suppose most old houses had fires in the bedrooms."

"Built in the days of cheap coal and cheaper servants," he told her.

185

"All I can remember is that lying there in the firelight was perfectly heavenly," she concluded, her voice trailing off as she remembered the peacefulness of it.

"There's a fireplace in my bedroom," Freddy said. "It was one of the selling points when I came here. One of those black leaded ones with a canopy. There's a cupboard alongside with coal and sticks, but I've never used it. Apparently you just buy a bag of smokeless fuel and a bundle of kindling wood and up it goes."

"You should have tried it."

"We could try it now. Make *proper* toast."

It was a big bedroom, easily accommodating a double bed as well as a *chaise-longue* and a couple of armchairs. Like the other rooms, it had shuttered windows, a central rose in the ceiling and corniced walls. The fireplace, which was already laid with paper, sticks and coal, had a blackleaded surround and bowed bars to the grate.

"You have to move the chimney plate out of the way first," Freddy said, reaching up the chimney. "It's to block the weather out when the fire's not on. There, that's it. You can perform the opening ceremony," he added, offering her a box of matches.

The flames leapt up immediately, the sticks crackled, the coals soon began to glow. They drew the two chairs up to the fire and sat in silence watching it until, after a little while, Freddy went out and returned with slices of bread, a jar of honey and some butter. He handed her a toasting fork and they took it in turns to dangle slices of bread over the fire until they began to turn golden, then brown, making satisfactory little crackling sounds in the process. She remembered how she had sat with her father long ago in the cottage in Netherby and he had brought in bread and honey because it was a good fire for toasting.

"Penny for them?" Freddy asked.

"I was just thinking, remembering earlier days."

"When you were married?" he asked and there was an unusually sharp edge to his voice.

"Oh, no. Student days. With my father in a cottage in the Dales; sitting by a fire like this, making toast."

He took her hand.

"You looked sad," he said.

She nodded, her eyes inexplicably filling with tears.

"Come here, you need a cuddle," he said, taking her on his knee.

And so she sat, comforted. And the cuddle became an embrace and the brotherly peck on the cheek became a lover's kiss. And the dressing gown fell off and it was the bed they were on and no longer the chair. And it was a different Freddy from the one she'd known for years. Or the same Freddy and she hadn't known him. And he was saying that he loved her and must always have done but not realised it. And to her surprise she was saying the same. And the fire cast the shadows of its flames across the ceiling and made patterns on the walls. And after passion there was peace; deep, perfect peace.

Mrs Crumb noticed, of course.

"So you're not going round to see Freddy this morning?" she enquired the following Saturday.

"No, we both have work to do, but I'm going this afternoon."

"Then I probably shan't see you until Monday, shall I?" Mrs Crumb said and, to her amazement, Judith felt herself blushing like a schoolgirl. Her, a divorcee of thirty-three.

"I've a lot of time for Freddy," Mrs Crumb went on. "Always had. And he's good for you. Makes you laugh. Well, I won't stop you working. I just called in to leave you this tile I brought you from Bosham."

She put the tile down between the mug from Lewes and the decorative candles from Hastings.

"Thank you, it's lovely," Judith said as enthusiastically as she could, and tried to look with deep approval at this latest addition to the clutter.

"Oh, I couldn't come back from a day's outing without bringing something for my lodger. Particularly as I can't be sure how much longer she'll *be* my lodger. No, don't look like that. As I say, I've always liked Freddy; she'll be a lucky girl who catches that one, I've always thought. There now, I'll leave you in peace."

Yes, I am lucky, Judith thought as she walked to Freddy's flat that afternoon. It was another grey and drizzly day, but as she walked the light seemed to sparkle on the puddles, passers-by looked benign; the world seemed a very cheerful place.

The outlines of things seemed clearer, everything brighter. As grief makes all things stale and unprofitable, turning even what should be joyful into sorrow and the merely sad into heartbreak, so this inexplicable joy illuminated everything, painting the dreary with beauty and excitement. She remembered the dead heaviness of grief after her father died as, almost with disbelief, she felt this vibrant joy casting its spell over everyday things and realised she had not felt as happy as this since he died – and had not expected to ever again.

We're both lucky really, Freddy and I, she thought, trying to rationalise it, as she rang Freddy's bell: we share the same career, neither of us wants marriage or children. We really make the ideal modern partnership: equal partners, that's what we'll be.

Freddy had lit the bedroom fire and there was a bottle of champagne by the bed.

"Freddy, what extravagance!" she exclaimed. "Is it for before or after?"

"After," he told her. "I'm more thirsty for you than for champagne at the moment."

So they lay again and watched the firelight flicker on the walls and ceiling as they made love. And afterwards they lay for a long time, close and still and everything was very quiet except for the little sounds made by the fire as it shifted and stirred in the grate.

"Shall we have the champagne now?" Freddy asked at last. "And then make plans?"

"What plans?"

"Well, I've been thinking. The obvious thing is for you to move in here. But then I thought really it would be better for you if we got somewhere else. Something new to both of us."

"Yes, but it seems a shame. You're so well settled in here and have all your things and—"

"But it's you I'm thinking of. Of course it would be *easier* to stay here, but when we're married—"

"*Married?* Did you say *married?*"

"Well, of course. Oh, I didn't ask you, did I? Judith, I'm sorry."

And suddenly he was out of the bed and kneeling on the floor. He took her hand and said, "Madam, will you do me the honour of being my wife?"

"Oh, Freddy, you idiot, do get up."

"Now what have I done wrong?"

"You've always said there was no point in getting married unless people wanted children, which we don't. You said it was better to be partners because partners are equal and you said—"

"That was when I was very young," he interrupted.

"It was last year, Freddy."

"Well, I was still very immature last year."

"You're ridiculous."

"Will you marry me?"

She lay on the bed thinking of all the reasons for not marrying him; she thought of her need for independence, her career, her sense of being married to the Bar. She thought of the disastrous marriage she'd once made.

But then, she argued back, she'd rushed into that marriage with Cedric in extraordinary circumstances and she'd done it out of pity, making the same mistake as her father had made. Certainly, she wouldn't be marrying Freddy out of pity. For what then? For companionship? But they could have that without marriage, that and passion too. Everything really. There was no point in being legally bound when you could make a perfectly sensible and civilised arrangement which you were free to bring to an end, without complications, without any legal knots to untie, if you decided you'd had enough of it. Thus her reason argued.

"Will you, Judith?" he was asking again.

She looked at him and somehow all these arguments, these pros and cons, seemed irrelevant. Love was saying something quite different; it was saying that this man whom she had grown to trust over the years, this man whom she loved, wanted to marry her. And although she couldn't understand it, really could not make rational sense of it, she realised that because she loved him, what he wanted had become what she wanted and if that included marriage, so be it. She'd just have to jettison some of her theories. Or perhaps it was simpler than that, and they both just wanted to be sure of each other for the rest of their lives. And anyway right now, as she looked at his anxious face, she wanted not to see hurt and disappointment on it; above all, she wanted her reply to make him happy.

"Yes, please," she said.

Thirty

T he odd thing was that nobody in chambers seemed in the least surprised by their astonishing news.

"I wondered when you were going to get round to it," Tim said languidly when they told him.

They were in his room with Geoffrey Craig and Charles Wrigley.

"Better late than never," Charles said. "The clerks have been having bets on it for at least six months."

"I don't believe this," Freddy said. "Do you, Judith?"

"No. We've just been good friends, haven't we? Honestly," she went on, turning to the others, "we had absolutely no idea ourselves until last week."

"Well, maybe it's a case of the onlooker seeing more of the game," Tim told her. "Anyway, congratulations to you both. All of us old married men are delighted."

And they all kissed her and shook Freddy by the hand.

"What was it the bard said?" Tim went on. "'*When I said I'd die a bachelor, I didn't think I'd live to be married*'?"

"Oh, spare us the Beatrice and Benedick treatment," Freddy objected.

Tim laughed.

"It's appropriate," he said. "Anyway, lots of congratulations once again. It's an awful bore, but I really have to leave you," he added, looking at his watch and making for the door. "A nice little case of breaking and entering in Epsom."

"And I've a bit of buggery to see to in Ipswich," Geoffrey said, following him out.

"And I'm off to the cells to visit one of the Playbells," Charles told them.

191

So they were left alone.

"It feels like months since I kissed you," Freddy said.

"Think of the *years* we've worked in these chambers together and it never entered your head," she said, laughing. "I mean what a lot of wasted—"

"Shut up," he said and kissed her.

"We ought to go and tell Tom," she said, after a while.

Tom was very correct.

"We have never, as far as I can recollect," he began, "had a married couple in chambers."

"Always a first time," Freddy told him breezily.

"Indeed, yes, sir. My friend George Gimbal once informed me that he had such a couple in his chambers, but the stresses were too great and it ended unhappily in divorce."

He paused and then said, "May I, on behalf of the staff, tender our congratulations?"

They thanked him and were relieved when his telephone rang so that they could escape to Freddy's room.

"That must be one of the least enthusiastic speeches of congratulation ever made," Freddy said, laughing as he held her in his arms.

"Do you think it's true about the couple in his friend's chambers?"

"No, and I don't believe in George Gimbal either. He doesn't exist. He's a figment of Tom's imagination. He's a useful invention, like Mrs Gamp's friend, Mrs Harris."

"I'll ask Mrs Crumb tonight. She's bound to know."

But Mrs Crumb, for once, didn't know.

"I've certainly never heard anyone else speak of him," she said. "I think your Freddy's probably right. You didn't get much work done today, I bet?"

Judith laughed.

"It was all lovely," she said. "But it was weird how they all seemed to know except us. Do you think that other people really perceive things about you that you don't know yourself?"

Mrs Crumb shook her head.

192

"You're too clever for me," she said. "But I'll tell you this. You have theories, Judith, you put your mind to things, but you can't live your life on theories; life's not so neat and tidy. But it doesn't matter, nature sorts it all out in the end. What do you want for a wedding present?" she demanded suddenly.

"Oh, don't worry about that. We're going to get married very quietly. I mean, neither of us has parents or any immediate family, so we'll just go quietly off to a registry office and then go away for a short holiday afterwards."

"But what about all your friends?"

"Oh, I don't expect they'll want to be involved."

"Nonsense, child," Mrs Crumb rebuked her sharply. "That's one theory too many. Of course your friends will want to see you spliced."

"Well, perhaps a few will come and we can ask them round for drinks or something afterwards at the flat. You especially, of course. We'll keep it simple."

So she and Freddy sat making lists by the gasfire the next weekend and the few friends turned out to be over a hundred and the drinks somehow became a buffet lunch provided by caterers.

"Amazing how things grow," she said.

"It's a lovely flat," Tim said to her as she and Freddy went the rounds of their guests. "You'll be staying here for a while, I suppose?"

"No, Freddy feels we should make a new start as soon as possible. In fact, we've just put in an offer for a dear little terrace house in Islington."

"Oh, I didn't know that."

"It only happened yesterday," Freddy told him.

"I don't expect you'll have much difficulty selling this place," Geoffrey said, looking around appreciatively. "Even in these hard times."

"You're right. We only put it in the agent's hands last month and there's already a couple who seem serious about wanting it. We've really been very lucky."

193

In fact, everything went wrong that could go wrong. The bottom had dropped out of the housing market and nobody seemed able to move. The people buying Freddy's flat, who had seemed to want it urgently, withdrew at the last minute because the sale of their own flat had fallen through. Then the people selling the little house in Islington rang to say they had to take it off the market because they couldn't get into the house they wanted to buy because its owners were stuck in a housing chain.

"We'll just have to start all over again," Freddy said, turning to her as he put the receiver down. "I'm sorry, darling, I know you loved that house. I think the best thing is to start looking again straight away. I'm free tomorrow afternoon. How about you?"

"I've a meeting in the cells with a mugger at two o'clock but I should be away by three."

They met outside Mobbs and Clangers. Freddy came up behind her as she was gazing at an advertisement in the window.

"Just look, Freddy," she said, sounding awestruck. "That lovely Georgian terrace house. And only a hundred and fifty thousand."

He looked at the photograph.

"Sorry, darling," he said, "but that's only the bottom bit. Look, it's the one-bedroom basement flat that you get for your hundred and fifty grand."

"Oh, and I was so hopeful – though I suppose I did think it was a bit too good to be true."

"It reminds me of the time I went to buy a new bath for the flat years ago," Freddy said, as they went inside. "There was one with a notice tied to it marked forty-five pounds. I thought I'd found a real bargain. Then the girl explained that that was only for the taps."

Inside the office, a condescending young man with sleek hair and a signet ring took what he called their particulars and tried to interest them in buying a disused warehouse in Hackney. It was, he told them, ripe for conversion.

"Bear with me," he said, when they had refused this offering, "while I surf the files for anything in your price bracket. I'll post any others to you, of course, hopefully on a weekly basis."

So they made their way home, stopping at every estate agent they saw, gazing at what was on offer in the window, leaving particulars of what they wanted in the office, emerging with fistfuls of brochures.

They were hungry and tired by the time they got back to the flat, but each had a hefty bundle of printed details of houses and Freddy and bought the evening paper for good measure.

"There seem to be plenty of houses on the market," he remarked, as they sat by the gasfire after supper, "it's just that none of them seems to be the one we want."

"We don't know that, Freddy. We've just got to work our way systematically through this lot. You take half and I'll take half," and she began dealing them out like cards.

"That's for the truly hopeless," Freddy said, bringing the wastepaper basket over from the corner by his desk. "And anything worth a second look we'll put on the stool for the other one to read."

"And we've got to do it seriously, Freddy," she warned. "Last time we always ended up reading out the funny bits and competing for the dottiest."

"I promise I'll be truly solemn," he said, kissing her.

They sat working diligently through the leaflets, the silence broken only by the gentle popping of the gasfire and the sound of paper being screwed up and lobbed in the direction of the wastepaper basket.

Then, "They don't have much respect for historical fact do they?" Freddy interrupted to say, "I mean, listen to this: 'Edwardian house believed to have been built in 1928'."

"I thought we were going to concentrate," she said. "Anyway, how about this? I've just had, 'Georgian up-and-over garage door'. And the one I've just chucked out had a medieval spike in the scullery."

"I don't believe it."

"It's true. At least they didn't call it a useful feature, which is how they usually describe something utterly useless. Here's one which says, 'Garden with useful pit'."

"That should attract the mass murderers."

195

"Don't be horrible."

"Do you remember the one we had last time? The piggeries in Gloucestershire?"

"Yes, it was my favourite," she said, laughing. " 'You'll find it hard to resist the appeal of these converted piggeries'," she quoted.

"We didn't find it very hard, did we?"

"And do you remember, 'Unique opportunity to acquire a semi in Bromley'?"

"Oh, let's have a break," Freddy said, getting up and coming to lean over her.

"No, Freddy, we've just got to plough our way through this lot."

So for a while they concentrated, reading silently to themselves, but then it was Judith who interrupted.

"*Private drainage* sounds very select," she said. "What does it mean?"

"It's estate agent jargon for *Sorry, no Main Drains.*"

"This is pretty refined too: 'There are courtesy lamps on this fine Gentleman's Residence'."

"Hand it over. It sounds just right for me."

"It's just under a million pounds," she pointed out as she handed him the paper.

"And it won't do," he said, smoothing it out. " 'Detached Gentleman's Residence'. I'm not detached any more."

"My father and I used to collect phrases like that. It started with blind dogs, I remember."

And suddenly she saw very clearly the cottage where they had sat together laughing by the fire. How long ago? Fifteen years it must have been. Sometimes it seemed like yesterday that they had laughed and talked together. At other times it seemed like a different life entirely. It *was* a different life, of course; that life when she had gone to buy the house in Colton Row. And now she and Freddy were doing the same. Only now it was real. But it had been real then, too. *Oh, but it had*, she thought, suddenly sad. Just as real.

Freddy glanced up, saw her expression and came quickly over to her.

"Cuddle?" he offered.

How was it that he always understood? she thought gratefully, as she made room for him in the big armchair.

"There, that's better. We'll look at the rest of them together," he said, picking up the pile of brochures. "Look at this," he pointed out. " 'Ideal granny flat upstairs'."

"I know what you're going to say: But we don't *have* an Ideal Granny."

He laughed.

"I saw a nice one the other day. It was on an escalator and it said, 'Dogs must be carried'. So, naturally I couldn't go on it because I hadn't a dog."

"Idiot," she said.

And she thought how alike they were, Freddy and her father. And it surprised her that she hadn't thought of it before. In many ways really. Even in this matter of being fascinated by words. Perhaps the legal mind is accustomed to being precise about words; can't help noticing their abuse or their absurd misplacements.

"Only about six more houses to go," she remarked a few moments later. "We're nearly through."

"I don't care if I never read a description of a pampas bathroom or a camel bidet or a low-level suite ever again."

"Do you remember when we were house-hunting last time and you didn't know what a low-level suite meant, and the girl was quite shocked?"

"Yes, she read it out for some reason or other and I remember thinking it was some kind of failed pudding. Maybe a Yorkshire pud that hadn't risen. Old Wives' Sod we used to call it at school."

"Well, that's the lot of them," she said, hurling the last of the brochures into the wastepaper basket. "Just the local paper to look at."

He spread it out for both of them to read. Suddenly she jumped, almost falling off his knee.

"Look, Freddy, look! Number Three Colton Row."

He read it.

"Sounds rather good," he said. "But they don't name their price."

"It *is* rather good," she assured him. "Oh, I don't believe it."

She told him about the house which she had once so nearly bought.

"The only thing is it just seems impossible. I can't believe it."

"Oh, I don't know, houses do come on to the market again and again," Freddy said matter-of-factly. "I saw the statistics somewhere. It was something like the average house changes hands once every five years – or was it three?"

"This isn't an average house," she told him, still awestruck. "This is Number Three Colton Row. They must be doing a private sale. There's a telephone number. Please let's ring now, this minute."

"All right, calm down."

"You'll have to do it."

"Why are you whispering?"

"Am I? I suppose I'm afraid of frightening it away."

She stood beside him as he rang, heard prices being discussed, heard him say he'd talk it over with his wife and ring back.

"It's five thousand above our limit," he said, after he'd put the receiver down.

"But, Freddy," she said, her voice still coming out in an urgent whisper, "when you think of the alternatives – the desirable piggeries in Gloucestershire, the unique semi in Bromley and the million poundsworth of Edwardian gentleman's residence built in 1928 and—"

"All right. You love it. We'll go for it."

"Oh, Freddy, I do love you."

"Me too."

So, still clutching each other, they rang back, had their offer accepted and celebrated with the last of the bottles of champagne left over from their wedding.

"Now all we have to do is sell this place," Freddy said, emptying the last of it into her glass.

*   *   *

The Ewe Lamb

Their luck seemed to change from that evening; within a week the couple who had withdrawn from buying Freddy's flat rang to say they'd found a purchaser for their own place and wanted to renew their offer. Meanwhile, buying Number Three Colton Row went ahead smoothly. And so it was that they moved into their new home exactly a year after they were married and celebrated their wedding anniversary by eating fish and chips with their fingers, sitting on the floor amid a litter of wrapping paper, teachests of china, and cardboard boxes of wedding presents. Judith looked at it all contentedly.

"We're really here at last," she said. "In our own home."

"You look quite radiant," Freddy told her. "Even with bits of shredded packing paper in your hair and fishy fat on your chin."

"You've got a great smear of something black down one side of your face," she said.

"Probably off the boiler. One of the men helped me to get it going."

"Weren't they good? By the way, they said they'd put the bed up for us."

"They did. In the wrong bedroom."

She laughed.

"We'll soon move it. Oh, Freddy, I love this house. Shall we prowl around it?"

They walked from room to room, contented with their lot.

"This is my favourite room, I think," Judith said as they stood in the little study, looking through the French doors into the walled garden.

"Judith," Freddy said gently, putting his arms around her. "The fact that once you hoped to live here with your father and then tragedy wrecked everything . . ."

"Yes?"

"I mean, doesn't that make it all a bit sad, cast a shadow?"

"Oh, no, absolutely not," she told him with utter conviction. "It doesn't hurt. It heals. I can't explain. He would have absolutely approved."

"Of me or the house?"

"Both of you, my darling."

199

She clung to him and soon the only sensible thing to do was to find their way to the unmade bed in the wrong bedroom and make love in a room which was uncarpeted and piled high with teachests of books and binbags of bed linen.

Afterwards he unwrapped the kettle and brought her up a mug of tea. Then he pulled a duvet out of a binbag and wrapped it round her.

"Oh, I am so glad we bought this house despite the extra thousands," she said, stretching luxuriously. "I mean, I don't mind economising to buy it, but I'd have resented having to economise for a house I didn't really love."

"Don't worry. On our combined salaries we can manage the mortgage. We've done the sums."

"And we've no dependants, now or in the future."

"Well, yes," he agreed, after a moment's hesitation. "I mean, no."

"Did you know that people like us are called TINKS nowadays? Have you heard that one? It stands for Two Incomes and No Kids."

He laughed and said, "How about bath and more bed? Tomorrow I'd like to make an early start on getting all the heavy moving done so you'll just have the finishing touches to see to on Monday."

'Finishing touches', she thought as she started on the kitchen on Monday. Finishing touches indeed! Just the small matter of finishing painting the top coat on the woodwork, scrubbing out all the cupboards, unpacking all the china and cutlery. But she thought all this without resentment, surprised at how much she was enjoying having a day off for domesticity. She'd never thought she had any kind of homemaking instinct. True, she'd longed to make a home for her father, but that was mostly for his sake. She'd wanted to make for him the home he'd never had with her mother. Without him, she'd been quite happy to lodge with Mrs Crumb; her brief marriage to Cedric being more of an unfortunate episode than a homemaking venture. But now she was surprised to find herself relishing it; she enjoyed arranging where everything should go, imposing order, having a system. She never would have thought she would get such satisfaction out of a boring thing like arranging a kitchen.

She'd heard people say that women had a nesting instinct because they were conditioned to prepare a place for their children. *What a load of nonsense*, she thought; she loved making this home for Freddy and herself but certainly that didn't include wanting to start a family in it. Her own childhood had put her off that sort of thing for ever. It was just the homemaking that she was enjoying. Tomorrow she would have to go back to the reality of work; make the most of this playing at houses, Judith, she told herself.

She was fitting saucepans into a drawer when the telephone rang at six o'clock.

"I'm Susie Cartwright and I live at Number Seven, two doors down from you," a cheerful voice said. "I saw your removal van arrive on Friday and I just wondered if there's anything you need?"

Judith, who had thought that neighbourliness was something which belonged to places like Netherby, not to London, was taken aback and tried hard to co-operate by thinking of something she needed. She couldn't.

"Then why not just come round for a cup of tea?" the voice continued. "And I can tell you about local doctors and plumbers and shops – unless you know all that already."

"No, we don't actually. I'd be grateful for anything you can tell me."

"Then come now. Jim's just got in and we usually have some tea at this time."

Susie Cartwright was a tall, big-boned young woman. Her hair, pulled back and secured with an elastic band, emphasised the large features of a broad face, innocent of make-up. Judith had an impression of bright brown eyes and a big mouth with large teeth, white and strong-looking. A colourful plastic apron covered most of her baggy skirt and jumper and she radiated a kind of disorganised goodwill.

"Come in, come in," she said, holding out both hands in welcome. "Mind all the clobber."

Judith negotiated the narrow hall which garaged two bikes, a double baby buggy, a small cart and various items of children's equipment, with the same sort of care she used to navigate her way across Mrs Crumb's drawing-room.

"Jim'll be down in a minute," Susie was saying, as she put the kettle on. "He always likes to get out of his City clothes the minute he comes home. The twins are up there with him."

The kitchen-dining-room, for the two rooms had been knocked through, was in such chaos, very like her own home had been at the weekend, that Judith at first assumed that Susie and her husband must also have just moved house. Then she realised that it was only the effect of two babies.

"They've just started to crawl," Susie said, opening a tin of tea-bags. "Into everything, they are. Oh, here they come. Jim, meet Judith, our new neighbour."

Judith saw a small, neat man, tidy despite the newly adopted pair of old jeans and sweater. His round, fair-complexioned face had a cherubic look, making him seem, she suspected, younger than he really was. He carried a baby on each arm.

"Sorry I can't shake hands properly," he said to Judith, proffering a finger. "They like me to carry them around when I get home."

The twins were identical girls, with big blue eyes, pink cheeks and fair hair. Four eyes studied her solemnly, assessing.

Jim secured each baby in turn into a high chair. Bowls of some sort of lumpy sludge were produced which he spooned approximately into the babies' mouths, whence it spread over their faces, on to their hair and into plastic bibs suspended round their necks. The bibs were stiff and had a kind of trough at the bottom. Now and then they dipped their fingers into this container, scooped up the detritus of their meal and dropped it lovingly on the carpet.

Judith watched, fascinated. They were like little birds as they sat with their mouths open, ready for the next spoonful. And the way they sorted out the food in their mouths was so clever: although they had only four incisors apiece, they managed to sieve out the lumps between their teeth, swallow what was smooth and eject the rest. Meanwhile, Susie produced cups of tea, bread and jam and the remains of a Christmas cake. It was surprisingly relaxing sitting there with them at the kitchen table among all the mess.

"I think I saw your husband going to work this morning," Jim said, wiping the stickier bits off his daughters.

He lifted the twins out of their chairs and set them down on the floor.

"We were making for the same tube. I work in the City."

The twins were enchanting. Even when she was talking, telling Jim and Susie about Freddy, about their work, about moving house, making notes of what they could tell her of local services, Judith couldn't keep her eyes off the babies. They crawled, one behind the other, out into the hall, disappearing behind a curtain. Then a little face would appear round the corner, looking up at them, laughing. The other would follow and they'd set off crawling with very deliberate movements of their little arms and legs, one behind the other, now and then plumping down on their nappy-padded bottoms, before setting off again on their progress round the kitchen.

Their parents, to Judith's surprise, didn't seem to find any of this particularly wondrous, just sat there drinking tea and eating fruit cake as if these miniature little beings were in no way extraordinary. One of them crawled over to her and pulled herself up by the chair leg.

"She wants picking up, if you don't mind," Susie said.

So Judith stooped down and picked up the little girl, who settled herself comfortably on her lap, pulled at her necklace and, when she lost interest in that, investigated first Judith's mouth with her fingers and then explored her nostrils.

"Don't let her be a bother," her mother said.

"She's lovely," Judith said simply, taking one of the tiny hands in hers.

The child's head, close to her face, had a warm, sweet smell. Gently she brushed her cheek against the soft fair hair. The smell was a country smell, natural as new mown hay. She wondered if all babies' heads smelled like this or was it special to just this one.

"You have a way with children," Jim remarked. "Do you have any of your own?"

"No."

"She's only been married a year. Give her a chance," Susie reprimanded her husband. "It's early days yet."

Judith wondered if she should explain that she didn't want any children, but decided that it would be tactless to say so in the hearing of the twins.

Besides, she wasn't sure now if it was entirely true.

This discovery shocked her. It was not the sort of feeling a career woman like herself should have. It wasn't a feeling she'd felt before. She was unsure what to do with it.

"Did you have a job before you had the babies?" she asked Susie instead.

"Oh, yes. I'm a dentist."

She was surprised. There was no reason why she should be, she thought. After all, Susie's teeth were a good advertisement for her profession. It was just that all this muddle hardly seemed compatible with a dentist's surgery.

"I was going to have the usual six months' maternity leave," Susie was saying, "but when it turned out to be twins I realised I'd need longer. I'll be going back next month."

"And the twins?" Judith asked, illogically shocked that this clearly domesticated woman with lots of maternal instinct should be going back to work so soon. She put her arm more firmly round the little body on her lap, as if to protect it.

"Oh, I'm going to have a very good carer for them. Marion will come in before we leave for work in the morning and one of us will be sure to be home by six. Marion says that suits her. She lives nearby. Careful, she's posseting on your clean blouse," she added, removing a trickle of yellow fluid with an expert flick of a face flannel.

"Oh, don't worry. It'll wash. But how will you manage when you go back to work? I mean, don't babies wake you up at night and so on?"

"Oh, you get used to it. It's not as if it's for ever, after all. And

I must keep up my job. Dentistry's one of those professions where you lose skill if you don't keep practising."

"Yes, I can imagine. The Bar's like that too."

"So you'll be in the same boat, won't you? But you'll manage like everybody else when your turn comes. You'll see."

Judith didn't reply. Of course she'd known that women did manage babies and careers, but she'd never even considered it as an alternative way of life for herself. She'd always intended to go on exactly as she was now: Freddy and her and the Bar. But here was Susie evidently taking it for granted that she'd have a family too. And to make it even worse, it was an assumption that she found herself unable to deny. No, she couldn't deny it, not with this little girl on her knee.

"Of course it'll be tough for a while," Susie was saying. "But what's the alternative? Childlessness just wasn't an option for us."

"No, of course not."

The baby was getting restless. Reluctantly, she put her down and watched her crawl across to her sister. Equally reluctantly, she decided it was time to leave. Fredddy would be home soon.

"Good luck with everything," she said, as she left. "I hope things work out well, with your Marion and everything."

"Oh, Marion's great," Susie reassured her. "A properly trained nanny. Very experienced. She once looked after triplets, would you believe? Twins will seem a walkover after that," she added, scooping up both babies as she led the way to the front door.

Judith stood for a moment on the doorstep, looking at this neighbour of hers with her baggy skirt and plastic apron and armful of babies, not sure if she felt compassion or envy.

"How any mother copes with triplets, I just can't imagine," Susie remarked as she opened the front door. She laughed as she added, "I mean, you've only got two hands and two boobs, haven't you?"

"And she's so cheerful," Judith told Freddy that evening when he asked her what their neighbours were like. "And utterly chaotic, but they're a lovely couple and I liked them both very much. You will too. And, oh Freddy, they do have two adorable little girls. Twins."

And she told him about how these tiny creatures ate and crawled and didn't despise a stranger's knee and he saw that her face lit up as she spoke.

"Not that I'd want them for myself," she added.

"Of course not, darling."

"Well, not for a long time, anyway."

"Of course not, darling."

"Would you mind not keeping saying, 'Of course not, darling'?"

"Of course not – sorry. I was just agreeing with you."

"You don't usually agree with everything I say."

"No, but on this particular topic, it's your choice. Until they develop some way of having babies extra-utero or whatever they'll call the technique, women have to bear all the pain and discomfort and ultimate responsibility, and I don't think men have any right to pontificate."

"Especially pontiffs?"

"Quite so."

There was a pause and then she said, "Of course, there's always the danger of leaving it rather late and then finding one had been wrong in thinking one didn't want children?"

He said nothing.

"The Fiona syndrome?" she persisted. "I mean, she took avoiding action, didn't she?"

"Yes."

"I mean, I might come to regret an earlier decision when it would be irreversible – too late to do anything about it?"

"You might."

"On the other hand, the thought of living in the sort of pickle poor Susie's in—" she stopped, thinking it was absurd to refer to Susie as poor.

"You wouldn't be. She has twins. You'd probably only be in half her pickle. If that. Being you, probably no pickle at all."

"But the Bar, Freddy. To think of missing cases, just when I'm building up a practice—"

206

"We'd get a good carer, of course."

"You're saying you want me to have a baby?"

"I'm not voicing any opinion. It has to be your decision."

Night after night they had these circular discussions and round and round went the argument in her head. After a good day in court, utterly absorbed in her work, she'd think she had no maternal instinct at all. At other times she only had to see a baby asleep in a pram to long for it to be hers. Sometimes the very idea of coping with a baby, with sick, with dirty nappies and disturbed nights filled her with horror. At other times panic filled her at the thought that she might never ever have a baby; she would leave it too late and regret it for ever.

At last one night she turned to Freddy, said, "I don't know, I just don't know," and burst into tears, whereupon, to her surprise, Freddy said quite sharply,

"Well, if you think you want a baby for God's sake lets's stop talking about it and just get on with it."

So they did.

Thirty-one

F or her fifteenth birthday, the family gave Joanna a magnifying glass.

"There now," Alice said. "You'll be able to look at all your
plants in detail."

"You'll see 'em all blown-up, like," Samson agreed.

So Joanna spent hours examining leaves, dissecting carpels,
identifying unknown flowers from a clearer view of their
anthers or stamens; absorbed in a way which Samson found
puzzling.

"I mean, when all's said and done, they're only flowers," he
said. "It's not as if they were animals."

"But she's always been like that, has our Joanna, mad about
plants from being a little 'un," his sister reminded him. "And
forever painting them too."

It was true; after she had started at the big school in Pendlebury when she was eleven, Joanna had taken to going walking on
the hills above the farm, no longer bringing back great bunches
of flowers but instead sketching them where they grew, or
painting carefully selected specimens when she got home.

"By, but that's better than the real thing," Samson had said
one day, admiring her handiwork.

"It can't be, Samson," she told him, laughing. "Nothing's
better than the real thing."

"It is here," he insisted, pointing. "You've got a better blue in
your picture than yon cornflower has."

"That's because the flowers are beginning to fade," she had
told him, but he wasn't convinced.

As the years passed, she had grown more adventurous. "I'm

going to go over Sawborough next Saturday," she had announced one day, "to see if I can find some gentians."

"Indeed you are not," her mother put in. "It's far too far to go
traipsing off on your own."

"We don't like you going off too far," Alice said gently, seeing
her disappointment. "There are plenty of flowers in the meadow
and you've always loved it there."

"But they're *different* flowers there, don't you see? Some sorts
grow on peat and some on the limestone, some in meadowlands
and some where it's marshy—"

"You can always go up on the tops with Samson," her mother
told her. "He's forever up there with the sheep."

"I know that and I *do* go with him. You know I do. But I like
to spend time and he always has to be up and going."

Of course she couldn't make her mother understand, she had
thought resentfully, she was far too old. And it wasn't just the
flowers; she wanted to get away on her own. Other girls in her
form at school did. All right, maybe they wanted to go to clubs
and discos with their boyfriends and she didn't care much about
that, but she, too, wanted to be allowed to go further afield. She
was thirteen then. For the first time her delicate face looked
sullen and she sulked for the rest of the week.

The problem had been solved by the field club. A notice went
up on the board outside the village hall that a Professor Cran-
berry, a retired naturalist who had come to live in Netherby,
would lead a walk every Saturday for anyone who wanted to join
him. He would tell them about the plants as they walked and
answer their questions. In the winter he would give lectures in the
hall.

There were only a few of them gathered on the village green
that first Saturday: two families with six children between them,
and Joanna. The professor was a sprightly little man with a
pointed white beard and very bright blue eyes. He wore shorts
and walked in a bouncy kind of way and when they were not
talking he sang to himself, or rather made a kind of ompety-
pompety noise as he bounced along.

He'd led them, that first day, up on to the hills beyond Boar's

Back and over to Sawborough, so that at mid-morning she could look down into the valley and make out Sloughbottom Farm in the distance. From these great and ancient heights it looked tiny, man-made and vulnerable tucked in next to its little wood. The professor explained how the hills were formed, how the limestone had been buried for millions of years and then the younger rocks had been eroded until everything looked the way it did now.

He knew much more than that kind of thing, though: he knew all the details. He knew where a particular plant could be found; not just its rough whereabouts on a hillside or in a field, but exactly where it grew.

'Behind that stone there, beyond the cairn, you'll find some purple saxifrage', he'd say. 'It might just be in flower now'. And they'd run up to the place, and there it was.

That first day he said they'd look for flowers that were good for you, that people used before there were any modern medicines. There was selfheal to cure sore throats and eyebright for sore eyes. Later he showed them plants that were good to eat, like the bright green leaves of brooklime which were as good as spinach. He dug in the earth beneath the white pignut flower and pulled up the root below, wiped it clean and gave it to them to taste.

He was always getting them to taste things; in the hedgerows he would pick out the young shoots of hawthorn. 'Bread and butter', he called them. Later when the dog rose brightened those hedgerows and dry-stone walls he told them how the hips, which were their fruits, were rich in Vitamin C and had been gathered in the war to make rose-hip syrup for children – and children had never been healthier either before or since.

Sometimes it was the other way round, he said, and it was the plants which did the eating. He showed them a sundew flower which curled up when he put a tiny insect on to its sticky leaves, crushing it and extracting from its minute little body the food which it needed for its own growth and which the surrounding soil was too poor to supply.

Once he gathered some red-stemmed meadowsweet whose leaves were dark above and pale below, and told them to sniff the little creamy-white flowers whose scent was the reason the plant had once been a strewing herb, strewn on the earth floors of the rooms of long ago to make the house smell sweet. And for a while she wished she had lived in the days of earthen floors with sweet-smelling rushes for mats, but then told herself not to be ungrateful and that Alice's patterned carpets were very nice too.

When she got home in the evening, Joanna, tired and happy, used to relay everything she had learned from the professor to her family as they sat in the kitchen. Her mother would either say, 'I could have told you that. My mam allus made peppermint tea with watermint and she cured my tonsils with selfheal and my gran used infusions of eyebright if any of us had a stye', or she would shake her head disapprovingly and say, 'I never heard tell of *that*'. So it seemed that the poor professor must either be reporting a commonplace or inventing a tale.

At the end of the second summer of field club walks, the professor took them up to the great limestone pavement high above the source of the beck, leading them up a steep and rocky path which wound its way between cliffs of scree. It was here, on the top of the world, after he had told them how the pavement had been formed in the Ice Age, that the professor mentioned quite casually that this was their last walk because he was going away. He had been asked to go to Madeira to lecture to tourists. It was an island with very unusual plant life, he explained, and would give him a great opportunity to study and write about its vegetation. It was only for five years, he said, as if that made it all right.

Joanna, who had thought that the walks would go on for ever, heard him with misery and disbelief. The others were similarly silent. In fact they were all miserable except the professor, who seemed genuinely surprised that they all cared so much. As they walked back, he explained that he and his wife would be keeping their cottage in Netherby and would come back and live here at the end of the five years. He made it all sound very reasonable, but to Joanna it felt like treachery. In five years' time he might be dead – and she would be quite old herself.

It puzzled her that someone who had seemed so much a part of their lives, who'd walked and talked with them, got to know them for two years, could then just go away. That wasn't the way of the farming people she'd grown up among; they stayed put. Then she thought that perhaps if you really cared about something, as the professor did, and wanted to study and pursue it, you just had to follow it.

They made a feeble attempt to keep the club going after the professor left, but without his enthusiasm and leadership it soon failed, so she walked on her own. One good thing, she realised, was that in those two years her family had got used to the idea of her going out on the hills and didn't raise the objections they had done before. Often as she walked alone she seemed to hear the professor's voice and there hardly seemed to be a place where she hadn't learned something from him. So, gradually she forgave him, even thought of him with affection and, when she realised that it had been the professor's idea that the family should give her a powerful magnifying glass, with gratitude too.

"Well, I told him that Judith had once said you might be a botanist," Alice told her. "And he said, 'In that case how about giving her a magnifying glass, a really good one'?"

So, on her fifteenth birthday Joanna peered through her new acquisition and thought how strange it was that a chance remark like Judith's, whom she couldn't remember ever seeing, should have had such a beneficial result.

Thirty-two

"And that," Judith said, showing Mrs Crumb a blurred grey splodge on a black piece of paper, "is a photograph of the baby."

Mrs Crumb looked at it, turned it upside down, tried again. "A photograph, is it?"

"Well, it's a photocopy of the scan, really. It was taken a month ago when the baby was only twelve weeks old, but if you look carefully you can make out the head and little hands and feet. Of course, it's only nine centimetres long."

Mrs Crumb tried again. She had read somewhere that up to a few weeks a human foetus is indistinguishable from that of a pig. She could believe it now.

"Very nice, Judith," she said at last. "Very nice indeed."

"Of course it'll be clearer on the next scan," Judith told her. "I'll bring you a copy of that when I have it."

"Thank you. And how will you manage when the babe's born? You'll stop working, I suppose?"

"Goodness, no. There'll be no problem," said Judith, whose confidence had been boosted by her pregnancy; the decision to start a family having at last been reached, she intended to carry this new venture through with the utmost efficiency. "We'll register with several agencies and have a choice of nannies. I'll start work again as soon as possible."

She got up, leant against the mantelshelf and said earnestly, "We're not going to be the sort of parents who opt out of life the minute they have children. I mean it's very boring when one's friends let their babies monopolise their lives and conversation."

"So you and Freddy won't be like that?"

215

Judith shook her head.

"Absolutely not," she said. "You know," she went on, sitting down again, "we women are so lucky in our generation. We can have a career and a family. Plenty of successful women barristers have children."

"And your Freddy will help a lot, of course."

"Oh, he's a great support already. He's going to come to the antenatal classes whenever he can. And he's got a handbook on what to do if the baby starts being born before we get to the hospital."

"That's very thoughtful of him, though I hope it won't be necessary," Mrs Crumb said, shivering at the idea of Freddy reading aloud, in his powerful barrister's voice, from some textbook while Judith writhed.

"And we're not going to be conned into getting too much equipment. Apparently these manufacturers make fortunes selling new parents all sorts of clobber they don't really need."

"Have you bought anything yet?"

"Well, we did go to look for a pram in a baby shop but there was a computer shop next door so we bought a PC instead."

"Well, it's early days."

"We thought that instead of getting a little cot, we'd get one of those big wooden ones and it can double up as a filing cabinet."

"I shouldn't think babies and files would mix very well. But you know best. Now you stay here and I'll bring in some tea."

"I'll come and help," Judith began, getting up. "Don't start treating me like an invalid."

"I'm not. Just stay there and be spoiled for once," Mrs Crumb instructed, as she took one of the many footstools that made crossing her drawing-room so hazardous and put it under Judith's feet.

Judith lay back in her chair and relaxed. It was really very pleasant, she thought dreamily, to sit here idly in her old lodgings and be mothered by Mrs Crumb. She'd never imagined pregnancy would be so agreeable; she'd never felt better in her life. She would certainly be able to go on working until the very last moment.

The Ewe Lamb

She was just so lucky, she thought as she counted her blessings; she had this fascinating job, a wonderful husband and soon she would have a baby. She looked at her life and saw that it was good. She seemed to have within her now an inner peacefulness that she had never known before, though perhaps she had had intimations of it sometimes at Netherby, as she sat by the beck or lay on the springy, sheep-cropped turf. Thinking of Netherby made her think that she must write and tell Alice about the baby. It was all right to tell people now. Alice would be pleased.

She thought about Alice's life and how well it, too, had turned out. Alice had really made something of herself and now her younger sister was clearly going to be successful and would have opportunities that Alice had never had.

"That's a joy, to see you relaxing with your feet up," Mrs Crumb said, coming in with the tea. "You ought to do it more often. No, don't move. You'll only get in my way," she added as she set about collecting up nests of tables, trays and cake stands from various corners of the room and rearranging them around Judith.

"I was teasing about the cot and the filing cabinet," Judith told her contritely.

"I thought you might be. Milk or lemon?"

"Milk, please. I'm stocking up on calcium."

"These egg and watercress sandwiches will be good for you too," Mrs Crumb told her. "Vitamins and iron."

So they sat and talked, Mrs Crumb enjoying plying Judith with good things and Judith enjoying receiving them.

"Oh, I nearly forgot," Mrs Crumb said, after they'd finished. "I brought you something back from St Ives."

She went over to one of her desks and took a parcel out of a drawer.

"It's a Cornish doll," she said, unwrapping it to show Judith. "You can save it for the baby. Wasn't it lucky that I chose it although I didn't know about the baby at the time? I nearly got you a Cornish pixie for the garden."

"It was sweet of you," Judith said, grateful for small mercies.

217

"And I'm really pleased about the baby," Mrs Crumb added as Judith got ready to leave.

"Thanks. So are we." She hesitated then, "Of course, I do know that I always said that I didn't want to get married and have children," she conceded. "But—"

"Well, never mind that now," Mrs Crumb interrupted. "Every generation has its theories, but they all end up behaving like their mothers."

That's one thing I won't do, Judith thought, as she put on her coat, hugged her former landlady and set off for home.

Thirty-three

A lice watched in amazement as Judith and Freddy unloaded the car.

She had helped them carry the pram – in two parts – and then the carrycot, into the chalet. That was no more than you'd expect, she thought, though personally she'd have used the top of the pram for the baby to sleep in. But there followed a Moses basket, two cases of baby clothes with packets of special soap to wash them in, a baby alarm, a padded mat to change the baby on and a big toilet bag of accessories. There was a steriliser, such as hospitals use, and several bags of disposable nappies. There was a large canister into which, Judith explained later, the soiled nappies, having been wrapped in pink, scented plastic bags, were fed. Apparently they emerged from the other end strung together like sausages.

Last of all appeared the poor little baby, who seemed somehow outclassed by all its equipment; after so much paraphernalia you'd have expected triplets at least, Alice thought, remembering Joanna's simpler homecoming.

Judith, she observed, looked strained and tired. She understood now why they had decided to come here for a break.

"You have a sit down," she told her. "And I'll make you a cup of tea."

Judith sat down obediently.

"Thank you," she said meekly. "Oh, I'm sorry, I haven't introduced you. Alice, this is my husband, Freddy."

Freddy, who had been disentangling his infant son from the little travelling seat in which his tiny frame was slumped, put him down in the Moses basket, came over and shook hands.

Alice observed a big, capable-looking man and was glad of it for Judith's sake. *She's going to need that sort*, she thought to herself, as she filled the kettle.

The baby began to cry; Judith jumped up nervously and went over to the cot.

"No," Alice told her. "You have your tea, and Freddy too. I'll see to the baby. I have an hour to spare before I need worry about getting the dinner. What's he called?" she asked, picking him up.

"Timothy. But—"

"Then Timothy and I will go for a walk around the garden while his parents have their tea."

And she carried the screaming baby outside.

"He hasn't got his mittens on," Judith said, getting up to follow them.

"Sit down, darling," Freddy told her. "Alice knows what she's doing and anyway it's at least seventy degrees out there. Now, why don't you make the most of the chance to go and lie down for a bit? Try and relax."

So she went into the adjoining room and lay on the bed, trying to relax. She knew she was wearing herself out with worrying. She hadn't expected this constant nagging anxiety. She hadn't worried about the baby when he was inside her, but now that he was out here with them, the world suddenly seemed fraught with dangers that threatened his vulnerable existence. Germs might attack his tiny throat and lungs, insects might sting him, snuffing out his frail life. She worried when he was wakeful at night and worried even more if he slept hard, terrified that he might have stopped breathing. He seemed to breathe so shallowly; she had even woken him up sometimes in a panic that he might have died in his sleep. So even sleep had become alarming.

She hadn't realised how difficult it would be just persuading him to take enough nourishment to keep him alive. When he was weighed she watched the scales with agonised attention and once, when he hadn't gained even an ounce, she actually burst into tears, there in the clinic in front of everyone. She read the baby books more avidly than she had perused even the most difficult brief. They were supposed to be helpful and reassuring, these books, but they managed, in their omniscience, to be somehow daunting. They made her feel even more inadequate.

Then last week he had had his first injection and she had gone along to the clinic quite happily but had then been horrified at how tiny his arm seemed compared with the great needle that was plunged into it so deeply that she thought it must come out the other side. And poor little Timothy had looked at her with such reproach, as if asking why she had let them do this to him, so that once again she had almost wept in her sense of over-whelming guilt. Oh why, she asked herself now as she drifted into an uneasy sleep, did she always feel so guilty, that she was failing him when all she was doing was trying to care for him who was so precious?

She awoke with a start, wondering where she was, and then, suddenly remembering, jumped out of bed, blaming herself for not setting the baby alarm, and ran into the sitting-room.

Freddy was sitting reading. He looked up and smiled.

"Had a good sleep?" he asked.

"Where's Timothy? Is he all right?"

"He's fine. He's had his bath and his feed and he's sound asleep. And we've got duckling for our supper."

"But we can't go over there and leave him."

"No. I'm going and Alice will bring yours over here so you can have it in bed. And all the other evenings she says Joanna will come and babysit while you and I go over for dinner."

"Joanna? Little Joanna?"

"Not so little. She's going to college in October."

It was Joanna who brought her meal over on a tray, hot under chafing dishes. She was fair like her sister, and of the same slight build. She was shy, as Alice once had been, and eager to please.

"I'm afraid I'm being an awful nuisance," Judith apologised, as the plates and dishes were arranged on the table by the bed.

"Not at all. And Alice says would you like lemon soufflé or apple pie for pudding?"

"Apple pie, please. I seem to remember she's famous for it."

"Oh, she cooks everything well, Alice does, since she went on that course two winters ago."

"It's awfully good of you to offer to babysit, Joanna."

"Oh, I'll enjoy it. I like babies. I'll push him out for you sometimes, if you like? I'll go and tell Alice about the dessert."

It was Alice who brought it over.

"I've finished my part in the kitchen," she said. "They can manage the rest themselves now. I've good help. So I thought I'd come and sit with you for a bit."

"That's lovely. Thank you. Do tell me about Joanna, while I'm eating. What's she going to study? I'd have liked to talk to her about it just now, but she was in a hurry to be off."

Alice smiled, "Yes, she would be," she said. "And she's shy, you know. She's going to study botany," she went on. "Do you remember you suggested that?"

Judith shook her head, mystified.

"Yes, you did," Alice went on, laughing. "When you were up here three or four years ago and I was telling you we were worried because Joanna seemed to spend so much time collecting flowers and drawing them and suchlike when we thought she ought to be studying, and you said perhaps she could combine the two by studying botany."

"Yes, I do remember vaguely now. How bossy of me."

"No, you just suggested it. It was something we didn't know about. She takes biology, but then she can specialise in plants and suchlike. There was a professor used to take them for nature walks and he encouraged her too. Of course the teachers at school were very good. She did really well in her A-levels *and* she won prizes for her flower paintings," Alice said, her voice casual but her face glowing with pride. "There, I'll take your plate."

She settled herself comfortably in a chair by the bed. She had put on weight, Judith noticed, and the fair hair was scattered with grey.

"I didn't bring coffee," she said. "I thought you might be worried about it keeping you awake."

"Yes, I don't sleep very well just now."

"You're anxious, maybe. And babies disturb your nights so

222

you don't settle even when they do. Perhaps you'd be better with drinking chocolate?"

"That would be nice, thank you."

"He's a lovely little boy," Alice said, when she brought in the hot drink. "You really have no need to worry about him."

"I know." She sighed. "Everyone tells me that, but I don't seem able to help it. I feel so inadequate somehow."

"Well, I've been thinking. You know, I think that nature puts worry into mothers when their babies are born, just like she puts in the milk. If she didn't, some of them wouldn't stand a chance. I help at the clinic in the village on weigh days and some of the girls have been so feckless, but once they have their babies, they're different again, suddenly responsible, because nature has sent in worry with the milk. But it seems to me that if you're already a thoughtful and caring person, maybe that extra anxiety nature gives you is a bit of an overdose. That's how I figure it, any road."

She thinks I'm thoughtful and caring, Judith realised, so perhaps I'm not so hopeless after all. She didn't reply for a while and then said, "It's odd that you, who've never had children, understand it all so well."

"Well, you see, I had the care of our Joanna when my mam was busy running the farm after our dad died. So I had to get into the way of looking after her."

"I wish I could get into the way of it."

"Well, I did have my mam there. You haven't yours, have you?"

"No, there are no parents on either side."

"Ah, well, you see, that makes it hard."

How strange that this new, perceptive Alice had seen something which should have been obvious to herself, too. Of all the times in her life, this was the one when she most missed having a mother.

"And, you see," Alice was saying, "in a way I'd been prepared for looking after a baby sister. On a farm you grow up looking after young things. You see calves and lambs born, you look after them when they're ailing. It makes it easier, it's a kind of preparation."

True, Judith thought. All her own training had been appropriate for her job but had nothing to do with mothering. That was something she had come to quite unprepared.

"But he's a fine little lad," Alice was saying. "And he's got parents who love him. What more does he need?"

"Oh Alice—" she broke off suddenly, her eyes filling with tears. Alice came and sat on the side of the bed and put her arms around her. And Judith leant against this girl whom she had once pitied, who had seemed so pathetically helpless, and was now her comforter. And she thought, *what a strange reversal of roles this is, and how arrogant I have been.*

"You're right, of course," she said at last.

"I'll leave you in peace now," Alice told her. "And your husband said to tell you to go off to sleep if you can. He'll creep in later and he'll see to Timothy in the night. So you can just relax and get a really good night's sleep."

After she had gone, Judith lay gazing out of the window, watching the sun set over the distant Sawborough. How was it that she hadn't noticed the view from this window before? It filled the picture window with fields, hills and the far mountain. She could hear the lowing of cows near the farm and the distant call of the sheep on the hillside. A climbing rose, moving gently in the breeze, stroked the window pane with its branches and a long-forgotten smell of cottage garden flowers – mignonette, was it, and night-scented stock? – wafted up from the border below. Reassured by the smells and sounds of her childhood, she drifted into sleep.

"I've been thinking," Alice said to them after breakfast the next morning, "your pram won't be much good for pushing along our lanes. It's more of a town pram, really. But I've had an old one in the loft for years so I've got our Samson to bring it down and give it a bit of a clean-up. It'll be just the job for pushing Timothy."

And so it was; in the days that followed, balmy days of sunshine and light breezes, they pushed the big-wheeled pram along lanes, over packhorse bridges, down tracks, even across fields. And Timothy looked about him and his cheeks filled out and grew pinker by the day. They fed him in the lee of dry-stone walls and afterwards ate their picnic while he lay on a rug and kicked in the sunshine. It was often evening before they loaded everything back into the big pram and bumped their way back to the farm.

Towards the end of their stay Freddy rang Tom Trapp, who said his case had been postponed. Another was on offer, which Freddy suggested should be covered by somebody else in chambers, to which Tom Trapp unwillingly agreed. And so they stayed an extra week, and by the time they returned to London, Timothy was sleeping through the night and so, restored in health and spirit, was his mother.

Thirty-four

J oanna Dowerthwaite stood in the doorway of her student room. In the new block, it was a typical modern box of a place, without character or charm, yet she, whose room at home, with its beamed ceilings and irregular walls, abounded in both, surveyed this featureless rectangle with wonder and delight. Her joy was tinged with disbelief; she still couldn't quite believe that she, Joanna Dowerthwaite from Sloughbottom Farm, was really here, that all those years of hard study had actually earned her the right to be in this college room.

She closed the door behind her and began arranging her things, taking her time about it because they were so few. It was Samson, taking an unprecedented day off work, who had brought her and her belongings here, though she'd told him she could manage by train, as she'd done when she came for her interview. But he had insisted on driving her, had helped her carry everything up out of the car and then stood, hugely out of place in her little room, unwilling to leave her in this unfamiliar world; fretting anxiously over her like that Judith had fretted over her baby.

She thought of him affectionately as she arranged the books and files on the flimsy little bookcase. Then carefully, like a child playing at houses, she unwrapped the mugs and plates which Alice had given her and arranged them in the cupboard by the basin in the corner. She untied the sheepskin rug and laid it on the floor by the bed, on which she had placed the three rather garish cushions given to her by cousin Clara. Lastly, she unpacked her case, arranging her clothes in a cupboard whose limited space was divided between a hanging area and shelves.

Then she stood back and surveyed the neatness of it all with satisfaction.

It was four o'clock and, a country girl who had been cooped up in a car all day, she needed fresh air. As she locked the door behind her, she realised that she'd never had a key of her own before. Well, she'd never needed one. Apart from that once when she came to the interview she'd never been away from home, even for one night.

There weren't many people about as she walked across to the porter's lodge. A few other Freshers, coming up early like herself, were ferrying cases and boxes and large plants up to their rooms, helped by solicitous parents. Preoccupied with their own affairs, they didn't stop to speak.

Outside the lodge, she hesitated. She'd like to go back to the Botanic Garden, which she'd briefly visited when she came for interview, but it was a long walk and she wasn't sure when it closed. So instead she walked towards the University Parks, which she'd only glimpsed from outside before. On her way she noticed a chemist's shop and, remembering there was something she would need next week, went in. To her dismay there was only a young man behind the counter. She couldn't bring herself to ask a man for anything so personal, so bought some toothpaste instead.

It was a gentle evening, as she walked through the main gates into the Parks; the sun, though low in the sky, still gave welcome warmth. There was no wind and the atmosphere was very calm and peaceful.

She seemed to have the place to herself as she walked along wide paths between trees and shrubs. She saw that leaves were already falling; mounds of them had been swept up and piled behind the bushes. There, she thought, they'll compost down and mulch the ground, feeding it, as the animals on the farm nourished the grass on which they grazed. Samson said that town life was unnatural, but even here, in this urban park, she could see the natural cycle of things. She'd tell him that, when she wrote, she thought, smiling at the remembrance of him.

Because the sun was so low in the sky it gleamed through the lower branches of the trees. She stopped and looked at a skimmia bush, amazed by the way the setting sun set the glossy leaves aglow and lit up the berries so that they really did shine like rubies. She took out the sketch book, which she always carried with her, sat on a bench and began to draw. She noticed that there were a few unseasonal little white flowers on its lower branches, the sort of thing, she realised, that you don't notice until you start to sketch with a more observant eye.

A man came and sat down on the bench next to her, a big burly man, thickset and wide-shouldered. She smiled, nodded, and got on with her drawing. He didn't say anything, but after a while she felt uncomfortable under his gaze and put down her pencil.

"Don't let me put you off," he said immediately, and his voice was deep, kindly, cultured. "I'll go if I'm disturbing you."

"Oh, no, please don't feel that."

He'd as much right to sit on a bench in a public park as she had, after all.

"Do a lot of drawing, do you?"

"Well, I'm interested in plants, that's part of my subject, so I do draw them quite a lot. I don't think I'm much good at it, but it makes me observe the details better and that's important."

He nodded.

"An undergraduate, are you?"

"Yes, I've just come up today, for the first time," she told him.

"My father was up at the university. But I didn't make it. Of course, in his day it was easier because there weren't all these women. They've taken the places men used to have."

"Oh, but surely it's a question of merit?"

He laughed. His teeth, like the rest of him, were big. One of the front ones, she noticed, was broken. There was still quite a lot of it, but a triangle was missing from one corner.

"Oh, merit!" he exclaimed. "I don't know about merit. You'd be surprised what methods some of these girls use to get a place."

"I think I'd better be getting back," Joanna told him, not liking the turn the conversation had taken.

"Have I upset you? I'm sorry. I shouldn't have spoken like that."

He sounded truly sorry, this strange man.

"That's all right," she said, gathering her things together and getting up off the bench. "It's getting too dark to draw now anyway."

She said goodbye and set off back the way she'd come. He got up and followed her.

"It's no good going back to the main entrance," he told her. "The gate'll be shut by now. You'd do best to go out by the other one. It isn't shut till later."

She stopped, surprised.

"Will it really be shut? I thought most parks don't shut until sunset?"

"You're new to Oxford, aren't you? We have our funny ways here. Sunset's an hour early; it's one of our traditions. But when the clocks go back at the end of the month, our sunset's at the same time as everyone else's."

"I've never heard of that," she said, laughing. "How extraordinary."

"Oh, you'll hear a lot of funny things."

He glanced at his watch. "Yes, the main gate will be closed by now. But I'll show you the way to the other one. We go back the way we've come, past the bench and you'll see a path off to the left, leading to the other gate which they don't lock until half an hour later."

"Thank you. I'm so grateful. I'd never have known," she said, walking beside him. "It would be awful to be locked in."

"Glad to help a lady any time," he said, putting his arm around her as they walked in step.

She didn't want to seem rude, but she didn't want his arm round her waist either, so just tried to walk further apart from him. But his arm was like an iron band.

"Don't you worry. I'll see you safely back. It's really not safe for a girl to walk alone in the evening. A girl needs a man with her."

"Oh, no, I'm quite all right. It's very kind of you, but really I'm quite all right."

"Oh, yes, you're all right," he said.

For the next few yards he didn't speak. She didn't know what to do. It wasn't a situation she'd ever found herself in before. She couldn't make him out at all. He seemed to think he was being kind and it would be churlish to ask him to leave her alone. But, oh, she did wish he'd go away.

She was relieved when he said, "It's just down here to the gate."

"Oh, thank you," she said, trying to escape his arm.

"I'll see you safely through it," he said, leading her off to the left. "It's just down this path."

It didn't seem much of a path to her. They had to push their way through bushes and under branches. But she could see a wall not far off so presumed that the gate must be in it. It would have been easier to walk in single file, but he kept his arm protectively round her as they stumbled through the undergrowth.

Their way was blocked by a pile of leaves.

"I think—" she began.

But suddenly she was down on the leaves. She didn't know what had happened. She thought he must have tripped over a branch and dragged her down with him as he fell. Her sketch book had flown out of her hand and the little bag with the toothpaste had gone too.

"No need to think," he said and his voice was gruffer now. "All you need is a man."

"Please get up," she said. "You're hurting me. I want to go home."

"You shall," he said. "Later."

This sudden change from friend to attacker confused and bewildered her. She opened her mouth to scream, but he was too quick for her; his hand was over her mouth before she could make a sound. She tried to bite the hand while kicking out with her legs.

"That's good," he said. "We all like a struggle, don't we? And what have we got in here? Let's look and see, shall we?" he added, pulling open her blouse. She pushed her hands against him, but he took her wrists and pinned her hands behind her back, lying heavily on top of her so that her arms were twisted and seemed to be being pulled out of their sockets. He had grabbed her bra and was pulling it up round her neck. He was clawing at her breasts, squeezing them in a vice-like grip that brought sickening pain, then biting hard. And all the time he kept one hand over her mouth as she sobbed and choked. *He's going to kill me*, she thought. *Please let me die quickly. Anything is better than this. Anything.*

"Open wide," he suddenly commanded. "We know you like to play games, you girls do. Put up a bit of resistance," he added whispering now in her ear. Then he deliberately bit it hard before dragging up her skirt and pulling it over her head, enveloping her so that she couldn't see or hear what he was doing. Only feel.

He swivelled round suddenly, and lay motionless on her chest, so that for a moment she thought it might all be over, but still she lay, rigid with terror, not knowing what he would do next, where he would strike. He seemed to be examining her. Then she felt his head on her bare stomach, felt his teeth bite, lower and lower. She thought of those big teeth, they were biting at her flesh now, tearing at her like a dog worrying sheep. She tried to hit his face with her knees, but he was too strong and heavy and she was totally in his power. With sick horror she realised she could feel his hands inside her, tearing her open, clawing frantically. It seemed to go on and on and she felt herself getting fainter and fainter. Then something huge was pushed into her and he was grunting and writhing. Then at last she lost consciousness.

The park keeper, walking his rounds that evening, noticed something white in the bushes. "Litter louts," he muttered, as he went to pick it up. Then he saw the body of a girl lying among the leaves, bloodstained and half-naked and beside her a little bag from which a tube of toothpaste had fallen and the white sketch pad which had first attracted his attention.

Thirty-five

H ow well everything is working out, Judith thought, as she sat in chambers this bright November afternoon.

Elsa had proved an excellent nanny, competent and intelligent, who filled Timothy's day with interest, with outings and with little games. He was six months old now, an enchanting age. She enjoyed every minute she had with him; how unlike those awful early weeks, she thought, shuddering as she remembered them. The turning point had been that visit to Netherby, those glorious three weeks on the farm: for that she would be forever grateful to Alice.

Going back to work had, perhaps, been a bit more difficult than she'd expected. She had a sneaking feeling of resentment that Timothy would see more of the admirable Elsa than of her, his own mother. He might even be unsure which of the two of them *was* his mother. It was illogical, she told herself; of course she was grateful that he obviously loved and trusted Elsa. All the same, she was pleased that he had started to crawl on a Sunday when she was there to witness it and meanly hoped that he would be considerate enough not to take his first step, when the time came, on a weekday.

She glanced at her watch: four o'clock. She had time to put in a good hour's work before she left for home. Elsa, who lived locally, stayed until six in the evening. She said she never minded staying later if they were delayed, but they made it a point of honour that one of them should be back on time, and so far had always managed it.

So long as you're well organised, Judith thought now, there really needn't be any serious clash between having a career and being a mother. It was just defeatism on the part of those women who said there was. Satisfied with herself and her tidily organised life, she turned back to studying the papers of a very untidy case of attempted murder.

It was as she was leaving that Tom Trapp knocked at her door. He was holding a brief.

"It's a rape," he said. "To prosecute."

"Thanks, Tom. I'll take it home with me."

They both had work to do that night after they'd put Timothy to bed and had supper. Freddy already had his papers spread around him when she opened the brief that Tom had given her: *R v Bradstone*.

She glanced at it.

"Oh, no, *no!*" she exclaimed.

Freddy looked up, alarmed at the horror in her voice.

"Oh, Freddy, Freddy."

He came quickly over to her.

"Look, Freddy, look. The name of the victim. There can't be two Joanna Dowerthwaites. And she was starting at the university in October. Oh, my God!"

She sat with her head in her hands, remembering the girl, her quiet manner, her youthfulness, her trusting country ways. And she thought of the terrible state of the rape victims in cases she had known.

"Oh, the poor child. Oh, my God," she said again.

He put his arms around her.

"I know, darling," he said. "I know. It's the most terrible of all crimes."

"What can I do to help them?"

"Well, you can't take the case, that's for sure. Never take on a case of someone known to you."

"No, I suppose I can't. But I could talk to them. They'll need all the help they can get. It's not their world, Freddy. They'll have no idea of the second rape the defence will put her through in court."

"Perhaps he'll plead guilty. Let's look at it."

After they'd read quickly through the pages, they turned to look at each other.

"He's as guilty as hell," Freddy said.

She nodded.

"The trial will be in Oxford, I suppose?"

"Yes. Oh, I do think it's wrong, Freddy, the way these cases are heard in places more convenient for the defendant than the victim. Do you remember the case I had of that girl who was raped on holiday in Surrey? The sixteen-year-old from Newcastle? She had to travel three times to court in Guildford, a whole day's journey from Newcastle, and three times the defence managed to get an adjournment. She couldn't face it again, so gave up the case."

"Let's hope there are no adjournments in Joanna's case."

"That depends a lot on the judge. I'll ring Alice tomorrow and see if she'd like to meet me for a talk."

"You'll have to explain that you can't take the brief."

"Yes. I think I'll ring now."

It was Alice who answered the phone. "Oh, Judith," she said, "it's good to hear you," and her voice broke. But she quickly recovered. "Joanna's not fit to travel," she said in reply to Judith's question. "But Samson and I'll come to see you. She'll be all right, left with our mam for the day."

"Where shall we meet?"

She didn't want to talk to them in chambers; it would be unethical if she was returning the brief.

She heard them conferring about a meeting place.

"Samson says he never wants to go to London, but could we meet at King's Cross station? Up here, folks think that King's Cross station is still part of Yorkshire."

"All right, I'll meet you off the train and arrange somewhere quiet where we can talk over lunch."

"The station'll do. Samson'll not want to leave the station and go into London."

"All right. There's a restaurant there. I'm afraid it's a long way for you to have to come."

"It makes no odds now," Alice said.

Accustomed though she had grown to seeing whole families of the victims of crime broken by a single vicious act, she was still unprepared for the change in Alice and Samson. It was heart-breaking to see the way that the life seemed to have gone out of them; to see on their faces that look of disbelief that people have when they cannot come to terms with what has happened, that wariness in their eyes.

They had obviously set great store by this meeting with her; she realised that they expected some miracle from one who understood the legal world but was also their friend. To her they could talk freely, these people who would normally have kept such matters to themselves. As they talked she felt the enormity of their grief: Joanna, still to them their little sister, had gone off with such hope and excitement, looking forward to a student life which was the culmination of all she had been working for these past years. She had been speeded on her way with the good wishes of all the village. They were proud of her. And two short days later she had been brought back in misery and – Judith sensed – dishonour.

"And the case has to be down in the south, does it, not some place nearer for us?"

"I'm afraid so. It's one of the reasons that some women drop their case."

"We'll not drop this case, whatever happens," Samson put in fiercely. "We'll fight for our Joanna to the end."

Judith hesitated. Then, "I have to warn you, Samson," she said, "that it won't be *you* who does the fighting. Joanna's the one who'll have to stand up in court to be cross-examined. She's the one who'll have to face answering endless questions, often very painful ones."

"And what about him? Will he be there?"

"Yes, in the dock."

"So she'll have to see him?"

"We'll try to avoid it. In the witness box she won't have to look at the dock. She can face the other way."

"She had to see him for identifying him, you know," Samson said. "And anyway, they knew by his teeth marks."

Alice, who had been pushing food round her plate, now gave up any attempt to eat.

236

"And all those questions," she said. "Will she have to answer them in front of everybody?"

"I'm afraid so. In open court. There'll be the judge and jury and two lawyers for the prosecution and two for the defence."

"And all the lawyers will be men, I suppose, except you?"

"Possibly. But Alice, I haven't explained clearly enough. I can't actually take the case. I'll help in any other way I can. You see, it just isn't done to be involved in a case with someone you know. It would make it too personal."

They both looked at her, dismayed.

"But we thought you'd do this for us," Samson said, baffled.

"I'm sorry. I did try to explain on the phone—"

"Joanna needs someone she knows and trusts."

"I know that. I can't tell you how sorry I am."

"Samson," Alice said suddenly. "Would you join that queue and get us three cups of tea? I want a private word with Judith."

Judith watched as he made his way towards the counter; a burly countryman, a stranger, out of place in a station restaurant crowded with urban travellers. Then she turned to Alice wondering what it was that she wanted to say that she didn't want her brother to hear.

Alice, pale, tense was clearly forcing herself to speak.

"Judith," she said simply. "It happened to me too. I know what it's like for Joanna."

"You mean . . . ?"

"Yes, I mean that. Years ago, when I was eighteen. The day I went down to the whist drive; the day I saw you out walking. It was that evening, in the copse."

"But you never . . . I mean, there was no case?"

Alice shook her head.

"The lads sorted him."

It was so sudden, so unbelievable, so unexpected. Judith could only look at her, shaking her head. It was Alice who went on speaking. She spoke passionately now, quite unlike her usual self; the words pouring out as if they had been dammed up for years.

"I don't want it to be for her like it was for me," she began, her voice low but intense. "I don't want her to be afraid of marriage,

237

I don't want her to miss out on anything she might have had just because of what was done to her. I want her to be whole, I want her to be able to trust a man again. I don't want it to be all shame and hidden. It's out in the open anyway, with the report in the newspapers. And if the law can help make it better for her than it was for me, then so be it. I know more about the law now; I know she can get justice. But, oh, Judith," she ended, her voice breaking, "we'll need your help."

Judith hesitated. She saw Samson approaching with the tea.

"Have you done?" he asked his sister and stood, looking anxious and touchingly helpless, as he held the flimsy plastic tray clutched in his great fists; waiting to know if he could join the womenfolk.

"I've said what I needed to say," Alice told him.

"And I've thought of something to say too," he said slowly, as he sat down. Turning to Judith he went on, "When you said, it's *not done* for you to take this case because you know us, do you mean it's not lawful?"

"No, Samson, but it's against convention."

"And does it matter all that much, this convention, I mean?" he persisted.

No, why should it? Judith thought suddenly. These were people she'd known since childhood. This was her friend Alice who had years ago been the victim of a terrible crime, and kept it hidden; who had had the strength to make a success of her life despite it; who had saved her from wretched depression when Timmy was born. This was Samson and Alice, who had looked after their younger sister, cherished and protected her, and now this dreadful thing had happened and they were turning to her for help. Alice had spoken so trustingly of getting justice, but they were going to be involved in a legal world which was totally foreign to them, whose ways were not their ways and whose words were not their words. Could she really let them turn to her in vain? Compared to their need, what did convention matter?

"No," she said, turning to Samson. "I think that this time it doesn't matter. I'll take the case."

Thirty-six

J udith's heart sank when she saw that the defence barrister was Colin Hacker, who had recently been making a name for himself as a successful defender of men accused of rape. Bitter because he had been passed over for the bench, Hacker was unscrupulous in cross-examination; as if it was his way of working off his spleen. He was particularly dangerous because he didn't come across as bitter. From the day when, as a young barrister, a judge had reprimanded him by saying, 'To cross-examine, Mr Hacker, does not mean to examine crossly', he had taken care not to alienate the jury by seeming to treat the witness roughly. He asked questions courteously, he could seem charming, even if it was in a somewhat supercilious manner. He could beguile witnesses into saying what they didn't really mean.

He was a dapper little man, always perfectly turned out. Now in his early fifties, he had been married twice, both marriages ending in expensive divorce. Judith often wondered if this had influenced his treatment of women in the witness box. Smoothly, courteously he contrived to turn that witness box into a dock; the victim into a criminal.

After the jury had been sworn in, Judith outlined the case for the prosecution and then, with gentle questioning, took Joanna through the events of that day; from her arriving in college until the time she was found in the Parks. Joanna, who had been carefully prepared for what she had learned to call her examination-in-chief, answered calmly, her voice quiet, her eyes not leaving Judith's face. But then she had to be handed over to the defence lawyer for cross-examination and was beyond Judith's protection and guidance.

"When you were unpacking in your room, Miss Dowerthwaite," Colin Hacker began. "Did you lock your bedroom door?"

"No," she answered, surprised. "I don't think I did."

"Wasn't that rather remiss? I believe your college asks all undergraduates to lock the doors to their rooms. In fact, I believe a notice is put to that effect in each room?"

"I didn't see it," Joanna told him, clearly unaware of what he was implying.

"I put it to you, Miss Dowerthwaite, that a young woman who was careful of her own safety would surely have kept her door locked, as instructed, rather than leaving it open as an invitation to any passer-by to come in?"

"Yes, I suppose so."

"Well, we will overlook that, and move on," he said in his most patronising voice, as if forgiving her, while at the same time letting the jury have the impression that she was not one who was over-careful of her reputation. "You walked to the Parks and after a little while sat on a bench."

"Yes, I was sketching."

"You sat down alone on a park bench in the late afternoon." He paused as if ruminating sadly on the morals of a girl who would do such a thing. "And then a man came and sat beside you."

"Yes."

"You didn't know that man?"

"No."

"Didn't you think it rather strange that he should come and sit next to you?"

"No. It's a public park."

"And then you talked?"

"Yes."

"Can you tell the court what was said?"

"He asked if he was disturbing me and should he go away."

"And what did you say?"

"I said it was all right for him to stay."

"So you *invited* him to sit with you?"

240

"No, I didn't. I just agreed that he could stay."

"Could you explain to the court why you did so? You could have told him to go away. You admit that he had offered to do so."

She hesitated.

"I suppose I thought it would be rude," she said.

She was beginning to feel confused; all these things that he was asking her about had seemed unimportant at the time. It was only the terrible thing which had followed that had given them this significance. But at the time she hadn't known that, hadn't know that one day questions would be asked about them in a law court. How could she have done? Or should she have been able to? For the first time she began to feel uncertain. Perhaps she had been stupid, had brought it all on herself.

She had managed so far not to look at the dock; now she made the mistake of doing so. She had not seen him since the attack, except once to identify him. Now just that one glance made her sick with horror. For a moment she thought she might faint; she gripped the ledge in front of her and looked towards Judith, who nodded encouragement. It was a reassuring look, a look which told her she was doing all right, not to lose heart.

They are all on my side, my brother and my sister and Judith, she reminded herself, and I mustn't let them down. I must just answer these questions, keep calm and not look at the man in the dock.

"And then you talked for a while?" she was being asked, evidently for the second time.

"Yes."

"Can you tell the court what was said?"

"We talked about drawing, I think. And he asked if I was up at the University and I said that I was and he said his father had been too but that he himself hadn't got a place because women were taking so many more places now."

"Didn't that strike you as a very strange remark?"

She hesitated.

"Yes, in a way, it did," she said slowly, "but then I suppose it's true, isn't it?"

241

"You must not ask questions, just answer them," he rebuked her. "You agreed that such was the case?"

"Not exactly. I remember I said that entrance must be on merit."

"And what did he say to that?"

"He said I'd be surprised at the methods some women used to get a place."

"And still you didn't walk away? You sat with this man, a total stranger, who made these suggestive remarks to you. I put it to you, Miss Dowerthwaite," and his voice was silky with understanding now, "that you gave him the impression that you, an inexperienced girl, away from home for the first time, quite enjoyed that kind of conversation; found it sophisticated, rather exciting?"

"No, I didn't. I did not," Joanna exclaimed bitterly and, as she remembered it all with sudden vividness, burst into tears.

"Would you like to have a break?" the judge asked. "We could adjourn for ten minutes."

"No, thank you. I'm all right," Joanna managed to say, getting a grip on herself, just wanting to get it all over without any more delays.

"Then," Colin Hacker went on, "he told you some tale about the main gate being already shut?"

"Yes, he said that they shut an hour earlier than the actual sunset time."

"And you chose to believe him?"

"I'd no reason to disbelieve him, but I did say that I thought it was extraordinary."

"Then you went with him into the bushes?"

"No, it wasn't like that. It wasn't like that at all."

"Perhaps you can tell us what it *was* like?"

"We walked along the main path and then he said there was a smaller one off to the left to a gate which would still be open."

"And how were you walking? One behind the other?"

"No, side by side. I wanted to go in single file, but he put his arm around me."

He looked at her as if shocked.

242

"You let a strange man put his arm round you? Is it your habit to let strange men embrace you in this way?"

There was a sudden eruption in the visitors' gallery.

"Stop this! Stop this, it's shameful!" Samson roared.

He stood there, bull-like in his rage. There was absolute silence in the court. Everyone looked at the judge.

"Sit down," he ordered Samson, "and be silent. Or leave this court."

Samson sat.

Colin Hacker repeated his question.

"No," Joanna said. "I didn't know what to make of it, but I thought he just meant to help me along, show me the way."

"Some may think that a very strange assumption, but we will let it pass. Then after a few steps through the bushes, you lay down with him on a pile of leaves, which was no doubt more comfortable for you than the uneven ground."

"No, I didn't lie down. He seemed to trip and drag me down with him."

"And what did you do?"

"I asked him to get up because he was hurting me."

"You didn't call for help?"

"I wanted to, but he had his hand over my mouth."

"And then he lifted up your bra?"

"Yes."

"With one hand? How could he do that without your co-operation?" Colin Hacker asked and then, turning towards the jury, he added with a knowing smile, "I'm sure that most men would agree that a bra is a most difficult article of a lady's clothing to take off. The average male has a real struggle to undo it. It would require at least that you raised you shoulders—"

"No! I did not, I did not."

"Very well, as you say, Miss Dowerthwaite. Let us agree tht you didn't actively co-operate. But you didn't fight very hard either, did you?"

"I couldn't. He was so strong. Stronger than me. He seemed like an animal and he," her voice shook in horror at the remembrance of it, "he was biting me."

243

"Yes, the defence concedes there was evidence of love bites."

Love! In such a context! Was he mad? Suddenly it seemed to her that the whole court was mad and she wanted to escape from it as she had longed to escape from her tormentor in the Parks. Helplessly, she began to sob.

The judge intervened.

"The court will rise for the midday break," he announced. "And give Miss Dowerthwaite time to compose herself. Miss Dowerthwaite, I will allow you to have lunch with your family, but must warn you not to discuss this case. Do you understand?"

Joanna nodded and whispered her assent.

"This court will sit again at two o'clock this afternoon," the judge pronounced.

They sat, the three of them: Alice, Samson and Joanna, at a little table in the corner of the canteen, uneaten meals pushed to one side.

"It's got to stop," Samson said. "They're making our Joanna out to be a criminal. And him in the dock just sits there and nobody says owt about him."

Alice, strained and pale with grief, said nothing. Joanna sat between them, composed now, but lethargic. She seemed like an animal that knows it just has to endure.

"We're not to discuss it, Samson," she warned. "I promised the judge."

"I'm not discussing it. I'm just saying," her brother told her.

"Judith did warn us that it would be a terrible ordeal for our Joanna in court, Samson. She said that was why so many women don't report what's been done to them. They can't bear all this."

"I reckon it's past bearing for our Joanna," Samson said. "It'd be better to withdraw than have her endure all this from that lawyer."

Alice shook her head, "No, Samson," she said. "We can't stop the case. It's out of our hands now. It's up to the prosecution."

"I can't but wish we'd never started it," Samson said.

"But if we hadn't, that man would be free to go and attack another girl."

244

"Samson," Joanna broke in suddenly. "I know I'm not to discuss the case, but nobody can stop me telling you this: I wouldn't stop the case even if I could. I'll not mind what they say or ask. I'll think of that other girl he might attack, that's what I'll do, and then I'll be able to bear anything."

"She's right, Samson," Alice said. "And I'm proud of her. It's the only way to get the man convicted."

"But it's a wrong way to go about it," Samson exclaimed. "After what our Joanna's been through, to put her through all this, it's . . ." words failed him and he said simply, "I could kill that lawyer."

Alice hesitated. Judith had explained that it was the defence lawyer's duty to try to get his client off, and the only way he could do it was to break Joanna; but she couldn't bring herself to say the words. The wrong that was being done to Joanna forbade any justification.

The usher summoned them back into the court.

"Tell me, Miss Dowerthwaite," Colin Hacker asked in his smoothest tones, "are you on the Pill?"

"Yes."

The jury looked surprised at her answer. It didn't fit the picture they had been given of this young virgin.

"The doctor said I should take it," Joanna began.

"Why?"

"Because I had – I had . . ."

She couldn't go on. She looked at the four lawyers, all men, she looked at the male judge, at the six men in the jury box, at the young men in the press gallery. She had to say it; she who hadn't been able to bring herself to buy a packet of sanitary towels from a male chemist.

"I had heavy periods," she whispered, "and not very regular. She said the Pill would make it better, and it did."

"Stop it," Samson muttered audibly. "Stop it. It's shameful."

Alice took her brother's hand.

"Ssh," she warned. "She's controlling herself and so must you."

245

The judge glared at them, but said nothing.

"You have told the court that one of his hands was over your mouth and the other pulling at your bra and that he was biting you. Can you tell the court what happened next?"

"His hands went down."

"Both hands? So his hand left your mouth and you could have called for help?"

"No, he'd turned about somehow, I couldn't tell exactly how, but his body seemed to be heavy across my face and chest so I could hardly breathe."

"And where were his hands exactly?"

She hesitated.

"Down below," she said.

"When you say, 'Down below', where precisely do you mean? Your feet? Your knees?"

There was a jeering edge to his voice. *He's enjoying this, bloody little sadist that he is,* Judith thought. Like Samson, she wanted to shout her outrage. And how can he pretend not to see the relative strength of that six foot man in the dock and this slight girl in the witness box?

Joanna remained silent.

"Do you mean your vagina?"

"Yes."

"That's where his hands were?"

"Yes."

"The traces of semen being outside the body, it would seem possible that there was no actual penetration."

"I felt it," she said.

"You felt *something*. I put it to you that what you felt was his fingers."

The usual ploy, Judith thought wearily; get your client off with indecent assault, which carries a shorter sentence than rape.

But Joanna was not to be shaken.

"It was his hands first," she said. "Then something else."

"For one who claims to be sexually inexperienced that is a fine distinction to make since you were unable to see what he was doing."

He smiled benignly at Joanna.

"Thank you for answering my questions," he said in his smooth, suave voice, "difficult though some of them may perhaps have been. I have no more questions."

He sat down and Joanna was allowed, pale now and trembling, to leave the witness box and be led away by the usher.

"The court will now rise," the judge announced. "Tomorrow we will hear the medical evidence. This court will sit at ten o'clock tomorrow morning."

"Call Dr Wendy Summers, Dr Wendy Summers."

The doctor who went into the witness box was a woman of early middle-age with a reassuring air about her. She answered questions precisely in a low but very clear voice.

"You are the doctor who examined the complainant on the night of October eighth?" Judith asked, after the doctor had taken the oath and stated her qualifications.

"Yes, I was called to the police station where she had been taken by a fellow student who had found her in a distressed state in college."

"Can you tell the court what you found on examining her?"

"The patient was badly bruised, her mouth was torn at one corner and there were bite marks on her body, particularly on her stomach and thighs, bad enough to have broken the skin in several places. Her left nipple was torn."

"And internally?"

"The hymen was ruptured and there was bleeding from the vagina which was torn and had to be stitched."

"And how would you account for this damage?"

"It seemed to me that it was the damage you might expect to find in a patient who has recently been raped. In consensual sex the vagina relaxes, but in rape it is tight and the walls tear. Being vascular, they bleed. I had to remove a haematoma in consequence of this."

"Thank you. I have no more questions."

Judith having finished her examination-in-chief, it was now the turn of the defence to cross-examine.

"Dr Summers," Colin Hacker began. "You say that there was bleeding from the vagina?"

"That is correct."

"How can you be sure that it wasn't menstrual blood?"

"Menstrual blood has a different appearance."

"I suggest to you that they can be confused."

"Not in my experience."

"I believe that there is an implement called a speculum which can be inserted into the vagina. If you had used one of these you could have ascertained if the blood came from the vagina or the uterus."

"That is correct."

"May I ask why you did not use this implement on the complainant?"

"You may not realise it, but it can be very painful to the patient. I did not consider it a suitable procedure to use on a girl who had never had an internal examination and who was deeply traumatised by the recent attack."

"I object, my Lord."

"Perhaps," the judge suggested, "you might amend your answer to the *alleged* attack?"

The doctor agreed.

"Dr Summers, in normal lovemaking, love bites occur?"

"Yes."

"Sometimes quite hard love bites, which leave marks, even break the skin?"

"I think that a woman would find such bites painful."

"But is not pain sometimes a part of sexual pleasure?"

"Possibly."

"Thank you. I have no more questions."

The contrast between the departing doctor and the park keeper who replaced her in the witness box could not have been greater. Where she had stepped into it looking brisk and neat, he shambled into the box like some walking compost heap that had been shovelled into a blue suit.

After the clearly spoken doctor, the jury had to strain to hear his mumbled responses to Judith's questions. What he lacked in audibility he made up for in volubility. He was at pains to point out that it was his diligent pursuit of litter which had led him to discover the girl lying in the bushes. The problem of litter evidently obsessed him and he was determined to make the most of his one little hour of glory to publicise his views to a lot of important people who had to listen. In so doing he contrived to elevate the sin of litter-dropping into the same order of things as the crime of rape.

His description of the state in which he found the complainant was, however, very important to the case and Judith dealt with him as patiently as she could. But she found it difficult not to be exasperated, especially as this was the wretched man who, instead of escorting Joanna to the police station, had taken her back to college, where she had fled to the bathroom and cleansed herself.

Hacker did not choose to cross-examine the park keeper who now shambled out of the witness box, making way for a police officer whose evidence was contrastingly clear and audible as Judith led him through the known facts of the case. This time Hacker did choose to cross-examine.

"When charged with the offence, could you tell the court what the defendant said?"

"He said," the policeman replied, reading out of a note book, " 'This is nonsense. The young lady willingly accompanied me into the bushes.' "

"Have you ever had dealings with the defendant before?"

"No, sir."

"He has a clean record?"

"Yes, sir."

"Thank you. I have no more questions."

It was the end of the prosecution case. It was now Colin Hacker's turn to present the case for the defence. He immediately called his client, his only witness. Sydney Bradstone was escorted from the dock to the witness box. Forewarned by Judith, Alice had taken Joanna away from the court, but Samson sat doggedly on, staring directly at the man in the witness box.

He saw that Sydney Bradstone was a big man, impeccably

dressed, very respectable-looking. And when he spoke, the man's voice was gentle, warm, reassuring.

He answered Colin Hacker's questions with quiet confidence. Yes, he had struck up an instant friendship with the young lady in the Parks. Perhaps he should have been more circumspect, he conceded, but she had been so eager, so clearly wanting him.

Judith listened with foreboding; there was no question that this was a voice to sow seeds of doubt in a jury's mind. Such a man, so kindly and so beautifully spoken, didn't sound capable of the kind of violence he was being accused of. Was it likely, they might ask themselves, that a man who had no criminal record, who had never committed a violent act, would suddenly, at the age of forty-two, behave in a manner so out of character with his past?

Colin Hacker's last question, cleverly worded, gave the defendant the chance to reply, "I am a man of integrity whose character is unblemished."

These were the words that rang in Judith's ears as she left the court for the luncheon adjournment and she knew that they rang also in the ears of the jurors.

She had decided not to see Joanna and her family over lunch. She needed time alone, to work on her cross-examination of Sydney Bradstone. It was vital that she found some weakness in this plausible man's defence. She knew all too well the unwillingness of juries to convict in rape cases, especially of a man with no record of violence.

As she made her way down the corridor she felt someone touch her arm. It was a small, fair woman of about thirty.

"Excuse me," she said with the careful enunciation of one who has taken elocution lessons. "But are you the lawyer dealing with the rape case?"

"You mean *R v Bradstone*?"

"Yes."

"I am. How can I help you?"

"I think it is rather a question of my helping you," the carefully manicured voice corrected her.

"Who are you?"

"I am Sydney Bradstone's ex-wife."

Judith didn't hesitate.

"Come in here," she said, pushing open the door of a conference room, and almost pushing the woman too. "Just stay here while I find my prosecuting solicitor. It's one of the rules that I mustn't speak to you without his being present."

"I'll wait," the woman said, sitting down at the table. "I won't run away. Don't you worry."

During the trial, Judith hadn't consulted very much with her prosecuting solicitor. Alan Comfort was an affable character and she liked him. But he was not a man of ideas; he was not one to think of a new route. His strength lay in following up facts, investigating the known way. Whatever he was asked to do was done thoroughly and promptly. She needed him now, and cursed herself for not having arranged to meet him before this afternoon's cross-examination. He might be anywhere in the building – or out of it.

Then, to her relief she saw his ample form coming down the corridor towards her, smiling benignly.

"Don't look so worried," he said. "Come and have lunch with me."

"No, thanks. And I'm afraid you probably won't get any lunch either. There's someone waiting to speak to us."

The woman was still sitting at the table.

"Mr Comfort," Judith said, "this is Mrs Bradstone."

"No, I'm not," the woman said. "I've used my maiden name since the divorce. Changed it back by deed poll, I did. Cost forty pounds and worth every penny. So please to call me Miss Sanderson."

"Certainly, Miss Sanderson."

"I'd have come sooner if I'd known, but it was just by chance that I saw the report in the *Oxford Times*. A friend always sends it to me now I've moved away to Bath. And I came straight over."

"Thank you. Now what do you have to tell us, Miss Sanderson?"

"He's guilty."

251

"We have to prove that," Judith told her. "He's claiming consent and that, backed up by his unblemished record, may move the jury to acquit."

"Unblemished record? Is that what he said? And they all believed him, I expect. Oh, he's plausible, that one. A proper gentleman I thought him when we met. He can win people round. But he's not going to get away with this."

"The police have no records on him."

"Not our police, maybe. This is what I've come to tell you. Four years ago, while he was working abroad, he was had up in Holland for indecent assault on two women. He'd got chatting to them after dark, one in the street and the other in a park. He admitted it in the end. He got three months in prison. In Scheveningen gaol, he was."

She paused.

"It was that conviction which got me my divorce. Couldn't have had better grounds, the solicitor said."

"And he's just told the court he had no previous convictions."

"He's a fucking liar."

Judith was accustomed to obscenities in court, obscenities from muggers, fraudsters, burglars, all kinds of villains. They had long ago ceased to surprise her. But this word spat out from the prim little mouth shocked her as none other had done.

"And I'm going to sit in that court and hear him get his come-uppance."

"No, you're not," Judith told her. "You *must not* appear in court. In fact you must disappear until the case is over. He mustn't get even a suspicion that you've been here. I have to use this evidence in a way which will take him completely by surprise. Just let me have your address or telephone number in case we need you. But go now, go while he's down in the cells. He must not see you."

"Anything you say," Miss Sanderson replied with surprising compliancy. "You're the expert."

And she shook hands and left them.

"Mr Comfort," Judith said, turning to the solicitor, the minute the woman was out of the door. "We've got to act quickly. Get in touch with the Dutch authorities immediately. Check her story. Get them to fax all the relevant papers."

"It shall be done straight away,"

"Yes, I know it will," she said, confident that he would make a swift and thorough job of it. "And I'm sorry about your lunch."

He smiled. "I'll make up for it at dinner time," he said, and was gone.

Judith sat for a moment planning her next move. Then she went to seek out the judge and ask for an adjournment. It was a beautiful day and the judge, mindful of the golf course, granted it with alacrity.

Joanna and her family were less happy with the postponement. She sat with them for a while, trying to allay their fears about the delay without giving away the reason for it.

"I hope it may be just one afternoon we've lost," she said.

"But will it start summat?" Samson objected. "Once you start delaying and shilly-shallying it goes on and on. And our Joanna can't be doing with it."

"No, I promise you," she said. "All being well, tomorrow – or at worst the next day – should see the end of it. There'll be my cross-examination of the defendant, which won't take long but is very important, then my speech to the jury, followed by the defence speech and finally the judge's summing up."

"Then we'll go for a walk now," Alice said. "Make the most of a bit of winter sunshine."

She watched them go with an aching heart. It wasn't just Joanna who, as Samson put it, 'couldn't be doing with it'. They'd all three of them had about as much as they could take. She sometimes found herself forgetting that the atmosphere in court, which was her natural habitat, was strange and stressful to outsiders. One look at those three faces reminded her of it.

She made contingency arrangements for seeing the judge the next day in case Alan Comfort got the documents they needed, then worked for a while on preparing her cross-examination. Finally, she gathered her papers together and said a prayer of thanks to the lady who had visited her at lunchtime, and set off for home.

She was glad to be getting away early. Timmy hadn't seemed well that morning; the cold he'd had for a few days showed no sign of clearing and his breathing had become wheezy, sometimes sounding quite rattling.

Don't start being an over-anxious mum again, she told herself as she drove home, there's probably nothing to worry about. Babies get colds and of course their breathing sounds noisy because they don't know how to clear their little throats or blow their noses. She'd asked Elsa to take him to the doctor, who would no doubt think she was being unduly fussy. She knew that her anxiety was made worse by the fact that Freddy, always the reassuring one, was away on a case in Birmingham.

Freddy had once expounded to her a theory that women are born with a great supply of anxiety waiting to be used, and that having a baby provides the ideal opportunity to deploy it. Dear, funny Freddy. When he rings this evening, she told herself, I must not worry him by sounding over-anxious.

She saw at once that Timothy was worse.

"The doctor says it's a chest infection," Elsa told her. "I've got the medicine he prescribed. He's had two doses so far. he'll need one before he goes to bed and another if he's awake at two, but the doctor said not to wake him if he's asleep. He wants to see Timmy again tomorrow morning, so I've made an appointment to take him at eleven o'clock."

I want to take him myself, was Judith's immediate reaction. I want to hear for myself what's the matter with him. *I want to be with him.*

She took a hold of herself, said calmly, "Thank you so much, Elsa. I'm sure he'll be much better after a good night's sleep."

But he didn't have a good night's sleep – and neither did she. He couldn't breathe easily, so kept waking up and crying. She tried to settle him with milk from the bottle; she carried him round the house, holding him close to her shoulder, patting his back, talking soothingly. She sang to him, she tried giving him warm water, but nothing seemed to comfort her miserable little boy. Sometimes he fell asleep in her arms, but the minute she tried to put him down in his cot he woke up and cried. So she sat nursing him on her lap while he dozed fitfully and she read some of her baby books, hoping for advice, but they just seemed to imply that babies don't cry without cause and good mothers should be able to find it. All of which made her feel even more inadequate.

By four o'clock she was almost as tearful as he was. I can't leave him tomorrow, she kept thinking to herself. But then she remembered Joanna in the witness box. Joanna needed her as much as Timmy did. She owed herself to both of them, pledged as she was to Timmy because she had chosen to have him and to Joanna because she had taken on her case. Thus she, who had thought that the claims of work and family could, by the application of a little intelligent planning, be reconciled, felt herself torn between them as she paced the bedroom, carrying the whimpering child.

At six o'clock Timmy finally fell asleep and she dozed for an hour before the alarm went off at seven. She didn't feel at all rested, but at least she had made up her mind what to do. It seemed she had to let one of them down; she was going to feel guilty either way. So it was a question of which one had the greater need. Elsa could do everything for Timmy that she herself could do. She could take him to the doctor, carry out medical instructions, nurse him, feed him. But nobody could help Joanna as she herself could do. The trial was at a crucial stage with this new evidence from Bradstone's ex-wife and she didn't yet know if that had been substantiated. Even if another barrister, experienced enough in this field, could be found at short notice, there would have to be a further adjournment of the case while he or she studied the brief. Joanna had had enough to bear without further prolonging her suffering.

Her first duty was to her client, Judith told herself, as she resolutely handed the care of her son over to Elsa at eight o'clock in the morning and set off on her journey to court.

She arrived early, but the solicitor was already there; on her desk was not only all the necessary documentation of conviction but also a police mugshot of a man who was undoubtedly Sydney Bradstone.

"Oh, well done," she said. "But that mugshot isn't a fax; it's far too clear for that."

"I happened to have a colleague flying in from Schiphol," the solicitor told her. "I managed to contact him last night and he agreed to act as courier. I met him at Heathrow early this morning. Yes, it's a good clear photograph."

"Thank you. I can't tell you how grateful I am."

"It's his ex-wife you should be thanking," he said. "It would never have come out without her telling us. The police wouldn't have enquired about convictions in foreign courts, not in a case like this they wouldn't. And they wouldn't have had access to divorce papers so could never have found out the grounds for the divorce."

Judith glanced at her watch.

"There's time to ask to see the judge in his private room before the court sits," she said. "Of course Hacker will have to come too."

"So he'll be put into the picture about his client's past convictions?"

"Yes, but he can't clue his client up because he's under cross-examination."

"Of course."

The judge saw them almost immediately and dealt with them briskly so that the court was able to sit at the appointed time.

"Mr Bradstone," Judith began. "You told the jury yesterday that you are a man of integrity with an unblemished reputation. I want to be clear what you meant by that. Are you saying that you have never been in trouble with the police?"

"You heard what the police officer said."

"But the jury must hear what *you* say. Have you ever been in trouble with the police?"

"No. Never."

"And you say, do you, that you have no previous convictions? I should like you to consider your answer very carefully."

"I don't need to consider it. The answer is that I have no previous convictions."

"Is this a photograph of you?" Judith asked, suddenly producing the mugshot supplied by the Dutch police.

The man in the witness box was visibly shaken.

"It may be, it may not be," was all he managed to say.

"Let me tell you this: it has been supplied to the prosecution by the Dutch police. Have you ever been to Holland?"

"May have. It's hard to remember. I've travelled a lot in my time."

"Then perhaps I can remind you."

Carefully she recounted the events that had taken place in Holland, from the time of his arrival there to the end of his prison sentence, so that Bradstone had no option but to admit that he had previous convictions and that he had tried to mislead the jury.

Judith had kept the cross-examination short and to the point. She did the same with her address to the jury. She stressed the evidence of the complainant, the victim, the only witness, the young student Joanna Dowerthwaite. She stressed the medical evidence of serious injury, and finally she stressed the fact that this respectable-seeming man in the dock, who had lied to the jury, was in fact a man convicted of violence whose imprisonment now would make the world a safer place for women.

When Colin Hacker addressed the jury, he began by trying to dismiss the new evidence.

"You are not here, members of the jury, to pass judgement on what happened four years ago in a foreign land. If indeed it did happen; for who among you would regard a verdict in a foreign court as being in any way comparable to a decision in a British court? I do not need to remind patriotic members of a British jury that they are part of a legal system which is the envy not only of Europe but of the whole world. No, you are here to pass judgement on what happened in an English park on the evening of October the eighth. You must put the rest out of your minds.

"I put it to you, members of the jury, that the complainant met a stranger in the Parks and let him pick her up. She encouraged him to sit by her on the park bench, even when he offered to leave. She accompanied him into a shrubbery where the couple proceeded to have sex. There was a certain amount of horseplay and some roughness. Perhaps there was more roughness than the girl had bargained for, more perhaps than she found pleasurable. But I put it to you, members of the jury, that the defendant had no way of knowing that she was objecting to his advances. She did not cry out or try to repel him.

"Members of the jury, there are many things a woman can do to protect herself against unwanted sex, if she so wishes. She can push the man away, she can keep her legs firmly crossed. It has been well said by an expert in this field that a woman's consent is necessary for sexual intercourse because, I quote, 'of the almost inexpugnable position she occupies on account of the topography of the sexual organs in the female body'."

And I, Judith thought, can quote another expert who said, 'Any lawyer who says there is no such thing as rape should be hauled out to a public place by three large perverts and buggered at high noon with all his clients watching'.

"The alleged victim," Colin Hacker went on, "did not give a clear signal of any kind to the defendant. Any man might be forgiven for taking her attitude for one of consent. And remember, the law does not find actual consent necessary, only that the accused may have *believed* that there was consent. It is a well-known psychological fact that women enjoy being seduced and therefore often start by saying 'no' when they mean, 'yes'. Members of the jury, I put it to you that since the complainant's protests, if any, were few and feeble, my client quite reasonably assumed that she was consenting to everything which they did together that afternoon."

He sat down. In the dock the defendant looked straight ahead. In the visitors' gallery, Joanna sat with head bowed, her sister on one side of her holding her hand, her brother on the other side glaring at the defence lawyer, whom he had come to loathe as much as he did Joanna's assailant.

"This court will rise for the midday break," the judge announced. "It will sit again at two o'clock."

The Dowerthwaites spoke little to each other over lunch. They were all aware that everything turned on what happened that afternoon and that there was nothing now that they or Judith or anyone else could do to influence events.

They saw Judith going into court as they made their way to the public gallery.

"Whatever happens," Alice said to her quietly, "we're grateful to you."

"The judge will be fair," Judith said, trying to reassure her. "He's a good judge."

The court was very still for the summing up; the jury leaning forward anxiously to catch every word which might help them reach the right decision.

After meticulously recounting the events in the Parks, the judge told the jury, "The identity of the defendant as being the person who was with the complainant that afternoon is not in dispute. And he admits that he had sexual intercourse with the complainant. The prosecution must prove that the complainant did not consent to sexual intercourse, and that the defendant knew it. This you can judge only from the evidence you have heard. If your view is that the defendant in all the circumstances may have believed that the girl was consenting to his having sexual intercourse with her, then your verdict must be not guilty.

"For this you have only the conflicting evidence of two people, the alleged victim and her alleged assailant.

"You may think that this was a quite unwarranted attack on an innocent girl or you may think that the defendant was led on into believing that she was the willing recipient of his advances."

The jury was not long in delivering its verdict of guilty. To Judith, who knew that juries can sometimes bring in inexplicable verdicts, the relief was tremendous. She looked across at Joanna and for the first time thought about her life after the trial. For Joanna sat unmoved; the verdict would not undo the damage done to her first by the rapist and then by the lawyers. The life seemed to have gone out of her. It was as if her youth was over; she would never again trust a man, nor ever walk carefree in a park.

If the verdict was satisfactory to the prosecution, the sentence was not; the judge sentenced the defendant only to three years in prison which, with remission, would mean he could be out again and roaming the Parks in a mere eighteen months.

"It's wicked, only three years," Alice said afterwards, when they sat in a little room near the court.

"It's not for me to decide," Judith told her, "but I shall advise that the case be taken to appeal. It's now possible to have a sentence increased as well as reduced, you know."

"And will it be?"

"I think there's a good chance. The appeal judges will have all the papers connected with the case. yes, I'm definitely hopeful."

"Well, we'd best be getting back to the farm now," Alice said. "It's a long journey. You'll be coming with us, love?"

"No," Joanna replied. "I'll go back to college. I've a lot of work to catch up on and there's only three weeks of term left."

"Well, if you're sure, love?"

Judith was amazed; she hadn't doubted that the girl would return with them to the farm to recover from the ordeal of the trial. It seemed that she was made of sterner stuff than any of them had realised. Not for nothing was she old Mrs Dowerthwaite's daughter.

"Then, er – I'll say goodbye," Judith said, in the awkward way of partings after trauma.

"Words aren't much thanks, but thank you for all you've done for us and our Joanna," Samson said gruffly.

Alice didn't speak, just went up to Judith, put her arms around her and embraced her. Then, "You saved us," she said simply.

Judith, of course, shook her head in denial, but on the way home she acknowledged to herself that there was some truth in the words. It would have been far worse for them if the prosecution had been conducted by a stranger, however competent. As Alice had supported her when she was verging on postnatal depression, so she had supported Alice's family now in their hour of need. She thought how strange it all was. Her life and Alice's were totally different, lived so far apart physically and metaphorically, yet at crucial times, when their paths had crossed, they had been able to help each other as nobody else could. Something deeper than life style or education bound them together.

She drove quickly. Now that the trial was over she could think of nothing but Timothy. She may have been hopeful about the appeal, but she was less so about her son. She thought of stopping to telephone on the way, but resisted the temptation. It wouldn't help Timmy and would only delay getting back. But she was nervous of what she would find and fumbled with the key of the front door when she got home.

Elsa heard her and came to open the door. Timmy was sitting on the floor playing with his bricks. She saw at a glance that he was much better.

"The doctor was pleased with him," Elsa said. "The infection is clearing up nicely. He still has a runny nose, but the medicine's already doing a good job on his chest."

After she had gone, Judith sat down on the floor with Timmy and played with the bricks before transferring him to the bath for more play. Then she sat quietly feeding him in the darkened nursery where he took plenty of milk and fell asleep in her arms. She held him for a while, thinking how lucky she was; in one day she had concluded a successful case and had come home to this perfect joy. I can manage both, I really can, she thought as she laid her son gently in his cot, but I'll never again make the mistake of thinking that it's going to be easy.

Thirty-seven

" It wasn't natural, all that carry-on in court," Samson said, as he sat by the kitchen fire with his mother and Alice this January evening. "Nobody should be bowed and scraped to like that judge was. All that rising and sitting and if your Lordship pleases."

It was the first time he had put into words the feelings that he had carried inside him as he worked on the farm this winter. Up here on the hillsides as he tended the sheep, mended dry-stone walls, dealt with all the everyday things, real things like animals and crops, what had happened in that southern court seemed like a mad dream. He had never been to an opera but imagined it would be like that; people all dressed up in wigs and funny clothes, speaking a strange language, unreal as a puppet show.

"Judith told me once that all that bowing to the judge isn't to glorify the man, but to show respect for his office, for his court. For the law really."

"They didn't show much respect for our Joanna."

Deep and protective were his feelings for his little sister. From the moment she came home as a tiny baby he had felt awe, respect, for her frailty, for her vulnerability. Of the three brothers, it was he who had taken over the role of father to the girl who had been born after her real father's death.

He felt responsible for her, it was as simple as that. And the fact that she had got all this education, that she was to move away to the south, didn't alter that, she still needed him. But he, her natural protector, had failed her. He had watched over her as a child, made sure she was safe on the farm and then, in her hour of need he had failed her. Where had he been when she was dragged into those bushes? Driving up north, unaware, in his van. He had let this thing happen to her.

Outrage and guilt had battled within him. And then he'd let them tear her apart in front of his eyes in that court and he hadn't been able to stop it. He'd had to watch the torment while the puppets in their gowns and wigs did their worst, and all in accordance with rules they had made up to suit themselves. He felt less of a man because of it, just as, in some strange way that he didn't understand, Joanna seemed less of a woman than she had been.

"She'll weather it," his mother said, as if reading his thoughts.

"Weathering hardens things – and folk," he pointed out.

"Ay."

"It was all law and no justice in that court," he persisted.

"Yes, I think in the end it was worse for our Joanna than it was for me when I was attacked," Alice agreed sadly. "I never thought it would be."

Her mother and brother looked at her uneasily. For nineteen years none of them had mentioned what happened to Alice that night, the night she had walked home from the whist drive. They had dealt with it promptly at the time: her mother had nursed her, her brothers had meted out punishment to her attacker. They had not felt the need to speak of it since; it was not their way. And now, sitting by the kitchen fire, this winter evening, Alice had broken the silence of years.

"I didn't have to go through what our Joanna did in that court," she went on. "Nobody questioned me about it. Nobody tried to make me out a liar. Nobody took notes so that they could write reports about it in the newspapers for everyone to read, just as if it was some tale about a burglary."

"But in the end," her mother pointed out, "both men did get punished."

"Nay, our Alice's right," Samson told her. "It was rough justice we gave that man, my brothers and me, but it was justice all the same. And it was quick and over and done with and no further damage to our Alice. They say there's better justice nowadays, but I don't believe it. It was all *wrong* what happened in that court."

It was a long speech from the usually taciturn Samson. It seemed as if Alice had unloosened tongues.

"He's right, Mam," she went on now. "I did get better justice. I know our Joanna's going to relive what happened her to that night in the park, just as I did. It seems to lodge in your mind and nothing'll shift it. You can feel it in your body still, as if your body isn't your own any more. She'll have nightmares, as I did. She'll be fearful of going out on her own. There's no preventing that. But she'll have other bad memories that I didn't have; memories and nightmares about being stuck up in that box on her own in court surrounded by strange men in wigs and being made to go over it again and again, being stared at all the time and then being asked questions fit only for a doctor's surgery."

Overwhelmed by grief and anger, she had to pause before adding vehemently, "At least what I suffered was private."

"Two of you, two in one family," old Mrs Dowerthwaite said quietly, voicing what they'd all been thinking during the past weeks. For the first time that either of them could remember, they saw tears in their mother's eyes. "I can't but ask myself why," she said.

She had aged recently. She tired quickly and had lost weight; her chin and nose were sharper so she looked haggard. Even her hair seemed sparser, the scalp visible where it was drawn tightly back into a bun.

"Well, there's one thing, Mam," Alice said, wanting to offer her mother some small consolation. "We were able to be with her, Samson and me. At least the trial was in the winter and not the holiday season," she went on, knowing that what they all needed was to bring the conversation down to the level of everyday, manageable things. "I'm sure I don't know what I'd have done if we'd had visitors expected."

"You'd have cancelled 'em," Samson told her.

Alice shook her head.

"No, I couldn't have done that. Not spoil their holiday. I was committed to them, like."

"You never mean you'd have put their holiday above our Joanna?" Samson demanded, outraged.

"I don't know what you two are argufying about," their mother, always impatient with the hypothetical, said. "It didn't happen that way and that's all that needs to be said about it."

Thus it was settled that the subject would not be raised again. And it never was.

Thirty-eight

J udith carried her coffee into the room which she had once
envisaged as her father's study and which was still her
favourite place in the house. Here, she and Freddy had a desk
apiece, walls lined with books, a view over the little garden. Here,
on a winter's evening like this, she loved to sit, shutters closed
against the night, by the old-fashioned gasfire.

Freddy was away in Switzerland but would fly in early tomorrow morning and they would all have a late breakfast together,
Freddy and she at the little pine table, Timmy in his chair alongside. This evening she would do no work, just relax with the paper,
happy to think that Timmy was asleep upstairs, that she was
through her first three months of pregnancy, that the baby would
be a summer baby, that Freddy was thrilled with the thought of
being a father once again, that Elsa was happy because she loved
tiny babies and that Timmy would be intrigued to have a baby
brother or sister, just sixteen months younger than himself. Judith
basked in all these certainties; it was one of those times when
contentment comes unheralded and settles peacefully on the soul.

The telephone rang.

"Is that Judith Delaney, as was?" a strange voice asked. It was
a woman.

Unreasoning fear seized her. Once before she had been sitting,
blissfully happy, awaiting her father, when a bell had rung and a
strange woman asked for her. This time it would be about
Freddy that she would speak. Even now the policewoman was
hesitating, trying to find the right words to break the news, just
like last time. Keep calm, she told herself, steel yourself for the
shock.

"Who are you?" she demanded.

There was another pause before the woman found words.

"I'm your mother," she said.

It wasn't possible. She didn't have a mother. She'd managed without a mother all these years. She didn't need a mother. She didn't want a mother. She had steeled herself for the wrong shock.

"What do you want?" she asked.

She could hear the hardness in her own voice.

"I just, just thought I'd like to be in touch."

In touch! This woman who had gone off to care for little foreign bodies in faraway lands, and who might just as well be dead as far as her daughter was concerned, why should she decide to ring her from Africa or wherever it was?

"Where are you?" she asked.

"In the telephone box on the corner."

"*Here*?"

"Yes. At the corner of your road."

There was another long pause, then she added, "I'm sorry. I can tell that I've upset you."

"What do you want?" Judith asked again.

"I was wondering, I mean, I'd like to see you, if possible?"

"What, *now*? After all these years?"

"I know it must seem—" the voice broke. "I mean, I just hoped . . . But, of course I understand if you don't—"

Her father had never blamed her mother, but she herself jolly well did, Judith thought. She was therefore surprised to hear herself say, "Well, since you're so near, perhaps you'd better come over."

An elderly woman stood on the doorstep. She was wearing a raincoat and hat of indeterminate shape and colour. She didn't look exactly poverty-stricken, but there was an air of shabby gentility about her.

She was smaller than Judith remembered her; time had turned her hair grey and her skin had the weatherbeaten, leathery look of the fair-complexioned who have spent too many years under a tropical sun. But it was the expression on her face which was most changed. She didn't look so hard, her eyes no longer had that veiled, wary look that Judith remembered from her childhood. They now had a vulnerable, even pleading, look. She realised that it was herself who looked wary now, her mother pleading, as she herself must once have done. She took no pleasure in this role reversal.

Did her mother expect to be kissed, she wondered? She, who had never demonstrated any affection for her own child? No.

"Come in," she said formally. "Perhaps you would like some coffee?"

"Thank you, that would be nice, if it's not too much trouble."

She might have been somebody calling with a collecting box, surprised at being invited in.

Judith took her into the study, shut the door on her and went into the kitchen. Her hands were trembling as she filled the kettle. If only Freddy was here. If only the woman – she still couldn't think of her as her mother – hadn't come this evening. She didn't want to be alone with her.

She tried, as she stood by the kettle, to get a grip on herself, sort out her own feelings, but the turmoil was too much. Anger was what she mainly felt; anger on her father's behalf. All her resentment was for him, not for herself. This woman had never been a loving wife to him, never made him a home. If she had, he might still have been alive. All the rage and hurt rushed back. She would never forgive what this woman had done to him. Never.

But she had to go back in there with her. No good expecting help from Freddy. Besides, it was really between the two of them. She would be polite and civilised. But give no leeway.

"How did you trace me?" she asked, in the tone of polite enquiry that anyone might use when making conversation. "Milk?"

"Please," her mother said, accepting the cup.

Judith offered sugar, which was rejected.

"It wasn't difficult. I guessed you might go in for law so I looked up the solicitors and barristers in the *Lawyers' Year-book* in the library."

"And what are your own plans?" she asked. "I believe you worked abroad?"

It's going to be perfectly manageable, she thought with relief, *if we just keep talking politely to each other like newly introduced strangers.*

"I'm retired now, back in England for good, but I'm doing voluntary work helping at a clinic with the babies two afternoons a week. And every morning I work at a nursery school. I have to work and really that's all I know, working with small children."

Oh, the irony of it! Keep calm, Judith told herself, but she knew that the polite veneer was beginning to crack.

"I'm sorry if I intruded," the woman opposite to her was saying, "I just wanted . . ." her voice trailed off.

"What?"

"I just wanted to know that you were all right."

"And if I hadn't been," Judith said sharply, anger at last finding vent, "it would have been a bit late, wouldn't it, for you to start showing an interest in your daughter?"

Her mother flinched, her face crumpled, her eyes filled with tears.

"I know. I'm sorry. I've often thought of coming, but I knew I wouldn't be welcome. How could I be?" she asked and there was anguish in her voice. "But I've worried all the time, and every day of this last year since I've been back in England I've thought about coming to see you."

"This last year? As if this last year mattered, or any of the last years. It's what you did *then* that matters. Why?" she heard her voice breaking as she asked, knew that her own face too was twisted with pain, her own eyes full of tears, as she remembered the frightened child she had once been. *"Why did you go?"*

Her mother shook her head; tears were running down her cheeks now and she was twisting a handkerchief round and round in her hands; workworn, they were, and speckled with brown marks. She scarcely seemed able to speak and when at last she did her voice was no more than a whisper, which Judith had to strain to hear.

"I couldn't manage any more, truly I could not. And I thought I had a calling."

"How very convenient."

Her mother bowed her head, nodded. "Yes, I realise that now."

She was silent for a while and then went on, "Judith, I know it's no excuse, but I realised as soon as I married your father that it was all wrong. He was too clever for me, him and all the people he worked with. He didn't realise it, but they'd have despised me if I'd tried to mix with them. It was just impossible," she ended hopelessly.

"You've no right to try to blame him," Judith burst out furiously. "He never blamed you. He was loyal in everything he ever said to me about you. He was the most tolerant and loving . . ." her voice broke and she couldn't go on.

"Oh, Judith, I'm not blaming him! But we belonged in different worlds. Then you were born and as you grew up, you grew more like him, more critical of me."

"Me? Critical? But I never—"

"Oh, you didn't need to say it. I saw it in your face, your clever little face. And I knew I couldn't manage, not against two of you. And then I found out that there were people out there who needed me, who would let me help them; who wouldn't be critical, wouldn't be cleverer than me. Wouldn't – oh, I can't explain. Oh yes, you're right, it was very convenient to feel called. But I was doing no good by staying. I just had to get away."

Too confused to reply, Judith sat in silence. Nothing was clear any more; the past was much less simple than she'd supposed, the rights and wrongs of things less black and white, human life messier and more muddled than she'd imagined. Her father had understood that; there must have been times, she realised, when he was worried by her own shallow certainties. She was certain of nothing now; she couldn't forgive her mother, but neither could she blame her as single-mindedly as she had done before.

"Well, I'll be going now," her mother said.

She groped on the ground for her bag. It was an elderly, fumbling gesture; she looked so old and sad that Judith felt for her a pang of pity that she would have felt for any other distraught old woman.

She reached out and picked up the bag for her.

"Thank you," her mother said.

She stood up and, speaking more firmly now, went on, "I'm sorry I came and upset you. I realise it was a mistake and all I've done is add to your distress. I'm truly sorry, Judith, especially as—" she hesitated and then added, "as you're pregnant, aren't you?"

Judith stared.

"Well, yes," she agreed, taken aback. "But I didn't think it showed."

Something approaching a smile lit her mother's face.

"I took up nursing out there and then midwifery. I suppose I got into the habit of observing early signs."

Judith found herself smiling back. After the storm, it was a calm moment of complicity, of understanding.

"We have a little boy," she confided. "Timothy. He's a year old. He's asleep now, of course."

"Oh, that's lovely. And he goes through the night, does he?"

"Yes, he does now, thank goodness. Ever since he was six months. Of course, we get the occasional bad night—"

"Oh, they all have those."

It was a relief to both of them to be back on safe ground.

They were quiet for a moment, then Judith said slowly, "Would you like to have a peep at him?"

She asked partly in order to keep up this new mood of calm, of civilised behaviour, but also, she had to admit to herself, because she wanted to show off her son to this woman who seemed so well informed about babies. No, it was more than that: she needed to have her mother see her baby. Strange as it seemed, it was now that she had a child of her own that she needed the mother that she had managed so well without for all these childless years.

It was her mother who hesitated.

"I wouldn't want to disturb him," she said.

"Oh, nothing disturbs him once he's asleep."

Treading softly, despite her assurance that Timmy slept soundly, they went upstairs and quietly crept into the room where the sleeping child lay. He was lying on his back, both arms outstretched above his head.

"He's lovely," the older woman murmured, awestruck.

"He always sleeps like that," Judith said, "with his arms up."

"It's good. It opens up his lungs."

The two women stood for a while, silently gazing down at the baby as he slept. He's in a different world from ours, Judith thought, watching him in his blessed unawareness.

Back in the study, her mother picked up her bag and stood awkwardly for a moment.

"I'll be on my way now," she said. "I'm sorry if I intruded. I know I shouldn't have come. Not after all these years."

"No, you did right," Judith said suddenly. "Look, I want to talk to Freddy about all this, but give me your number and I'll get in touch."

Freddy took the news with surprising calmness.

"Well, I've always thought that if she'd died, you'd have been informed somehow or other," he told her as they sat over a late breakfast in the kitchen, his travel bag still unpacked on the floor. Timmy, in his high chair was being fed spoonfuls of mashed banana and baby rice.

"Let him have a go on his own," Freddy suggested.

So she gave the loaded spoon to Timmy who lifted it carefully from the plate, raised it very deliberately towards his mouth, but then turned it upside down so that the contents fell back on to his plate instead. Since he wasn't hungry, he enjoyed repeating the process several times.

"He's only messing," Judith remarked. "He might as well get down."

So Timmy was sponged, wiped dry, de-bibbed and set down on the floor with his toys.

"Now we can talk," Freddy said, pouring them more coffee. "Quite honestly what do *you* feel about it? I mean, that's all that matters."

273

"That's the trouble," Judith said, sighing and crumbling the remains of a croissant in her fingers. "I feel different things every hour. I don't think I can forgive what she did, yet seeing her with Timmy, she somehow seemed a different person. Oh, I don't know; it's just odd suddenly to have a mother."

"And odd that Timmy now has a grandmother," Freddy pointed out.

"Well, if she's as unreliable as a grandmother as she was as a mother, he'd be better off without her," she told him sharply.

He put his arms round her.

"Poor darling," he said, stroking her hair. "It was awful for me when I lost my parents when I was still at school, but at least they had no option when they died. I can't imagine how dreadful it would have been if they had *chosen* to go away and leave me."

"There were reasons why she did, Freddy," Judith explained, coming to her mother's defence now that she was being criticised by Freddy. "I'd like to understand. It's better than being bitter."

"Of course," he said, kissing her. "And there are some people, you know, who make a better job of being grandparents than they did of being parents. If she's one of them, perhaps we shouldn't deprive Timmy of the only grandparent he's got. But it's your choice entirely. Send her packing if you'd rather."

Judith pushed the plate of crumbs aside.

"No," she said decisively. "We've got to give it a try. How about asking her to go out with us this weekend?"

And so it was arranged. They picked her up the next morning and she drove with them to the park. Timmy attached himself to her in the unquestioning way of small children, letting her push him on the swing, hold him as he went down the little slide, replace his shoes which always fell off at regular intervals.

Freddy treated her gently, Judith noticed. She was more pathetic, he admitted afterwards, than he had expected. It was quite a shock, he said, for a man to find he'd got a mother-in-law, and he'd imagined something more formidable. She simply didn't look like a woman who would abandon her child. We

274

none of us know what we might do if pushed beyond our limits, Judith told him.

She herself was, of the three of them, the least at ease. She couldn't help but feel strained with this woman as she tried to reconcile the mother she had been with the one she was now. She found it simpler to let her talk to Freddy, play with Timmy.

It was a bright February morning, but after they had had a picnic lunch on a bench while Timmy, replete, slept in the buggy, the sky clouded over and the air turned damp and chill.

"Shall we go and walk round the pond?" Freddy asked, getting up.

"It's a bit cold for him to be out now," Judith objected.

"Have you tried the soft play centre?" her mother asked tentatively.

They shook their heads.

"Never heard of it," Freddy told her.

"There's one called Wonderland, not far away. It's great for children. I've taken some of my charges there."

So they let her guide them as Freddy drove to Wonderland, which turned out to be a kind of juvenile paradise where small children swung, climbed, bounced and slid and where little ones like Timmy could scrabble about in a great box of plastic balls.

There were tables where parents and grandparents sat and relaxed over cups of tea. *We must look just like the other three-generation families*, Judith thought, looking about her. But we're not like them, not really. She stayed there with her mother, sipping tea, not talking, still ill-at-ease in this new situation; not sure if she had enough forgiveness in her to welcome her mother into her family.

Freddy had taken Timmy off for a ride in a miniature bus; they both watched as it weaved its way among other tiny cars and lorries being manically driven by ecstatic toddlers.

A young couple carrying twins, stopped by their table.

"It's Mrs Delaney," the girl said. "I've told you about her, darling. The children adore her."

They shook hands.

They looked at Judith, expecting introductions.

Judith saw that her mother hesitated to state her relationship with her, fearing to offend her by making such a claim. Such humility was pitiable; she saw that the decision had to be hers.

She stretched out her hand.

"I'm her daughter," she said.

Thirty-nine

O ld Mrs Dowerthwaite died in the spring and was buried alongside her husband in the cemetery up the hill. Their two funerals, however, could not have been more different. Most of the village came to the church for this one and afterwards drove up to the farm for tea. The visitors staying there had become friends over the years, had grown fond of the old lady and so joined in the family observances.

Joanna came home for the funeral. Alice surveyed her anxiously when she met her off the train in Pendlebury, raking her face for signs of stress or depression. She saw that Joanna was looking more relaxed now and had even, she thought as she hugged her, begun to put back on some of the weight that she had lost. She'd had some of that counselling that everybody had nowadays. Well, it seems to have suited her, Alice thought. And then the fact that the light sentence meted out by the trial judge had been increased on appeal – thanks to Judith – to ten years had done more than anything to raise her spirits. She need not fear seeing him ever again. So the world had become a safer place thanks to what Joanna had gone through in that witness box. At least she could feel that some good had come out of it, *and that's a feeling which helps you to bear the unbearable*, Alice told herself.

Later, she found herself wondering how the others bore it; the ones who didn't have a Judith, kind and knowledgeable, to help them through the humiliation of the court ordeal and who didn't have parents, brothers and sisters to love and comfort them and help them rebuild their broken lives. How did they manage to go on living in the everyday world? But these thoughts came later;

for the moment she thought only of Joanna and gave thanks for her survival.

Judith drove up alone to the funeral, leaving Freddy in charge of Timmy. She had decided to stay at The Curlew, not wanting to intrude too much on the family. As she drove up the M1 she wondered why it had seemed so important to her to come all this way; why she hadn't even considered not coming. After all, she hadn't known old Mrs Dowerthwaite well, had hardly seen her. Yet she had always felt her presence, never doubted that it was her will which had kept the family going; that it was the old woman's strength which had found its way into her daughters.

Not that Mrs Dowerthwaite was so very old, but she had always seemed so. It was impossible to imagine her as young or even middle-aged. A life of unrelenting toil had aged her and no doubt being out in all weathers, combined with hard water and carbolic soap, had given her face that ancient, weatherbeaten look, as stern and indomitable as the bleak landscape of millstone grit and limestone scree which surrounded her.

The strength of the hills was in her, Judith thought, realising that one of the reasons she had come was because she needed to pay tribute to that life of endurance and to a mother who had been rocklike, always there; unlike her own mother. But also, she wanted to see how the rest of the family was faring; she had only seen Joanna once since the trial and very pale, thin and wan she had seemed. She hadn't managed to look Judith in the face, this girl who had once been so open; as if to do so would bring back unbearable memories of humiliation and shame. So Judith had felt it was better not to see her for a while.

She worried about Alice, too; would she have been able to take up the threads again? Without her mother, would she be able to continue with the life she had made for herself up here on the farm, as if the horror of what had happened to her sister had never been? And Samson. She had been surprised at the warmth and compassion she had felt for Samson during and after the trial. Inarticulate, outraged; what greater contrast could there have been with articulate types like Colin Hacker who had long ago lost any capacity for outrage?

The Ewe Lamb

She remembered how, years ago as a girl of twenty, she had pitied Alice and despised Samson, thought him boorish. She felt a shiver of shame for her judgemental younger self as she parked outside The Curlew that night.

The funeral was at twelve o'clock the next day, so after breakfast she packed and went for a walk. There wasn't time to climb up the hills; instead she walked along the more homely lanes around the village. Honeysuckle and sweet briar roses were already beginning to flower on the dry-stone walls on each side of the narrow lanes. In parts the walls were so high that they hid from view the cattle that were feeding on the other side. Only by the gentle sound of the grass being tugged as they grazed, did she know that they were there.

It was very quiet apart from this little sound and the occasional plaintive call of a lamb and the deeper, grumbling reply of a sheep. She walked slowly, sometimes letting the long grass of the verge trail through her fingers, pausing now and then to breathe in the sweetness of the air or look up at the hills, at wooded Westerbirt and sheep-cropped Enderberg.

It was so quiet that she heard the sound of the beck long before she rounded the bend and came to the ancient slate bridge which took the lane across the stream. She saw that the old bench was still there on the near bank and that a plant like coarse rhubarb still grew at the water's edge. The beck was wide and shallow here, very clear as it rippled over the pebbles.

She stood for a while on the warm slate, looking upstream towards the dalehead, whence it flowed rapidly between narrow banks, sometimes dropping in little slate-backed waterfalls, lazing for a while in a tawny pool and then rushing off again, white and foaming, to drop steeply in another miniature water-fall. And thus it made its way down to the meadow where, its rapid descent achieved, it spread itself between low and marshy banks. Slow now and shallow, it slid between the stone pillars of the bridge upon which she stood. For a long time she gazed, mesmerised by the flow of it, and then at last she turned and followed the beck as it looped and curved its leisurely way downstream towards the village.

She was warm after her walk and the little church was pleasantly cool as she sat on a back pew and watched the people coming in. She recognized some: Tom and his wife from the post office; Myra who helped at the pub, and some she remembered from her childhood and then realised it was their children she was seeing. The bereaved family came and sat in the front pews, as was the custom, and Mrs Dowerthwaite's coffin was carried in by her three sons and a big lad who, Judith thought, must be the eldest grandson; all of them looking very solemn and not quite at ease in their best suits.

After the service was over, they took up their burden again, lifted it up on to the bier and pushed it up the hill to the cemetery. Some of the congregation followed by car, most on foot, talking quietly among themselves. When they reached the graveyard, Judith stayed back and waited by the old wooden gates while the family stood around the freshly-dug grave and watched the coffin being lowered into the ground. "Dust to dust, ashes to ashes," the familiar old phrases were carried to her on the breeze.

Afterwards, back at the farm, everyone relaxed, as if acting out the opinion that life must go on. Farmers talked of the collapse of cattle prices, women exchanged news, talked of meetings and enquired about each other's children.

Alice had been lavish with the funeral feast – part-lunch, part-tea. Cold meats and salad, pies and tarts and puddings were laid out on the big table in the stone-flagged kitchen. What had been a sombre congregation relaxed into being cheerful guests, a little subdued perhaps as befitted the occasion, as they helped themselves and carried their laden plates to tables set ready for them indoors and out, while Clara bustled about replenishing teacups.

Judith found a seat for herself on a bench in the sunny little courtyard where Alice had her herb garden. A pale green aromatic plant grew alongside the slate seat; she let her fingers slide through its feathery leaves and then sniffed them as she had seen Alice do, shutting her eyes as she did so, so sweet was the scent that lingered on her hand.

Joanna approached, offering cake.

The Ewe Lamb

"What's this shrub called?" Judith asked, hoping to persuade her to come and sit for a while and talk.

"Southernwood," Joanna told her.

She hesitated for a moment and then sat down.

"Some people call it lad's love," she added.

Judith saw that the girl was looking much better now; that she held her head high again and looked directly at you, as she always used to do.

"How are you getting on, really, I mean?" she asked after they had talked generalities for a while.

"You mean my studies?"

"Both."

Joanna smiled.

"I'm enjoying the work," she said. "And as for the other, well, I'm mending."

"She's more than mending," Alice told her, coming up and putting her arm around her sister. "She's doing grand and we're all proud of her."

"I've had a lot of help," Joanna said. "Polly – that's my counsellor, well, more my friend really, now – has been wonderful. We've talked for hours. Then there's Simon—"

Judith saw Alice look up suddenly; evidently this was the first she had heard of Simon.

"He's studying agriculture and quite a lot of our work overlaps," Joanna explained. Then she laughed and went on, "We met in the tropical palm house at the Botanic Garden, of all places. He was researching which plants are useful for food and I was, well, I was just interested in the plants, I suppose."

Judith nodded. Once it might have been an occasion for teasing, but not now, not with Joanna.

"We've been to some lectures together and we're going to the horticultural research station next week."

"And you like him, this Simon?" Alice asked.

"Oh, he's great. And do you know, at first he'd always ask someone else along, Polly or another friend of mine, if we were going anywhere a bit quiet? Just in case I felt nervous of being alone with him, because he knew what had happened to me. I

281

didn't realise of course. I just thought he liked my friends, but he admitted it to me last week, when nobody could come with us."

"That was very thoughtful," Judith said.

"But not necessary," Joanna told her, "because I feel quite safe with him. Though I suppose," she added, "that I might not have done at first."

Alice said nothing, just nodded; looking, Judith thought, a little abstracted.

After Joanna had gone, she said suddenly, "I want her never to be ashamed, Judith. Nothing that's done to you should make you ashamed, only what you do yourself."

They looked at each other, understanding. No more was said, but the sentence and the way Alice said it, stayed with her as they lingered in the little courtyard, sitting on the slate seat by the sweet-scented bush which people called lad's love.

She understood now why Alice hadn't married and as she felt her own child moving inside her, she thought sadly that this was something that Alice had never known, and it seemed to her that although Alice had made a success of her life here on the farm, she must feel unfulfilled; this woman who would have made such a lovely mother. Yet she seemed unembittered.

"I must be going, Alice," she said at last, making herself stand up. "It's a long drive back to London."

"Thank you for coming. We're very grateful, Samson and me."

"You're managing?"

"Needs must. Besides, we owe it to Mam."

She reached out and put her arms round Judith.

"Now, you take care of yourself and the one you're carrying," she said. "And don't forget to come back and see us as often as you can. And bring your little ones."

"Oh, Alice, of course we will. More than anything I want them to know and love this place."

"Ay. They'll be better for it," Alice said simply.

As she drove home, she thought about those words. It was true; she had always found this a healing, strengthening place. It might be London where she must live and work, but it was here that she really belonged and where she knew that one day she would return. There was a permanence here; the hills were changeless and so, whatever the superficial alterations of time and fashion, was the character of the people who lived among them. That was what bound her and Alice together.

She thought of the last time she had been up here, how miserably depressed she'd been when she arrived; she shied away from even the memory of those wretched weeks of feeling hopelessly inadequate after Timmy was born. As she got nearer to London, she found herself for the first time wondering if her own mother, when the infant Judith was born, had also suffered from depression, made worse in her case by being the untutored wife of a clever academic. She, too, had had no mother to turn to. Nor had she had an Alice for a friend. Perhaps rather than sink into depression, she had fought back with anger and resentment.

It must have been infuriating, she realised now, to watch that baby grow into a clever and difficult little girl, maddeningly devoted to a father who was hardly ever there. Was she perhaps so frightened by her own bitterness towards her child, that she had no alternative but to leave, comforted by religious instruction to give up her family and follow her Lord?

She knew this was something she would never be able to discuss with her mother, however much closer they had now become, so she would never know with certainty. But at least she was beginning to understand. And so to forgive.

After all the guests had gone, including Clara, who was always the last to leave any do, Alice went up to the cemetery to tidy the flowers and see that everything was in order. She walked between the gravestones, reading the familiar names. Some were hard to make out, mossed over by time. But JOSEPH DOWERTHWAITE 1920–1976 RIP was still clear cut, though the stone was patterned with little rosettes of lichen, pink and green and grey.

She wasn't much of a one for praying, but she stood looking at the tombstone and prayed that her mother also might rest in peace. She remembered how much she owed to her; how her mother had looked after her on that night of terror in the farm wood. She remembered her loving care, her wordless grief. And, when they realised that Alice was pregnant, it was her mother who had saved her from the humiliation of village gossip and the shame of her brothers by pretending that the child was her own. So she had been able to keep her baby, hadn't been forced apart from it by abortion or adoption, and little Joanna had restored joy and hope to her life.

She thought now about Joanna, who called her sister; she was glad that she had never told her the truth. She had considered it; she knew that there was a theory that children should be told the truth about such things. But she was a practical person who didn't set much store by theories. Now, more than ever, it was best that Joanna should never know that she was born of a rapist's attack. Better by far that she should feel herself the wanted child of a loving family. What did it matter whether she was Alice's daughter or her younger sister, when she was equally loved either way?

So Alice stood, her hand resting on her parents' headstone, feeling the slight roughness of the lichen which encrusted it, and thought how strange it was that she could look back on it all now more calmly than she would ever have dreamed possible; with sadness, but without the earlier horror. It was as if that dreadful event had been mossed over by time, which gently softens anguish into sorrow.

It was a mild evening. She went and sat for a while on a grassy bank and gazed across at the distant fells. It was a tranquil scene. In front of her lay the village, its grey houses clustered around the church, while further away a few farmsteads lay scattered among the fields where sheep grazed and looked from here indistinguishable from the boulders which surrounded them. And beyond it all were the hills which ringed the village, as if holding together in their embrace the farms and houses and all the people in them.

It's a grand view you get from the cemetery, Alice thought; we're lucky in Netherby to have such a lovely outlook when we die.